Stuart Neville has been a musician, composer, teacher, salesman, film extra, baker, and a hand double for a well-known Irish comedian. His first novel, *The Twelve*, was one of the most critically acclaimed crime debuts of recent years, and won the Los Angeles Times Book Prize for best thriller. He lives with his family in a small town near Belfast, Northern Ireland.

You can discover more about the author at www.stuartneville.com

THOSE WE LEFT BEHIND

DCI Serena Flanagan hasn't heard the boy's name in years. Not since the blood on the wall and the body in the bedroom. Not since she listened as he, no more than a child, confessed to brutally murdering his foster father. But now Ciaran Devine is out of prison and back in Flanagan's life. And so is his brother, Thomas — the brother she always suspected of hiding something. When Ciaran's probation officer comes to Flanagan with fresh fears about the Devines, years of lies begin to unravel, leading to a truth stranger than anyone could have imagined . . .

STUART NEVILLE

THOSE WE LEFT BEHIND

Complete and Unabridged

CHARNWOOD
Leicester

First published in Great Britain in 2015 by
Harvill Secker
London

First Charnwood Edition
published 2017
by arrangement with
Penguin Random House UK
London

A catalogue record for this book is available
from the British Library.

ISBN 978-1-4448-3177-1

Published by
F. A. Thorpe (Publishing)
Anstey, Leicestershire

Set by Words & Graphics Ltd.
Anstey, Leicestershire
Printed and bound in Great Britain by
T. J. International Ltd., Padstow, Cornwall

This book is printed on acid-free paper

For the agents, editors, publicists and many more passionate book people who help create the illusion that I know what I'm doing. I'd be lost without you.

Prologue

The pillow is cool on Ciaran's cheek, damp from sweat. Sunlight makes a glowing rectangle on the wall. It lingers flickery green behind his eyelids when he blinks.

He does not want to look at the wall on the other side of the room, or what lies in the corner there, beneath the window. He does not want to see that. After all the shouting and the noise and the cracking and the hot and the wet, he doesn't ever want to look at it again.

The mattress rocks. Warm air finds the tiny hairs on the back of Ciaran's neck and waves them like the grass on the dunes, back when they were little, and things weren't so hard and angry. A bare arm slips around his waist, the hand taking his. The chest against his back, all warm and cuddly, bony knees tucked behind his.

Ciaran sees the red points of blood on both their wrists. Join the dots. Make a picture.

His hands are sticky with it.

'Are we going to jail?' he asks.

'Probably.'

Thomas squeezes him tighter, his mouth close to Ciaran's ear. The teeth held behind his lips for now.

'Will they send us to the same jail? Or different ones?'

Thomas holds his breath as he thinks. After a while, he says, 'Dunno.'

Ciaran feels something cold and heavy where his heart should be. 'If it's different ones, will they let us visit each other?'

'Dunno.'

'I hope they do.'

Downstairs, a hammering on the door. More noise when all Ciaran wants is soft quiet. The letterbox squeaks open.

'Jenny? Jenny!'

Ciaran thinks it's the old man from next door, the grey one who looks cross and small-eyed at the brothers when he sees them over the hedge.

'Jenny? David? Are you there? Can you hear me?'

Thomas's chin rests on Ciaran's shoulder.

'David? David! I've called the police. Come and open the door if you're there.'

Far away, high above everything, a wailing noise, rising and falling. Like some terrible animal galloping to their hiding place to gobble them up. It gets louder.

Ciaran wants to cry. He wants to take it back. He wishes it hadn't happened at all. His shoulders judder as the tears come. He closes his eyes.

'Shush.' Thomas's lips are soft against his ear. 'We'll be all right. I'll look after us. Don't worry.'

The wailing comes close, falls and dies, the sound of tyres on the driveway outside. Car doors opening and closing.

Ciaran opens his eyes, sees the blue light dancing on the wall.

'They're here,' he says.

He doesn't know if Thomas hears him. His brother keeps on talking, his words dripping into Ciaran's ear like warm oil even as the front door rattles on its hinges.

1

When Paula Cunningham heard the news about the boy's release, she knew the case would fall to her. She had felt no surprise when Edward Hughes called her to his office. The file had been waiting for her on the boss's desk, half an inch of reports, assessments and evaluations. It pulled a bitter curse from her throat.

City centre traffic hummed and rattled beneath Hughes's window, car horns sounding, someone whistling for a taxi. She turned the pages while Hughes chewed a pen at the other side of the desk.

A single photograph of Ciaran Devine at the front, hollow eyes and blank face, a little boy long gone.

They'd used the same picture in the Sunday red top she'd read at the weekend. SCHOOL-BOY KILLER TO BE RELEASED, the headline had screamed above a half-page story.

She knew as soon as she saw it. Just knew.

'Any way out of this?' she asked.

Hughes shook his head. 'None at all. The young fella needs your experience.'

'What about Terry Grimes?'

'Terry's tied up. It's your case, and that's all there is to it. You can handle him. He's been good as gold on his temporary releases. Tom Wheatley at the hostel says he was no bother at all when he stayed over.'

The boy would have had excursions accompanied by one of his case managers. Shopping trips, a meal at McDonald's, a walk in the park. Finally, they would have allowed him a night in the hostel off the Saintfield Road, in the south of the city.

She pictured him sitting in the small, clean room, perhaps counting coins in the palm of his hand, trying to grasp the simple acts other people took for granted. Going to a shop counter, asking for what he wanted, saying please and thank you.

Cunningham remembered taking a lifer called Brian to a newsagent's. He had mumbled, 'Polo mints, please.' The shopkeeper had set the sweets on the counter. Brian, who had strangled his girlfriend to death after a drinking binge, had grabbed the packet, dropped a twenty-pound note in its place, and walked out of the shop.

When she'd caught up with him, his change in her hand, Cunningham asked why.

Brian had stood there on the pavement, blinking tears from his eyes, before he said, 'Cause I don't know what they cost.'

Remove a man from the world for years then drop him back into it, expecting him to simply pick up where he left off. It doesn't work. He'll be lost. And Ciaran Devine would be no different.

Cunningham had entered the Probation Service twelve years ago, not long after gaining her MSc in clinical psychology. As a postgraduate student, she had spent summers working on the wards of psychiatric units, then a year in

5

Maghaberry prison, counselling inmates. She had learned things in those days that would stay with her until her last breath, like the terrible cost of casual violence, and how poorly the system dealt with those who inflicted it.

In all those dozen years, Cunningham wasn't sure if she'd ever done any good.

She let the air out of her lungs, wished for a cigarette. 'All right,' she said. 'When's the ADR?'

'He gets out Wednesday. That gives you a week to prepare.'

'Jesus, how am I supposed to prepare for this?'

Hughes put his forearms on the desk. 'In a thorough, diligent and professional manner.'

Cunningham glanced at him over the open file. He probably thought he was giving her his serious face, but he looked more like a prissy matron. Edward Hughes was on the large side, yet he had a countenance more like that of a schoolboy than a man well into middle age.

'What about the brother?' Cunningham asked.

'Thomas? He's kept out of trouble since his release. He's not supervised any more.'

The newspaper had also carried a picture of Thomas Devine, smaller than that of Ciaran, tucked away on the second page. Older, leaner, darker. Handsome like his brother, but in a sharper, more jagged way.

An image flashed in her mind: the boys escorted towards the side entrance of the courthouse, blankets over their heads, a uniformed policeman at each arm, followed by the detectives who got the confession, brilliant camera flashes, screams of hatred from the onlookers.

No one knew the boys' names then, the press ordered to keep quiet.

'He didn't go for a Mary Bell order?' Cunningham asked.

A new identity, a lifetime of secrets, named after a little English girl who did two unspeakable things almost half a century before.

'Thomas gave it a go,' Hughes said. 'The judge threw it out. He didn't reckon they were under sufficient threat.'

The names had appeared in the papers more than a year and a half ago when Ciaran had turned eighteen. His minimum tariff of six years had expired, but he continued to be held at the Secretary of State's pleasure. The local Belfast journalists salivated over a potential release, stored up their bile and outrage. Politicians gave stiff-lipped opinions that amounted to nothing.

'God help him,' Cunningham whispered.

She hadn't meant to say it out loud. She glanced up at Hughes, expecting a reproach.

He said, 'God help the both of you.'

2

Detective Chief Inspector Serena Flanagan punched in her key code and entered the station's core. A walled compound containing a cluster of red-brick buildings, small windows, a fortress in the heart of Lisburn, built to shield its occupants from bullets and bombs. Flanagan avoided all stares, averted her eyes as she made her way to the second floor and the office she hadn't seen in four months. Whispers followed her through the corridors and stairwells.

'Ma'am,' a voice called.

Flanagan pretended she hadn't heard it, kept walking, her door only a few yards away now.

'Ma'am.'

She stopped, gave a silent curse, and turned.

Detective Inspector John Hoey, a coffee in one hand, a sheaf of papers in the other. Flanagan offered a smile, a nod.

'Good to see you back,' he said as he approached. 'How are you feeling?'

'Not bad,' she said. 'Looking forward to getting to work.'

'I see your hair grew back.'

Flanagan had turned to leave, but his words stopped her. 'Excuse me?'

'From your treatment.' He raised his coffee cup, pointing a finger at her head. His face dropped. 'Oh. Is it a wig?'

Flanagan took a breath. Gave him a patient

smile. 'I didn't have chemotherapy,' she said. 'Just radiotherapy. So I didn't lose my hair.'

'Oh,' he said. 'Oh, good. I was wondering, will you be getting your team back together?'

'Yes,' she said. 'As soon as I get caught up, see who's still available.'

'I'd like to be considered,' Hoey said. 'Just so you know. If you need the numbers made up.'

'I'll bear it in mind,' she said. 'Thanks.'

Flanagan turned, left him there, and headed for her office. She let herself in, closed the door behind her, leaned her back against it.

Aside from Hoey's crass stupidity, she thought, that wasn't so bad. She'd been dreading the return for weeks. The looks of pity. The expressions of sympathy. They would come, that much was certain, but she felt that perhaps she could at least be gracious in response.

Six weeks after her surgery, she had been in Tesco browsing loaves of bread. She had nudged her trolley against another shopper, turned to apologise, and recognised a work colleague of her husband's. Heather Foyle, she was called, a maths teacher.

Heather had stared at Flanagan, eyes and mouth agape, visibly struggling to find a few words.

'For Christ's sake, I didn't die,' Flanagan said before wheeling her trolley to the checkouts, her face burning, regret already souring her stomach.

She had called Heather later that evening to apologise, battled through the no-don't-mention-its, tried to explain herself against the tide of

9

condescension. Even then, when she knew she was entirely in the wrong, aware that Heather Foyle was simply being a good person, Flanagan had to stamp on her own anger. She had never experienced the pity of others until her breast cancer diagnosis, and it was more unpalatable than she had ever imagined.

So far, only Hoey, his clumsy words and his expedient sympathy as he fished for opportunities. She could take that. There would be more to come, and she would smile and say, I'm fine, thank you, and ask after the enquirer's wellbeing, and most definitely not shout at him or her to shut up, just leave her alone, let her get on with living.

Flanagan's office remained as dim as she remembered, sunlight muted by the tinted glass in a window so small it served little purpose. And hot, too. She crossed the room, opened the window to its full extent, which was no more than a couple of inches. For her own protection, her superiors would have said. This building looked like a small prison from the outside, and often felt like one within. Across the rooftops, she could just see the spires of Christ Church. Flanagan counted herself lucky; most of the views from this station were of walls and wire fences.

She took off her jacket, slung it over the back of her chair, and sat down. The quiet of the room seemed to press on her, a physical sensation, as if the silence hardened the air.

Three framed photographs sat on her desk, one portrait of each of her children, and another picture of the family. One of those terrible posed studio shots that she disliked, but Alistair had insisted. She'd turned the frames face down the last time she left the office. To keep the dust off them, she'd told herself, but part of her believed it was to shield her family from the goings-on here.

Flanagan set each of them upright and was startled by how young Ruth and Eli looked, how much they had changed, and she felt a strange sadness for the smaller children they'd left behind in these images.

A sharp rap of knuckle on wood made her jump. She exhaled and said, 'Come.'

Detective Superintendent Stephen Purdy opened the door. A stocky bespectacled man with a shock of pure black hair that some speculated was a wig. Flanagan had inspected it as closely as she could and found no evidence to back up the claim, though she suspected he dyed it.

'It's good to see you back,' he said. 'How are you feeling?'

'I'm fine, sir, thank you,' she said, hoping he wouldn't ask her to elaborate.

DSI Stephen Purdy was not an idiot like Hoey. He lacked emotional intelligence, found casual conversation difficult, but he was not stupid. He would know not to push her on her illness.

'Good, good,' he said.

She indicated the seat in front of her desk as she sat down.

'No, I'm not stopping.' He hovered there,

11

looking as comfortable as a mouse in a cattery.

It was up to Flanagan to set him free. 'What can I do for you?'

'Ah, well, first of all I wanted to welcome you back.' He dipped his head and waved a hand in a bowing gesture. 'And to get you started on some work.'

Flanagan had noticed the file under Purdy's arm when he entered her office. He placed the manila folder on the desk and tapped it with his index finger.

'This was sent over from B District. You know DCI Thompson's retiring in a few weeks? He's leaving a lot of unfinished business behind him. Between you and me, his MIT had become a bit of a shambles. These are the loose ends from the last few cases he's left open. The ACC wants you to work through them, see what's still worth following up, what's better off dropped, that kind of thing. He thought it might keep you occupied while you get settled in again. I can let you have a few DCs if you need the help. There's a new DS, Ballantine, she's very capable. Now that Calvin's abandoned us, she might make a good starting point for a team.'

Detective Sergeant Calvin had been Flanagan's assistant on her Major Investigation Team. He'd suffered a shoulder wound before she had taken leave for her surgery, and that had been enough for him. The Police Federation had helped him push for a medical pension, and then he was off.

'I don't imagine she'll want to start off pushing paper around for you,' Purdy said, 'but we all have to do it sometimes.'

Flanagan felt a growing weight inside. A file full of busywork and drudgery, sweeping up someone else's mess.

Purdy saw the disappointment on her. 'Come on,' he said. 'You've been out of action for weeks. You can't expect just to land back here and dive into a hot case. It'll be a month or more until you've got a proper team established again. I can't have you twiddling your thumbs for all that time.'

She waved at the file. 'I know, but this . . . '

Purdy gave her his sternest look, usually reserved for the lower ranks. 'It's not exciting work, I know, but there are victims in those pages that still need someone to speak for them.'

'Of course,' Flanagan said, feeling like an admonished child. 'You're right. I'll get working.'

Purdy nodded and said, 'I'll leave you to it.' He stopped at the door. 'Oh, I meant to say. You heard about the Devine boy?'

'That he's due for release, yes.'

'Wednesday,' Purdy said.

'That soon?'

'I'm not supposed to know that. They're keeping it quiet to stop the press going after him. A call came in last week from the probation officer who's been assigned to him. She wants a word with you. I told her to come by today, late morning. All right?'

She remembered Ciaran Devine, a child then, a young man now. A little over seven years ago, the first awkward signs of puberty about him, sitting across the table from her in an interview

13

room. She was the only one he talked to. He called her by her first name. Even when he confessed, she struggled to picture this small boy doing that terrible thing.

She had voiced her doubts, but the boy had confessed, and that was enough.

Ciaran had sent her a letter after his and his brother's convictions. It came via the station. She had blushed when she read it. It still lay at the back of a drawer in her bedroom at home, even though she should have destroyed it.

'All right,' Flanagan said.

'Good. Here's hoping he stays out of trouble.'

As Purdy left the room, closing the door behind him, Flanagan pictured Ciaran Devine's thin fingers, the tiny cuts on his skin. She pushed the image from her mind and opened the folder in front of her.

⋆   ⋆   ⋆

Flanagan met Paula Cunningham in the reception area at twenty-five minutes past eleven. A little less than average height, slim build but not skinny, perhaps a decade younger than Flanagan. Businesslike in her manner.

Stop it, Flanagan told herself. Every new person she met was subject to the same kind of snap judgements, as if they were a suspect in some investigation only she knew about.

She gave Cunningham's ID a cursory glance, nodded, extended her hand. They shook.

'Thank you for seeing me,' Cunningham said. 'I know you've just returned to work. I'm sure

14

you've a lot to catch up on.'

'Surprisingly little,' Flanagan said. 'My office okay?'

'Absolutely.'

They did not speak as Flanagan led Cunningham beyond the locked doors and up to her room. Cunningham took a seat. Flanagan sat opposite.

Cunningham looked up at the window over Flanagan's shoulder. 'Doesn't it get claustrophobic in here? So little light.'

'You get used to it,' Flanagan said. 'So you wanted a chat.'

'Yes,' Cunningham said, pulling a notebook and pen from her bag. 'About Ciaran Devine.'

Moleskine notebook. Parker pen. Good quality, but not flashy. Functional. Plain shoes with a small heel. Not much jewellery, minimal make-up.

Stop it, Flanagan told herself again.

'What do you want to know?' Flanagan asked.

Cunningham opened the notebook, readied her pen. 'I understand you conducted most of the interviews with Ciaran.'

'That's right. You should be able to access the transcripts that were submitted by the prosecution.'

'Yes, I have them. But I wanted your impressions of him. What did you feel about him?'

Flanagan looked away, hoped her discomfort didn't show. She examined the back of her left hand. Her wedding and engagement rings. The small scar from when, as a child, she'd tried to crawl beneath barbed wire into the field behind her grandfather's house to see the pony with the sagging belly and matted coat.

'Well, my first impression,' Flanagan said. 'My first impression was the blood on the wall.'

Purdy, a DCI then, led her through the house. A detective sergeant for almost five years, Flanagan had seen many murder scenes. The ugliness of the act, the indignity of it. And the intrusion of strangers into the victim's home, his or her life laid bare in all its banality and oddness. Evidence of personal habits that would shame the victim if he were alive to know they had been discovered. Slovenliness, loneliness, addiction. Sudden and violent death rarely visited those with stable lives, with loving families, with purpose to their days. More often than not, murder happened on drunken nights between friends brought together by their mutual dependencies, petty arguments exploding into bloodshed, kitchen knives buried in throats, heads cracked open by heavy objects. No planning, no intent, only rage unleashed.

But this was different. Purdy had told her about it on the drive over. A prosperous middle-aged couple on a good street on the outskirts of the city, one son of their own, fostering dozens of less fortunate children over the years. Now two of them had apparently turned on David Rolston.

They pulled up outside the house, saw the two marked cars blocking the road. Through the tinted glass, Flanagan saw them, a boy in the rear of each car, waiting to be brought to the Serious Crime Suite in Antrim station by the officers who had arrested them. An hour ago, they had been children. Now they were killers, their lives burned away by one terrible act.

In a downstairs sitting room, Purdy and Flanagan met the two uniformed officers who'd found the body, and the boys just feet from it. Good furniture in the sitting room, a three-piece suite, well used but fine quality. A large flat-screen television, well-stocked bookcases, tasteful ornaments on the mantelpiece. Over the fireplace, a large landscape painting in oil. Somewhere along the north coast, Flanagan guessed, a local artist. Probably at least fifteen hundred pounds. Photographs here and there. A handsome couple, their one son smiling with them. Decent people, people of substance. Flanagan took it all in within seconds, building an image of the lives destroyed, and felt a small and aching mourning for them.

The uniformed policemen looked grey like ghosts, the younger of them struggling to contain his emotions.

'From the start,' Purdy said, 'just as it happened.'

The older officer spoke. 'We got here a few minutes after the call. We found the neighbour on the doorstep, the one who'd dialled 999. He said he'd heard a commotion, a lot of shouting and banging, then it had all gone quiet and no one was answering the door. We tried knocking too, but no response. We were able to force a window and get in through the kitchen. The neighbour had told us the noise seemed to come from upstairs, so we went straight up there. We found the body in the master bedroom, and the two boys lying on the bed. I checked for signs of life, not that there was much point.'

Flanagan saw the reddish-brown beneath his fingernails, in the creases of his knuckles.

'Then we took the two boys into custody and called for the second car.'

The younger cop lost his grip on himself as his colleague spoke. He sniffed and rubbed his hand across his eyes.

'Your first killing?' Purdy asked.

The young cop nodded and wiped at his cheeks.

'Cry all you want. I'd be more worried if it didn't get to you.' Purdy turned to Flanagan. 'Let's take a look.'

As they left the room, the older cop called after them. 'It's bad. Just so you know.'

Purdy and Flanagan exchanged a glance, then made their way up the stairs, Purdy leading. More paintings on the walls, smaller than the one in the living room, but probably valuable nonetheless. And photographs. Flanagan looked at David Rolston's face in each as she passed, him and his loving family ageing frame by frame, knowing the life she observed had ceased to exist.

Purdy entered the bedroom first, stopped, breathed in and out once, a long sigh of an exhalation. Flanagan imagined him expelling a little of his soul, a piece of him for ever lost.

19

She had prepared herself for the smell. Always the same. But she could never have been ready for the devastation she saw when she looked into the room.

One side appeared normal. The neat conservatism of any middle-class couple, the decor clearly chosen by the wife. Tasteful floral wallpaper. More good quality furniture and fittings. One antique dressing table, probably an heirloom.

But the other side of the room, beneath and around the window. Walls slashed and smeared by madness and hate. Red arcs across the wallpaper. Spattered on the window, drops too fine to be visible from outside.

There, where he'd retreated into the corner, what remained of David Rolston. One arm hooked up and over his head at an unnatural angle making him look like a rag doll that had been thrown in a childish rage. Skull fragments. Flaps of skin, strands of hair. One eye gone, the other open and dull.

On the stained carpet, between his splayed legs, a cast iron bookend in the shape of a cat. Its pair remained on the dresser beside the body, books spilling onto the floor.

'Dear Christ,' Purdy said. 'Children did this. Children.'

Flanagan's hand went to her stomach, an instinctive motion. She had not yet told anyone other than her husband that she was pregnant. She said a silent prayer that this horror would not seep through her flesh and touch the growing life within.

Flanagan first met Ciaran Devine in his cell at Antrim Serious Crime Suite. The doctor had finished his examination, passed her in the corridor. A custody officer held the cell door open for her. Ciaran was sitting on the bench that served as a bed when she entered.

So small.

He looked up at her, startlement in his eyes. He had not expected a woman, she realised. His blood-soaked clothes had been removed, replaced by standard issue dark navy sweatshirt and joggers. Too big for his skinny frame, they sagged on him, the cuffs draping over his hands, revealing only his fingers. Slip-on plimsolls like Flanagan had worn as a child at school gym classes. Blond hair cut close to his scalp.

The custody sergeant had told Flanagan about the bruises, both fresh and fading, on Ciaran's arms. Some of them like teeth marks. Self-harm, the custody sergeant had said. The boy had a history of it. Young for that, the sergeant observed. Flanagan told him biting was the most common form of self-harm amongst younger children. The custody sergeant had shrugged and said, young for killing people too.

Ciaran's hands shook. Tears ready to come at any moment. He had been as calm as could be expected so far, the custody sergeant had told her, even when he was booked in. But Flanagan could tell the boy's composure was a thin veil that might slip or be torn away in an instant. The staff in the custody suite had a nervous resolve about their work. They hated to have children locked up. So many dangers, so much to go wrong.

Flanagan took a breath, reminded herself once more that Ciaran was a child undergoing an experience more terrifying than most adults would ever have to endure. She gave him a shallow smile and spoke with the friendly but firm voice she had practised and refined over many hours.

'Ciaran, I'm Detective Sergeant Serena Flanagan. I'll be interviewing you in a little while, once your social worker gets here. Right now, I have to take a DNA sample.'

She showed him the clear plastic tube in her hand, the cotton swab inside.

'Is that all right?' she asked.

He blinked, and a tear rolled down his cheek. 'Where's Thomas?' he asked.

Not even a whisper, barely a croak in his throat.

'Thomas is in another block, in a cell like this one.'

'Can I see him?'

Flanagan shook her head. 'No, I'm sorry, you can't.'

Ciaran's control began to break. His hands danced in his lap, fingers grabbing at air, at cloth, at skin. His shoulders rose and fell as his breathing quickened. Panic creeping in, taking over. Panic blots out reason, lashes out, causes harm. It must be held at bay.

Flanagan crossed the cell to him, hunkered down so her eyes were level with his.

'Ciaran, listen to me. I know you're frightened, but I need you to try to stay calm. I know this is a scary place, but you're safe here. You're going to be all right, I promise. I'll make sure of it.'

'I want Thomas,' he said, his voice a despairing whine.

'You can't see him, I'm sorry.'

He brought his hands to his face, bent over, curling in on himself. Weeping like the lost child he was. Even though she knew he had been involved in the most brutal violence, even though the blood still dried on his palms, Flanagan felt a piercing sorrow for this boy.

She did the only sane and reasonable thing she could imagine: she dropped the plastic tube and put her arms around Ciaran, gathered him in close to her. Rocked him as his tears soaked through her jacket.

Dear God and Jesus help him, she thought.

★ ★ ★

An hour later, in a cold interview room, Flanagan sat opposite Ciaran and a social worker. Michael Garvey wasn't the brothers' case worker; rather he had the misfortune to be on call for out of hours duty. Flanagan had sat at an interview table with him many times before, but never for anything like this. Garvey looked pale and uneasy. She couldn't blame him.

Flanagan composed herself and arranged her notes on the table. No sooner had she released the boy from her embrace than she regretted the impropriety of it. She instructed herself to firm up, remember the victim, not to let her empathy cloud her judgement. This interview was the First Account. No time to be distracted.

She studied the boy for a moment. Ciaran Devine, only twelve years old. Father killed in a hit-and-run by a joyrider just yards from the family home when Ciaran was four years old. His mother had died five years ago from heart failure caused by endocarditis, not uncommon among heroin users. She'd lost custody of her boys eighteen months before that, mental health issues compounded by drug and alcohol abuse. The brothers had been shunted around the care system ever since, had nobody but each other.

A shitty start to life, Flanagan thought, but no excuse.

She and the social worker went through the ritual of opening sealed cases, examining blank CDRs, before she inserted them into the audio recorder. She cautioned the boy, and Garvey double-checked that he understood.

Then Flanagan began.

'Ciaran, do you understand where you are?'

'Yeah,' he said, the word no more than an expulsion of air.

'The detained person has replied in the affirmative,' Flanagan said. 'Try to speak up, Ciaran, so the microphone can hear you. It's important. So where are you?'

'The police station.'

'Yes. The Serious Crime Suite at Antrim Police Station. How old are you?'

'Twelve,' he said.

'And what is your brother's name?'

Ciaran hesitated. He knew she was aware of the answer. But he couldn't know about cognitive interviewing, the information funnel, the art of beginning with vague, open questions, narrowing down over time to the hard root of truth.

'Your brother's name, Ciaran,' she said.

'Thomas.'

'How old is he?'

'Fourteen,' Ciaran said. 'He'll be fifteen in May. He didn't do it. It was me.'

Flanagan inhaled. Garvey put his hand on Ciaran's thin arm.

She gave the boy a smile she intended to be reassuring, but it felt tight on her lips. 'We'll come to what happened to Mr Rolston in a while. Right now, we need to — '

'Thomas didn't have anything to do with it,' Ciaran said, his voice rising. 'It was me on my own.'

Flanagan looked to Garvey. He stared back at her, his eyes wide. He turned to the boy and said, 'Ciaran, you're entitled to have a lawyer here. Do you want me to get one for you?'

Ciaran did not react to the words, as if they were spoken to some other boy in some other room.

Flanagan leaned forward. 'Ciaran, I want you to think very carefully about what you've just said. It's very important that you tell the truth. Even if what you said is true, Thomas was still there with you when it happened. He'll still be in trouble for it. You won't spare him anything by lying about it.'

'He was there in the room,' Ciaran said, staring at his hands. 'But he didn't do it. It was all me.'

'Ciaran, I saw the blood on Thomas's clothes. He was as covered in it as you were. You'll not convince anyone he wasn't at least alongside you when it happened. But now's not the time to — '

Ciaran looked up at her, and she noticed for the first time how blue his eyes were. 'I'm not lying,' he said. 'He tried to stop me. But I didn't want to stop. He didn't do it. It was me on my own.'

'The time is eleven minutes past six,' Flanagan said. 'I'm suspending the interview now.'

She reached for the audio recorder, hit the stop button. She left Ciaran alone with the social worker, headed out into the corridor and found Purdy leaving the room where he had been watching a video feed of both the boys' interviews.

'What did Thomas say?' Flanagan asked.

But she already knew the answer to that question.

3

Cunningham walked across the open ground towards Phil Lewis. Lewis waited with his hands in the pockets of his corduroy trousers. He wore a shirt and tie beneath a V-neck sweater. He looked like he worked in just about any public sector job, that smart but slightly frayed look all but the highest paid civil servants tended to have.

Except for the heavy bunch of keys chained to his belt.

Buildings clustered around them, flat roofs, high walls and fences, enclosed yards. Behind the main complex stood a trio of greenhouses set in their own gardens.

Young men looked up from their digging and planting to watch her. Some looked closer than others, let their gaze linger beyond casual glances. Many of the boys were unnaturally bulky; a fervent gym culture thrived among the inmates, passing their hours of tedium lifting weights. A dangerous combination: the petulant immaturity of young offenders and the physical strength of grown men. Cunningham ignored the burning sensation their attention left on the skin beneath her clothing. She tightened her grip on the folder under her arm, the ever-present cigarette craving drying the back of her throat.

Lewis extended his hand as she approached. His fingers were soft and cool on hers. He didn't look at the visitor's tag she wore clipped to her jacket. They had met many times before.

'He's in the Offender Management Unit,' Lewis said.

She followed him towards the blue two-storey prefab building.

'How is he?' she asked.

'Quiet,' Lewis said. 'He's always quiet. He's a decent enough young fella, considering.'

Considering.

Jesus, Cunningham thought. Considering he'd killed a human being.

'Is he using?' she asked.

'No, not that we know of. Thomas, his brother, kept him out of the way of all that. Kept him clean.'

'Not even cannabis?' She couldn't mask the surprise in her voice. Lock up a young man for hours upon days upon weeks, pen him in with dozens of other boys, all as bored as him. There were only so many ways to pass the time.

'Not even a bit of blow,' Lewis said. 'There was a worry he might start once Thomas left us, but he didn't. Or if he did, he kept it well hidden.'

'When did he last see his brother?'

Lewis paused at the door, pursed his lips as he thought.

'Maybe a fortnight ago. He was getting fidgety 'cause he hadn't seen Thomas for a few weeks. They had an hour together, and Ciaran settled down after that. He always does. You'll want to make sure they see each other as soon as possible. Thomas always seems to put Ciaran back on track. You ready?'

Lewis hit four digits on the keypad. The red light turned to green. He pushed the door inward, held it for her, followed her inside.

The corridor's low ceiling made it feel like a tunnel, the fluorescent lighting bleaching the life from everything it touched.

'This way,' Lewis said.

He led her to another door, another keypad.

A rectangular window set into the wood, segmented by wire mesh. Two figures at a table, one broad and round-shouldered, the other thin like a blade. Both sat with their hands folded on the wood. Neither spoke.

The larger man looked up when Lewis knocked the glass. Cunningham recognised him as Joel Gilpin, a senior prison officer who'd worked the Maze and Maghaberry before coming to the Young Offenders Centre.

Lewis tapped in the same four digits and entered the room. Cunningham followed and closed the door behind her, stayed there as Lewis approached the table. The lock whirred and clicked as it sealed them in.

Lewis placed the fingertips of one hand on the table, some clandestine signal that the life of the young man in front of him had now changed. 'Ciaran, this is Paula Cunningham, your probation officer.'

The young man looked up from the tabletop. His eyes met hers for no more than a moment. Long enough to send a crackle from the back of her skull to the base of her spine. She shivered as she exhaled.

'Hello, Ciaran.'

The tip of his tongue appeared from between his lips, wet them, retreated.

'Hello,' he said in a voice so small Cunningham couldn't be sure if she'd heard it at all.

He wore a T-shirt with some meaningless logo splashed across the chest, cheap jeans and a light hooded cardigan. The kind of clothes you'd buy in a supermarket or a chain store, with made-up brand names that any teenager would refuse to wear. A holdall lay in the corner.

'Do you mind if I sit down?' she asked.

His narrow shoulders rose and fell in a timid shrug. He brought his thumb to his mouth, teeth working the nail. Cunningham noted the stubs of keratin at the tip of each finger, the red raw skin.

Lewis remained standing, his back against the wall, while she took the seat opposite and placed the file on the table. She sat still, let the silence thicken, waiting for him to glance up at her once more.

When he did, she asked, 'Has everything been explained to you? About what's going to happen?'

Ciaran nodded.

'Good,' she said, offering a firm smile when he gave her another fleeting look. 'As soon as I've signed the forms, I'll take you to my car, and I'll drive you to the hostel. Okay?'

Ciaran nodded.

'I'm told you've had two stays in the hostel.'

She waited, listened to him breathe.

'Ciaran, I said you've had two stays in the

hostel. Is that right?'

He shifted in his seat, understood she expected a response. He nodded.

'How did you like it?'

'S'okay,' he said.

'Good. So you've met Tom Wheatley, the manager there. You know their rules. What they expect of you.'

'Yeah,' he said.

'Good. Shall we go?'

4

Ciaran wants to walk behind her, to follow, but she won't allow it. When he slows his pace, she does too. Mr Lewis and Mr Gilpin stay back, their footsteps echoing on the shiny floors. Ciaran feels them there, like shadows trailing from his heels.

Once the probation woman has given her visitor's card back to the front desk, once they're outside in the cool air, once Mr Lewis and Mr Gilpin have been left behind, she stops walking.

Ciaran stops too, shifting the bag's weight on his shoulder. He can't look at her as she turns to him. He turns his head away, shy, wishing Thomas was here to tell him how to be.

Thomas always knows how to be. What to say. What to do.

'Ciaran,' she says, 'I'm not going to lead you to my car. You are going to walk with me to my car. Beside me. All right?'

Ciaran's stomach feels weird, like wriggly worms are eating him from inside. He looks back to the door he's only just walked through. He wants to go back to where he knows how things work. But he can't.

He feels all shaky frightened. Thomas would tell him to grow up, not to be a scaredy-cat, a cowardy-custard.

Thomas isn't scared of anything. But Thomas isn't here to keep the scared away.

'All right?' the woman asks.

Ciaran swallows, feels the pressure like little balloons in his ears, thinks of later on. Thinks of his brother. 'All right,' he says.

She nods. 'Come on, then.'

She walks. He keeps pace with her, his gaze on the tarmac as they cross the car park. From the corner of his eye, he studies her. She isn't tall, but she walks as if she is. She walks like she practises it, like how she walks matters a lot.

The breeze is strange on his skin. And the light. Ciaran can feel the light, as if he could split apart the colours, his skin knowing one from another. He is outside in the world, and he doesn't know how to feel.

They approach a small car. The badge says Nissan. He can't tell which model. He doesn't know anything about cars. Thomas does. Thomas likes cars. Thomas has bought one. He told Ciaran two weeks ago. He promised to take Ciaran for a spin.

'To the seaside?' Ciaran had asked, hope bursting in him.

'Maybe,' Thomas had said, and Ciaran had gone all dizzy and floaty behind his eyes.

The probation woman digs in her handbag, cursing under her breath, until she finds a key. She presses a button. The car makes a mechanical clunk. She opens the boot, and he drops his bag inside.

'Get in,' she says, pointing to the passenger door.

Ciaran does as he's told. He almost always does. He's a good lad. All the guards say so. The dashboard presses against his knees. The car smells clean, but litter has been stuffed into the pockets and cubbyholes.

The woman lowers herself into the driver's seat.

An important question occurs to Ciaran. 'What do I call you?' he asks.

'My name,' she says. 'Paula.'

'All right.'

She starts the engine, and the radio shouts all blaring loud before she reaches for the volume control.

Ciaran looks out of the passenger window, back towards the buildings he has left for the last time. He supposes he should feel something more, something big, as they drive away. Happiness, excitement, anything. But he doesn't. Even as the car cuts along the tree-lined driveway towards the main gates, and all he can see is wood and the leaves going brown and yellow and orange, even then he feels nothing.

The gate to the main road comes into view.

And the men with cameras.

Paula says, 'Shit.'

She slows the car to a stop.

Ciaran winds his fingers together in his lap. He sees the men gathering on the other side of the gateway, huddled in groups, chatting. Some of them smoking cigarettes. He remembers seeing men like them years ago, through the windows of the police van.

They notice the car. Just a few at first, but soon they're all crowding towards the opening, pushing and shoving. Ciaran thinks of piglets fighting over their mother's teats. He wants to laugh, but he holds it in.

'It was supposed to be kept quiet,' Paula says. 'Someone must have tipped them off. They weren't here when I came in. You can cover your face if you want. Maybe put your hood up.'

He raises the cardigan's hood and drops his gaze to his hands.

The car moves off. The men swarm as it pauses in the gateway. Camera lenses clatter on the glass. Lightning fills the car. Ciaran gathers the fabric of the hood around his face, the flash-flash-flashing cutting through the weave.

Paula sounds the horn, inches the car forward, curses the photographers.

One of the men shouts Ciaran's name. Asks if he has anything to say to the family of David Rolston.

That laugh is still pushing to escape him, making his lips all stretchy, swelling up inside his chest. He pinches the hood together to cover his mouth.

The car lurches forward onto the road. Paula accelerates hard, jerks the steering wheel, straightens their course.

'I'm sorry about that,' she says.

Ciaran says nothing. He fears if he opens his mouth the laughter will spill out of him, and she will think bad things about him. When the urge dissolves in his throat, he pulls the hood back and watches the road ahead.

Within a few minutes, they have passed through the avenues and crescents of semi-detached houses that Mr Lewis had called the

Four Winds. That name put a picture in Ciaran's head, of walls of air rushing through the streets, going north, south, east and west. It made this cluster of houses sound like somewhere strange and far away when really they were just ordinary homes for ordinary people. That had been a month ago, the last time Ciaran had been allowed to stay a night at the hostel. Mr Lewis had told him he could take a walk to the shops nearby if he wanted. Ciaran hadn't dared.

The car halts at the junction with the big road with all its lanes of rush-rush noisy traffic. Ciaran looks up at the signs to see what the big road is called. He's not sure he understands what they say. They say A55 and Outer Ring. Which is it? Both? He doesn't like this junction, the cars coming from every direction, moving like bullets. A lorry rumbles past, and Ciaran feels the force of it through the soles of his shoes, through the carpet, and the car's metalwork. He feels the displaced air rock the Nissan on its wheels. He wonders what it would feel like if the lorry hit them. The bang, the impact, the glass flying, he and Paula shaken inside the car like those dotty-red crawly ladybirds he'd trapped in a jar when he was little. Thomas had taken them from him, had shaken them hard to see if they would die.

He swallows and closes his eyes.

The car moves, the engine note rising in pitch.

When Ciaran opens his eyes again, they have crossed the junction. The big shopping centre passes on their right, the hostel on the corner to their left.

36

'After we get you checked in,' Paula says, 'we'll take a walk over. You can buy some things.'

'What things?'

She shrugs as she flicks the indicator on to turn left. 'I don't know. What do you need?'

Ciaran thinks about it as they round the corner and she pulls the car up to the gate.

Two photographers point cameras from the footpath. They approach the car. Another man watches from across the road, a notepad and pen in his hands. The gate opens, and Paula drives through. She watches the men in her rear-view mirror.

Ciaran struggles to find a want for anything at all. But he will try very hard to think of something.

★　★　★

He places his bag on the single bed. The room is white and shiny clean, apart from the smears of grey above the heater and the little blue patches on the walls where someone had put up posters with that sticky stuff that isn't Plasticine and taken them down again.

'What do you think?' Paula asks. 'Will it do?'

She leans against the door frame, her arms folded across her chest.

'It's not the room I stayed in before,' he says.

'Probably someone else is in it. Is that a problem?'

Ciaran considers. He liked the room he had before. It was an odd shape. But this one will do. He says no, it isn't a problem.

'So you know the rules,' Paula says. 'Back here by nine every night. No alcohol. No drugs. They can search the room at any time. No visitors.'

No visitors? He feels those worms in his stomach again, wriggling, chewing on his insides. 'What about my brother?' he asks.

'You can see him whenever you like,' she says. 'But not here.'

'Can I call him? Can I see him today?'

'Whenever you like. You can call him from the payphone downstairs. But why don't we take a walk first? We can go shopping.'

Ciaran looks towards the window. He sees the blocky buildings of the shopping centre across the road, the cars streaming in and out.

'What about those men? The photographers?'

'They've got what they wanted. They'll be gone by now.'

'But I don't need to buy anything.'

Paula smiles. She has very clean teeth. 'A cup of tea, then. There's a café at the Marks & Spencer's. You could get a sandwich if you're hungry. Did you have any lunch?'

His stomach growls, the worms chased away by her words.

5

Flanagan expected DCI Thompson to be hostile. Instead, he appeared defeated.

She and DS Ballantine travelled to Ladas Drive station in east Belfast and found Thompson waiting in the canteen, nursing a cup of tea in the furthest corner, well away from eavesdroppers. Flanagan fetched a coffee from the counter and placed it on the table alongside the file full of Thompson's unfinished business. Ballantine declined a cup.

DS Ballantine was a tall woman, Flanagan guessed late twenties, blonde hair, with an athletic build. Earnest and eager as Flanagan had been in her younger days, and just as full of ambition. She'd been told to take notes and keep her mouth shut, and had her pen ready as soon as she sat down.

'I'm not out of here for a month yet,' Thompson said, 'and they've put me out of my office already. I'm having to share a desk with a bloody media officer. How the hell they think I'm going to be any good to anybody sitting there, I don't know.'

Flanagan offered him as cheery a smile as she could muster. 'Well, you've got your retirement to look forward to.'

A little more colour drained from Thompson's grey face and his eyes grew distant.

'Have you anything planned?' she asked.

39

'Mostly staying out of the wife's way,' he said. 'Apart from that, a big long stretch of nothing. What are you, forty, forty-two?'

Flanagan cleared her throat, smiled, and said, 'That's a personal question. But I'll be forty-six in a couple of months.'

'How far into your contract are you?'

'Almost eighteen years. But I'm not really counting.'

'So you've got twelve years still to serve,' Thompson said. 'Like a prison term, isn't it? A fucking life sentence. Murderers get less, for Christ's sake. No chance of an early release for us unless you get shot or get your bloody legs blown off in some booby trap. And what about you?'

Ballantine seemed startled that a question had been sent in her direction. She blinked and looked to Flanagan.

'What, you need permission to answer a question?' Thompson asked. 'So DCI Flanagan's as hard as they say?'

'I'm five years in,' Ballantine said.

'I see. Still fresh, then. Don't worry, you'll have the shit kicked out of you soon enough.'

Ballantine turned her gaze down to the blank page of her notebook, her face taking on a faint red glow of embarrassment.

Thompson turned his attention back to Flanagan. 'You were on the Devine brothers case, weren't you?'

'That's right,' Flanagan said.

'I hear he's up for release. Makes you wonder why you bother, doesn't it? Wee bastard like that,

40

hardly inside long enough to get his coat off, and now they're turning him loose. If it was up to me, scum like him and his brother would never see the light of day again.'

Flanagan did her best to keep a friendly tone. 'Well, the courts have to keep emotion out of — '

'We had a dog one time, a wee mutt, as pleasant a thing as you ever met. Then one day it bit our youngest on the face. He was lucky, he could've lost an eye, but he wound up with just a bit of a scar on his cheek. Anyway, the night it happened, I took that dog, and I put it in the boot of my car along with a towel soaked in chloroform. Came back the next morning, it was dead. You think that was cruel?'

Flanagan swallowed. 'It's not for me to — '

'Yes, it was cruel,' Thompson said. 'But that dog never bit anyone again.'

Flanagan cleared her throat and asked, 'Shall we crack on?' She took her notebook from her bag, opened it to the list of questions she'd drawn up, hoping she could use them to sweep up the mess Thompson was leaving behind. Now she focused on the page to avoid looking at him.

'Can we start with the Milligan assault?' She opened the file to the first photocopied A4 sheet. 'That was, what, nine months ago? Now, I've got a list of interviewed witnesses — all male — who were at the bar that night. Seventeen in total. Sixteen of them said they were in the toilets when the assault happened, and they saw nothing. The seventeenth, the barman, said he was in a stockroom. And it just so happened the CCTV was switched off that night.'

Thompson's shoulders slumped. 'That's right. So?'

'Well, there's a floor plan of the bar in here. I believe the toilet is about ten feet by five, it has two urinals, one cubicle and a washbasin. You accepted the account of sixteen men who said they were all in there at the same time.'

'You know where that bar is?' Thompson asked.

'Yes.'

'Then you know what kind of street it's on, the kind of area it's in. I could walk up and down that street bare-bollock naked with my arse painted red and my hair on fire, and no one would see a bloody thing.' Thompson smiled at his own imagery. 'What, you think those witnesses would've suddenly remembered who put that poor bastard in intensive care if I'd just asked them a bit nicer?'

'No, but I've questioned as many uncooperative witnesses as you have. There are ways and means, pressures to apply. I'd like to be sure you explored every possible avenue.'

Thompson's smile dropped away, his eyes darkened. 'Just who the fuck do you think you are?'

Flanagan opened her mouth to speak, but he slapped the table, rattling cups and cutlery. Ballantine flinched.

'Who do you think you are, talking to me like that?' Thompson said. 'Accusing me.'

'I'm not accusing you of any — '

He stood, his chair sliding into the wall with a clatter. People all around looked up from their sandwiches and drinks.

'Thirty years,' he said, his voice rising, his finger wagging at her. 'Thirty fucking years I gave this bloody service. Now they're done with me, they're going to throw me away like a shitty rag. And now, here's you.'

Flanagan placed her hands flat on the table, adopted as soothing a tone as she could manage. 'Please, why don't you just sit down and we can — '

'Who are you? Tell me that. Who the fuck are you to come here and accuse me of not doing my job?' His hands shook. His eyes red and watery. 'I think of everything I gave up for this. All the abuse I got on the streets. All those mornings I crawled on my hands and knees in the frost and the rain, looking under my car to see if some bastard had put a bomb there. What for? You tell me, what for?'

Flanagan glanced around the room. Saw the other police officers look away. Ballantine stared at her notebook, her pen's nib frozen half an inch from the paper.

'Eighteen years, you said. If eighteen years isn't enough to suck the will out of you, try thirty. See how you feel then. Tell me if you think it was worth it once your whole bloody life's been wasted.'

Thompson stood by the table, breathing hard, his hands opening and closing. Flanagan held his hateful stare, refused to look away. She watched his anger burn out, leaving a shell of a man in front of her.

'Christ,' he said, his gaze flicking around the

silent room, the florid colour washing away from his sagging cheeks. 'Jesus Christ.'

He wiped the back of his hand across his eyes, his palm across his mouth.

'I'm sorry,' he said, the words choking in his throat. He walked away.

Flanagan closed the file and put her notebook back in her bag as murmurs rippled around the canteen. Ballantine stowed away her notebook and pen, got to her feet.

'Where are you going?' Flanagan asked. 'I haven't finished my coffee.'

She lifted her cup, took a sip. She would not leave until the last drop was gone, no matter how hard they stared.

6

The photographers have left. No one pays any attention as Ciaran and Paula use the pedestrian crossing. She presses the button at the first section, the word WAIT lighting up until the shrill beep-beep-beeping and the green man tells them to go. At the second set, she keeps her hands by her sides.

After a while, she says, 'You'd better do the needful or we'll be here all day.'

For a moment, Ciaran wonders what she means, but then he understands. He reaches across and puts his finger on the white plastic button. He feels the gouges in the otherwise smooth plastic, and something gritty and sticky. He wipes the tip of his finger on his jeans.

They cross the final section and walk around the building. Through the windows Ciaran sees the Sainsbury's supermarket, all shiny bright oranges and whites. The worms return to his stomach, nagging and itching with worry.

The high ceiling, the aisles that stretch away as far as he can see. Such a big place, so few walls and doors.

He takes a breath, holds it in his chest as Paula guides him through into the main building. The noise comes all jangly rushing from the entrance to the supermarket. Voices and machines, electronic screeching beep-beep-beep, children shouting mummy-I-want-I-want-I-want.

And the people. So many faces, and Ciaran knows none of them. They stream in and out of the shops, push and shove and bustle, counting money out of their pockets and purses, clutching bags, talking and laughing, voices hard and scratchy in his ears.

He stops walking. Hard panicky breath, in-out-in-out-in-out until his head goes light. Paula carries on a few steps before noticing.

'What's up?' she asks.

He tries to keep his words free of the shaky in his throat. 'Can we go back to the hostel?'

'Why?'

'Just. I want to go back.'

'The café's only down here,' she says. 'We'll be there in a minute and you can get a cup of tea.'

He takes a step back, his thighs quivery with fear. 'I don't want a cup of tea.'

She takes a step forward. 'A Coke, then. What about a sandwich?'

He shakes his head. 'I don't want anything.'

She smiles, beckons, her teeth shining and sharp, her nails red. 'Give it fifteen minutes. That's all, just time for a cup of tea. Come on.'

His fingers curl. He jams his hands down deep into his pockets. 'You can't make me.'

Her smile softens, her sharp teeth hidden. 'That's right. No one can make you do anything. Anything you do, you choose to do it for yourself. No one else is responsible but you.'

Ciaran wants to scream at her, tell her she's wrong, show her she's wrong. But screaming never does any good. No one likes it when he screams. So he swallows instead. 'I want to go back. I want to call my brother.'

'Ciaran, let's — '

'I want to call my brother.'

Paula flinches and steps back. People stare. How loud had he spoken? He can feel the words burn, even after they've left his mouth. What had he shown of himself?

'Don't raise your voice to me, Ciaran,' she says.

He feels heat in his eyes, a thickening in his throat. He doesn't want to cry like a baby. Not here. Not in front of this woman. Thomas wouldn't want him to cry. Thomas would shake him and tell him he's a big boy now.

'I'm sorry,' Ciaran says. 'I didn't mean it.'

'Mean what?'

'To . . . I don't know.'

'To get angry?'

He closes his eyes, wishes all the people away. They're still there when he opens them again. 'I want to call my brother,' he says.

Paula stays quiet for a moment, then nods and walks past him. 'All right.'

Ciaran follows her, the heat spreading out from his eyes across his face.

A man lingers by the supermarket's off-licence. The same man who had been watching at the hostel, a notepad and pen in his hands. He's young, only a couple of years older than Ciaran. His face is familiar. Ciaran thinks about it as he and Paula walk back towards the road and across to the hostel. Neither of them speak on the way.

By the time they get back, Ciaran remembers who it was.

But he doesn't think about that any more because his brother is waiting in the common room for him. Thomas, his only and best big brother is waiting for him, like he always said he would.

7

Cunningham waited on the threshold of the lounge, watching, as Ciaran entered.

Thomas stood with his back to the wall. Three other young men sat gathered around the television, watching a cartoon, mumbling and chuckling to each other.

Ciaran stopped in the middle of the room, frozen in mid-stride, as if locked in some spell. Thomas studied him for a moment, then pushed away from the wall, as thin and graceful as Ciaran was skinny and awkward. He crossed the room and wrapped his arms around his brother.

Ciaran wept, free and unashamed sobs. He returned his brother's embrace, and Thomas squeezed tighter.

The three seated boys moved their attention away from the television, sniggering at the display of emotion.

Thomas turned his head towards them. 'What are you looking at?'

No anger in his voice, just a plain question.

The biggest of the three boys held his stare while the other two turned back to the television. 'I'm looking at you pair of homos,' he said.

Cunningham looked back over her shoulder to Tom Wheatley's open office. She waved her hand and he looked up from his paperwork. She inclined her head towards the room. Wheatley got to his feet and came to Cunningham's side.

'Look all you want,' Thomas said to the boy 'When you're not looking, that's when I'll come for you.'

The boy stood, the other two paying attention now.

'What was that?'

'You heard me. But I'll tell you again if you want.'

Wheatley stepped past Cunningham and into the room. 'All right lads, settle down,' he said, his Liverpool accent showing no sign of fading after years living in Northern Ireland. 'We don't need any drama.'

The boy stared for a few seconds more, then returned to his seat, smirking to his friends.

Wheatley came back to the doorway, nodded to Cunningham. 'Call me if you need me.'

She patted his arm as he passed.

Ciaran brought his sobbing under control. 'I have to stay here,' he said.

'Same as me when I got out,' Thomas said. 'Doesn't matter. We can still see each other every day.'

'They won't let you come to my room,' he said to Thomas. 'I can only see you down here.'

Thomas took Ciaran's face in his hands, wiped the tears with his thumbs. 'Don't worry, we've got the whole city. You can come to my place any time you want. They can't stop you. So long as you're back by nine.'

'Can we go now?'

'Yeah. We can go in my car.'

They embraced again, and Thomas said, 'It's all right. I'm here now. I'll look after you.'

Cunningham stepped inside, approached them.

Thomas looked up from his brother's shoulder, his face expressionless.

'You must be Thomas,' Cunningham said, though she knew full well.

She felt Thomas's gaze cut through her like an iced blade. Then, as if someone had thrown a switch, a polite smile broke on his face. He moved away from Ciaran's arms and extended his right hand towards her.

'I'm Paula Cunningham,' she said, 'Ciaran's probation officer.'

'Nice to meet you,' he said, giving her hand a firm but gentle shake.

As if he'd rehearsed it, she thought. She watched Ciaran from the corner of her eye. He seemed to almost melt away, absorbed by the air around him. As if someone had cut out the shape of a boy from the world, leaving only a shadow behind.

'I hear you've done well over the last couple of years,' Cunningham said. 'I think you'll be a good example for Ciaran. I'd like you to see as much of each other as you can. Phil Lewis at Hydebank told me you were good for each other.'

Thomas put a hand on Ciaran's shoulder. Ciaran sparked back into life.

'He's my brother,' Thomas said. 'He's all I've got. I'll always look out for him.'

He smiled again, his lips closed tight. Cunningham imagined him drawing a curved line beneath his nose. She pushed the thought away.

'Good,' she said. 'I'll leave you two to catch up. Remember, Ciaran, back here by nine, and I'll see you at the office tomorrow at eleven. All right?'

Ciaran nodded and looked at his feet.

Thomas nudged his elbow. 'Say thank you.'

Ciaran said, 'Thank you.'

'You're welcome,' Cunningham said as she backed towards the door.

The cold, slippery feeling would not leave her stomach as she drove home.

8

The car is red and old and smells stinky of cigarettes, but Ciaran knows Thomas doesn't smoke. Thomas guides the car through evening traffic, heading towards town. Joy bubbles inside Ciaran, but he keeps it secret. Thomas has taught him to bury his feelings deep, wrap them up tight in a bundle, not to let anyone use them to hurt him or his brother.

'What do you think of her?' Thomas asks.

Ciaran doesn't answer straight away. He's not sure of the right thing to say.

After a while, he says, 'She's all right.'

Thomas nods. 'Yeah. She seems all right. But watch her. They're all the same. Probation officers. They all want to send you back inside so you're not their problem any more. Mine wanted to send me back too, I could tell, all the questions he kept asking me. He pretended he cared about me, but he was a liar. They all are. I played along until my supervision was up and I didn't have to bother with him any more. You do the same. Do what she tells you, but don't trust her.'

Ciaran stays quiet.

'You don't want to go back inside, do you?' Thomas asks.

'No,' Ciaran says.

'If they send you back, I might not be allowed to come and visit you.'

Ciaran chews at his thumbnail.

'You don't want that, do you?'

'No,' Ciaran says.

'She'll send you back. So you have to be careful.'

'Yeah,' Ciaran says. 'I'll be careful.'

'It's like that cop you liked, what was her name?'

'I don't remember,' Ciaran says, but he does. He hopes Thomas is too busy watching the road to see the lie on him.

'Yeah, well, she was the same. They're nice to you, pretend they're your friend. But they'll turn on you. They always do. You listening?'

'Yeah,' Ciaran says.

Soon, Thomas pulls into a side street. He goes quiet as he navigates through the rows of terraced and semi-detached houses, most of them old. He halts at an ugly square block of a building, red bricks, three storeys.

'Here we are,' he says.

Ciaran gets out of the car and follows Thomas to the building's entrance. A row of buttons on a panel, numbers next to each of them. The door looks like the doors they have at Hydebank and the hostel, wire mesh embedded in glass. Thomas opens it with his key and steps inside. Vinyl tiles on the floor and stairs, cold and echoing. Like the places where Ciaran and Thomas spent almost all their lives.

Thomas climbs the stairs. Ciaran follows, four flights, up to the second floor. The door says 2C. They go inside. The first room Ciaran sees is the one where Thomas sleeps. The bed is neatly made. The walls are bare.

Thomas lies down on the bed, stretches out. He lifts his hand up to Ciaran.

Ciaran lies down, his back to Thomas. Thomas's chest presses against him, his legs behind his. Their hands join, their fingers tied together. All is silent for a while, only the sound of their breath. Not even the noise of traffic.

No boys in the corridors or rooms, no shouting, no staff barking at them.

Thomas's lips warm at Ciaran's ear. 'We'll be all right,' he says.

Ciaran closes his eyes.

'Just you and me,' Thomas says. 'Like it was before. No one else. I'm going to keep you safe. And you're going to keep me safe. Nobody's going to hurt us. All those bastards out there, they can't touch us. And if they try . . . '

The thought hangs in the air above them, unspoken.

Ciaran takes a breath, and says, 'I saw Daniel today.'

Thomas's body stiffens. 'Who?'

'Mr Rolston's son.'

Quiet for a time, then, 'Where?'

'At the shopping centre. He was watching me.'

'Did he say anything?'

'No.'

'If you see him again, you call me straight away. All right?'

'All right,' Ciaran says.

'We're safe now. Just remember that. We're safe.'

Ciaran can't hold it back any more. The tears

come, hot and thick, wetting the pillow against his cheek. Thomas holds him tighter, whispers beautiful words that glitter in Ciaran's mind like silver.

★ ★ ★

Thomas has fallen asleep. Ciaran listens to his deep, steady breathing for a time before he slips off the bed. The alarm clock says 19:35. He leaves the bedroom, explores the flat.

There is a small table in the kitchen. A laptop computer sits on it. Ciaran knows how to use a computer. He had classes when he was inside. He opens the lid, presses the power button.

The computer asks for a password.

Ciaran thinks for a moment, then enters his own name.

The computer rejects the password.

Ciaran thinks again. He tries once more, swapping the letter I for the digit 1. C-I-A-R-A-N.

The computer's desktop appears, along with its rows of icons. Ciaran finds the one for the internet browser and clicks on it. Google is the home page.

He types a name into the search field, concentrating on each letter.

Serena Flanagan.

A page of results, most of them news stories from the BBC, the *News Letter*, the *Belfast Telegraph*. He reads the headlines as best he can, remembering what he learned in Hydebank, taking his time. Some describe a big case and a

56

shooting at a shopping centre in town. He clicks on a link. There's a photograph of the place where it happened: Victoria Square. Ciaran doesn't know it. Maybe it opened after he went away.

A hand on his shoulder. Ciaran's heart leaps. He looks around and up. Thomas standing over him.

Thomas says, 'What are you doing?'

Ciaran closes the laptop. 'Just looking.'

'That woman cop,' Thomas says.

Ciaran drops his gaze to the floor. 'Yes.'

'That's all right,' Thomas says. 'Look if you want. But I need to get you back soon. Ten minutes, all right?'

He walks away, leaving Ciaran alone with the computer and the dead things that live on inside his head.

Flanagan stood behind the unattended desk in the custody suite, watching the CCTV feed from the boy's cell. She observed as he woke and dragged himself upright, looked away while he used the toilet.

Ciaran returned to the vinyl-covered pad that served as a mattress and sat with his head in his hands. Flanagan wondered at the turmoil that raged between his fingers, inside that young skull. The impossible wish to take it back, the terrible future he had made for himself.

'You'd never believe it to look at him,' a voice behind her said.

She turned to see the overnight custody sergeant, John Richie, wheeling a trolley laden with several trays of buttered toast and mugs of steaming tea. He rolled it to the desk then folded his arms, watching the screen. End-of-shift fatigue darkened his eyes.

'How's he been?' Flanagan asked.

'Quiet,' Richie said. 'Not a peep out of him. Same for the brother.' He shook his head. 'A kid like that. You'd never think he had it in him. The older one, maybe, but not him.'

'Nothing's for sure yet,' Flanagan said.

'But you have the confession.'

'True, but I'm not accepting it for now.

There's still work to do.'

'What, you think he'll change his story?'

Flanagan nodded towards the trolley. 'Do you mind if I take his breakfast to him?'

Richie pursed his lips. 'I'm supposed to bring the food.'

Flanagan gave him a smile. 'I'm just helping out, chipping in, team spirit and all that.'

Richie sighed and said. 'Yeah, all right, if you want.'

Flanagan lifted a tray from the trolley and followed Richie into the block. He stopped at the door to Ciaran's cell, opened the hatch to peer through, then slipped the key into the lock. Flanagan thanked him as he stepped aside. He closed the door over, leaving it ajar by a few inches.

Ciaran watched her enter, frozen in place, as Richie's footsteps receded along the corridor.

'Breakfast,' Flanagan said. 'You hungry?'

Ciaran did not answer.

She set the tray down next to the boy, tea lapping the rim of the mug, then sat on the far side of it.

'Don't worry,' she said, 'this isn't an interview. Nothing's being recorded. No lawyers or social workers needed. Strictly speaking, the custody officer should bring you your breakfast. I just wanted to see if you were okay.'

Ciaran sat quite still, his hands in his lap. He stared at the floor, as if to look at her might burn his eyes.

'Are you okay?' she asked.

He reached for a piece of toast, took a bite.

Flanagan kept her silence as he chewed, and when he took a sip of tea.

'It needs more milk,' he said. 'I like it milky.'

'Okay,' she said. 'I'll remember for next time. 'Did you get much sleep?'

Ciaran shrugged and took another sip. After he swallowed, he asked, 'Can I see Thomas today?'

'No, not until the investigation's complete.'

Ciaran returned the mug to the tray, pushed it back towards her.

'What's wrong?' she asked.

'Don't want it,' Ciaran said.

'All right,' she said. She lifted the tray and moved it to the floor, leaving nothing but air between them. She allowed a stretch of time to pass before she spoke again.

'Why did you kill Mr Rolston?' she asked.

Ciaran's lips tightened.

'Like I said, this isn't an interview. I'm not recording anything you say. I'm not taking notes. I just want to understand. Why did you want to hurt Mr Rolston?'

Ciaran took a breath. Flanagan tried not to tense.

'Mr Rolston did things to Thomas,' he said.

'What kind of things?' she asked.

'He came into our bedroom at night,' Ciaran said. 'After everyone was asleep. He held Thomas down. He put his hand over Thomas's mouth so he wouldn't make any noise.'

He recited the words as if reading them from a page. As if he'd practised them.

'Did you see this happen?' Flanagan asked.

60

'I heard it.'

'How often?'

'Every night, near the end. It didn't happen when we first went to live there. It was a few months before it started.'

'Did Mr Rolston ever touch you?'

'No,' Ciaran said. 'Only Thomas.'

'So you hurt Mr Rolston because of what he did to Thomas.'

Ciaran nodded.

'Will you say that on record? Later this morning, when the social worker's here, and I interview you under caution, will you say all that?'

Ciaran did not reply.

'Have a think about it.' She reached for Ciaran's hand. 'All right? Just think about it.'

His skin soft on hers. Shocking and warm. She squeezed his fingers. The bones beneath the flesh. Seconds passed before she realised he was holding his breath.

'The best thing you can do for you and your brother is tell the truth,' she said. 'Will you do that? It'll be easier for everyone. For you and Thomas. And for the Rolstons.'

Ciaran remained silent, breathing only when she released his hand. She got to her feet, the skin of her fingers cold where his had been, and looked at the watch on her wrist. 'We'll be starting in about half an hour. Think about what you want to say.'

She closed the door behind her.

Richie watched her as she passed. He nodded towards where the bank of CCTV screens was hidden on the other side of the desk.

'That boy doesn't need his hand holding,' Richie said. 'What he really needs is a good kicking.'

Flanagan did not respond as she exited the custody suite.

9

Flanagan arrived late for the support group's coffee night, but no one seemed to notice. A dozen or more women, most older than her, a few younger. All of them survivors.

The café had closed for the day, but been reopened exclusively for the group. The owner had lost an elder sister to breast cancer two years previously, and this small gesture eased the grief once a month. Coffee and tea were free of charge, and whatever cakes and pastries hadn't been sold that day were for the taking. And if they were sold out, the owner provided more, quietly, at no cost. Flanagan suspected that was the main reason some of the women still came.

For most, though, it was the camaraderie of this circle of friends. And they were friends, from all ages and backgrounds, brought together by a disease that knew no prejudice. Protestant, Catholic, or otherwise, all of the labels these women carried through their daily lives were left at the door.

Flanagan saw Penny Walker at the table in the corner, talking with a younger woman she didn't know. She checked her watch: a good ten minutes to catch up with Penny before the group discussion began. Flanagan lifted a coffee from the row of filled cups on the counter and crossed the room.

Penny saw her approach, stood and smiled,

but a glassiness to her eyes caused a cold dread in Flanagan's stomach. They embraced. The younger woman seemed to intuit that Penny and Flanagan had things to discuss. She melted away, joined the others.

'So?' Flanagan said, sitting down.

'Not good,' Penny said.

Penny Walker had been the first to befriend Flanagan after her diagnosis and surgery. A tall and slender woman of sixty-two, she had worked for the Arts Council of Northern Ireland before taking early retirement on medical grounds. She and Flanagan spoke at least once a week, often more. Had Flanagan been asked before her diagnosis if she would ever engage with a group like this, she would have said never. But now she found this gathering of women the only place she didn't feel her disease was a chain around her neck, a leash by which others held her.

'Oh no,' Flanagan said.

'It's metastasised,' Penny said. 'My liver, now, and spreading.'

Flanagan reached for her friend's hand.

'Two to three months, I'm told, maybe more with chemo.'

'Shit,' Flanagan said. 'Will you?'

'No.' Penny shook her head. 'No more treatment. It's time to let go.'

She said it with a hollow finality. Flanagan didn't argue. Penny had looked permanently exhausted since Flanagan had first met her. She had reached the point so many of the terminally ill do, where surrender is more bearable than fighting on. Flanagan had wondered many times if she would ever have that choice to make, and if she would have the courage or the wisdom to choose correctly.

She reached for Penny's cheek, touched it with her fingertips. Penny leaned her head into Flanagan's hand.

'You've been a good friend these last few months,' Penny said. 'Thank you.'

'Not at all,' Flanagan said. 'You helped me more than I helped you.'

Penny smiled. 'Well, who else would do it?'

Flanagan had met Penny's husband, Ronnie, a large dishevelled man who talked in rambling circles about books and music, the poetry of John Hewitt, the songs of Van Morrison, his visits to Belfast's Maritime Club in the sixties. A good man, but childish in his emotions, Penny had said. He'd coped poorly with his wife's illness, fretting over how he would manage without her. He had demanded that Penny teach him how to cook so that he could do it for himself in her absence, but he displayed little ability. Flanagan knew: she had once endured a lasagne he'd prepared. It had been in the Walkers' beautiful little house in Hilden, the northern part of Lisburn, near the brewery that shared its name.

'Will you tell the others?' Flanagan asked.

'This evening,' she said, 'near the end. I don't want to bring everyone down.'

Flanagan understood. Bad news for one was bad news for all. Even within the few months she had lived with cancer, two women she had come to know had died. Every one who fell reminded those still standing that they could be next. They all waited for the illness to return, every ache or pain surely a signal of another growth. Flanagan was the same. She examined herself for more lumps at least once a day, often more. The terror of a recurrence had taken root in her mind, and no amount of reassurance from doctors or soothing words from counsellors would weed it out.

'How's Ronnie taking it?' Flanagan asked.

'Not well,' Penny said. 'Since his diagnosis he's gotten more and more childish. Like he's given up on himself.'

'Diagnosis?'

Penny's shoulders fell. 'We haven't told anybody yet. It seems too much to share. He has Alzheimer's. Early stages, it only shows in the little things. He'll make himself a cup of tea and forget to drink it. Sometimes I just find him standing in a room, staring into space. God help Julie. She's going to have to care for him when I'm gone.'

Flanagan had met Penny's daughter a few times. A pleasant woman, but with a constantly serious demeanour.

'We've talked about it,' Penny said. 'When she and Barry get married, Ronnie will live with them for as long as they can cope. But it's not fair, really, is it? She should be looking after kids of her own, not being saddled with her father. But she's a good girl.'

Penny remained quiet for a few moments, her eyes glistening with memory, before she said, 'You know, I can't complain.'

Flanagan raised her eyebrows. 'Yes you can. I bloody would.'

'It's twelve years since I was first diagnosed,' Penny said. I had seven years clear before the secondary, and that's been kept at bay for five. And it's been a good twelve years. I've travelled all over. I always wanted to, but there never seemed to be the time before I got sick. Work, then Julie when she came along, and Ronnie and all his oddities. And they were all excuses. The only thing ever stopped me getting on a plane was me. Now I've seen Paris, Rome, Barcelona, New York, you name it. Most of it without Ronnie dragging at my heels, thank God. I've lived more in the last twelve years than I did in the fifty before that. I think I can settle for what I've got.'

Flanagan reached over and took Penny in her arms, prayed she would have such strength if the time ever came for her.

When they separated, Penny said, 'We're going to take this weekend away. Me and Ronnie. We'll head up to Portstewart before the students take it over. We had our honeymoon there, you know. I booked it this morning. A little cottage overlooking the Strand. We'll have some good wine and some good food. Just one last time.'

Flanagan took Penny's hands in hers. 'It might not be the last time.'

'No,' Penny said with an almost imperceptible shake of her head. 'There'll never be another.'

* * *

Alistair was in bed reading when Flanagan got home. She looked in on Eli and Ruth on the way to the bedroom. Almost nine, Ruth had fallen asleep with a scattering of books around her. Flanagan cleared them away and turned off the light beside her daughter's bed. Eli, five, a little bull of a boy, his legs hanging over the side of his bed. She gently hoisted him up and in, covered him with the duvet, then bent down to place a kiss on his cheek. He huffed, rubbed his palm across his face, and burrowed into the bedclothes.

In her own room, Flanagan removed the holster from her belt, opened the wardrobe, and placed the weapon inside the electronic safe that was bolted to the base. It whirred and clunked when she pressed the close button.

'How was the meeting?' Alistair asked, looking over his glasses as she draped her jacket over the chair by the window. He never spoke until her Glock 17 was stowed away, as if she was not his wife until she was unarmed and the evidence of her work's dangers was hidden from view.

Flanagan sat on the edge of the bed. 'Penny's got two to three months.'

'Jesus.' Alistair put his book down and stroked her shoulder.

'She's very stoical about it. More than I could ever be.'

'You don't know how you'll respond until you get there yourself. And with any luck, you never will.'

Flanagan kicked off her shoes and set about undoing her blouse. 'But it's always going to be there. Just hanging over me, waiting to drop.'

He nudged her with a knuckle. 'That sounds like self-pity. Stop it.'

'Oh, let me have a bit of a wallow.'

'Never,' he said. He leaned over and kissed her.

Flanagan exhaled, let the sorrow flow outward, deflating her body. That done, she undressed, pulled on her pyjamas, and slipped in beside her husband. Alistair picked up his book and found his place. He did not respond when she brought her body close to his. The paper rustled as he turned the page.

She rested her chin on his shoulder, her hand on his stomach, beneath his T-shirt. She splayed her fingers, felt the hairs move under and through them, his warm skin, the softness of the paunch he kept threatening to do something about.

Alistair cleared his throat and kept reading.

Flanagan brought her lips to his ear, kissed him, soft, feeling the warmth of her own breath. She kissed him again, and he turned his head to return the gesture. Lips warm, the tickle of his beard. Deeper and longer. She heard the book drop to the floor, and he turned his body towards hers.

She hooked a leg around his waist, pulled him in closer, her arm around his neck. His hips moved in reply to hers. The hardness of him pressed against her, through their nightclothes. Shy at first, then more insistent. Warmth there between them, and her hand followed, seeking him. He pulled away, but she drew him back. His hand moved from the small of her back, down, firm and eager.

Flanagan reached for his other hand, held it for a moment, her thumb kneading his palm, then brought it to her breast.

Alistair let it stay there for a time as the heat drained from him, as his body became still, his lips dry. He went to lift his fingers away, but Flanagan brought them back, tried to kiss him again. But it was too late. He had gone.

'It's past eleven,' he said. 'We've both got an early start.'

'So?' she said, keeping the anger and the hurt from her voice. 'We'll be baggy-eyed, that's all.'

He untangled himself from her and lay back on the bed. 'I'm tired, love.'

'You know, you don't have to touch me there. I can keep my top on. You can — '

She watched as Alistair blinked, his mouth moving, seeking the words to reflect his heart. He sighed as his desire to tell her the truth was defeated by his quiet nature. In the end, he said, 'I'm tired, love. Let's get some sleep.'

He rolled over, his back to her, and pulled the duvet up to his chin.

'It's just a bit of scarring,' Flanagan said, 'hardly anything at all.'

He stayed silent.

'I'm not some disfigured monster, for Christ's sake.'

She listened to his breathing for a time until he said, 'You know I don't think that.'

'Then why won't you touch me?'

'It's just . . . I'm tired, darling, that's all.'

70

He reached across to the bedside locker and flicked off the light, the darkness quieting them. Flanagan retreated to her side of the bed.

Eventually sleep outran her anger, falling on her warm and heavy. Alistair's voice, soft against her ear, woke her.

'You know I love you,' he said.

'I know,' Flanagan said. 'Same here.'

He kissed her once, leaving a cold place on her skin.

10

Daniel Rolston rewound and watched it again.

The car nudging out of the gateway, the pressmen holding their cameras to the windows, the blue-white flashes, the shouting. The woman drove, her displeasure clear on her face. In the passenger seat, Ciaran Devine, holding his hood closed over his face. Hiding. The coward.

'You can't hide from me,' Daniel said.

He felt foolish as soon as the words came out of his mouth. Foolish and weak. Talking to himself in the living room of the flat he shared with his girlfriend. They had moved in together six months ago, renting a one-bedroom in a repurposed linen mill near the city centre. The rent stretched their budget, but back then, it seemed the right thing to do.

Daniel had been angry for days. No, that wasn't true. He'd been angry for years, and afraid. But the anger had been dormant for so long he'd grown so weary of it. And then he'd seen the newspaper, and the anger blossomed anew, like a tree bursting from the ashes of a forest fire.

All he'd ever wanted was for the brothers to tell the truth. Once the grief and rage at the destruction of his family had sunk into the background of his being, the remaining wound was the lie they'd told. He would never have believed a lie could hurt so much had he not lived in its shadow for so many years.

And to think, Ciaran had been a sort of, almost, friend. Just for a little while.

Daniel watched the car drive away from the photographers.

Then, an old image of the house he grew up in. The policemen coming and going.

He lifted the remote control and hit rewind again, watched the house disappear, the car reverse through the gates. He pressed play.

The woman. She'd been with Devine at the shopping centre. Who was she? Some relative? Or some official assigned to look after him?

He watched the car pull away from the men once more, smoke from the exhaust left in its wake. His thumb found itself on the pause button, froze the image of the vehicle's tail. With his free hand, he lifted his notepad from the coffee table, compared the car's registration, even though he knew it matched.

The creak of the door startled him. He dropped the notepad onto the couch, hoped Niamh did not see.

'What are you watching?' she asked, her words blunt with sleep. 'I didn't hear you come in.'

He had no answer for her.

She sat down beside him, ran her hand across his shoulders, down his back. 'Come on to bed.'

'In a while.'

Niamh rested her head on his shoulder, the fabric of her pyjamas rubbing against the polyester of his work shirt. His tie hung loose at his collar. They sat silent for a time.

'What about now?' she asked.

'I've stuff to do,' he said. 'I haven't done the dishes yet.'

'Sure there's hardly any to do. I can — '

'I'll do them,' he said, his voice harder than he'd intended. He waited, wondering if she would return his anger, scowl at him and leave. The disappointment when she didn't surprised and shamed him.

Instead, she said, 'Go and do them now, then. Stop dwelling on this.'

Niamh pointed at the television. She knew exactly what he'd been watching, had texted to tell him it was on the news, that she had recorded it for him.

'I'm not dwelling on anything.'

'Where were you this evening?'

'Out,' he said.

'Out where?'

'I went to the cinema.'

'What to see? I might've wanted to come too.'

'You never want to see anything I want to see.'

'Maybe this would've been an exception.'

Daniel hoped she would leave it at that, but she asked, 'Did you go looking for that boy?'

He stared at the chipped surface of the coffee table, a blocky piece made from particleboard that they'd bought from Ikea.

She would not take his silence for an answer. 'Did you?'

'He's not a boy,' Daniel said, his voice crackling in his throat. 'He's a — '

'You promised me,' she said, more sorrow than anger in her tone. 'Jesus, Daniel, you promised me you wouldn't do it.'

'I just wanted to — '

'We can't go on like this. You have to stop dwelling on it.'

'I'm not dwelling on it.'

She reached for the remote control, still in the grasp of his right hand. 'Then give me that.'

He whipped it away, pushed her with his left arm, rocking her against the armrest. Niamh stared at him for long seconds, her lips pinched tight, her nostrils flaring with each breath.

'I'm sorry,' he said. 'I didn't mean to — '

'Go fuck yourself.'

She said it with no passion, her voice flat and dead. She stood and left the room, closing the door behind her, the wood whispering in the frame. He felt the draught of it on his face, carrying her faded perfume with it.

Daniel pressed the stop button and the television returned to some late night panel game, second-rate comedians cracking jokes about the week's news. He turned the volume down until they were mute, opening and closing their mouths like cattle chewing cud.

Ciaran Devine was out, like his brother two years before him. And there wasn't a thing in the world Daniel could do about it. When the Probation Board had contacted him this time, he hadn't even responded. It had done no good when Thomas Devine was up for release. He had emptied his heart to them, told them exactly what the brothers' actions had cost him, but it made no difference. They had let him go anyway.

At the time, Thomas's release hadn't been much more than a ripple on the surface of

Daniel's life. He wasn't happy about it, but what could he do? Nothing, he told himself, quite reasonably. He'd had no desire to track Thomas down, to confront him, to ask him why.

But then, weekend before last, Ciaran's photograph on the front of the newspaper. Daniel had been in the newsagent's, getting the papers when he saw the headline on one of the local weeklies.

He remembered shaking, dropping the newspapers he'd already selected. His bladder suddenly aching for release. He was a child again, that disorienting shock of the world shifting beneath his feet as his mother told him what had happened. All over again, the years between then and now compressing into nothing.

Why had Ciaran's release hit him this way, and not Thomas's? Daniel couldn't explain it to Niamh, though he did try. She had hugged and comforted him as he tried to articulate it, but his thoughts got ground up in his anger until he could make no sense of them, let alone share them with someone else.

Nine months those boys spent in his parents' house. His house. Except it was never really his house.

Something had gone wrong when Daniel was born, his mother had tried to explain it to him, something to do with her womb. He had almost died inside her. It left her unable to have more children. Whenever he tried to complain about another foster child coming to his home, to eat at his table, to share his toys, his mother reminded him that his birth meant he would have no brothers or sisters, so she wanted to care for the children that most needed it. As if their invading his family were a punishment for the ruin he'd left in her belly.

'Not every child's as lucky as you,' she would say, and she would give him that cold stare. And he would try to embrace her, and she would shrug him off and tell him not to be fussing round her, he was a big boy now.

So he would be polite and smile as another boy or girl arrived. He would help him or her carry their bags to his or her room. Show them his PlayStation, his games, the garden, how to work the TV and the DVD player.

Each newcomer would stay anything from a few weeks to a year, but only ever one at a time.

Until the brothers came.

Daniel had turned fourteen a few weeks earlier. He had more than two years on Ciaran, but only six months on Thomas. And Thomas was taller, with hard hands. It wasn't so bad when the foster kids were smaller. They would stay out of his things and out of his way. But not the bigger kids. They came from the rough areas, knew how to fight, didn't cry when they got hurt. They knew Daniel for a weakling the moment they saw him, and they knew everything that was his was now theirs.

'Don't be selfish,' his mother would say. 'Look at all the things you have. Learn how to share.'

But there was no sharing. Not with the older kids. There was only taking.

Thomas had made Daniel's position clear two

days after arriving. Daniel had found him in the kitchen, taking a biscuit.

'You're supposed to ask,' Daniel had said. He lingered in the doorway, feeling his own kitchen had become their territory, and he an intruder.

Thomas and Ciaran had been respectful and polite since they'd taken the spare bedroom. Especially Ciaran, who stuck by his brother's side like a ghost that haunted the living. He had sat there at the table, eating the biscuit his brother had taken, staring at Daniel. Smaller than Thomas, but stringy thin like him. Always watchful, as if he was merely a spectator in this world.

Thomas didn't answer. Pimples scattered across his face, a dark and bitter smell about him.

'You're supposed to ask,' Daniel said again, firmer, meaning his authority to be noted.

Ciaran's gaze moved back and forth between them both.

'Who am I supposed to ask?' Thomas said.

'Mum or Dad,' Daniel said. 'You can't just take stuff.'

'Your ma and da aren't here,' Thomas said. He finished the biscuit, wiped his hands on his T-shirt, and opened the fridge.

'Mum's just gone to the shop. She'll only be a minute.'

Thomas took a sealed packet of sliced ham from the fridge and set about opening it.

'That's for our lunch,' Daniel said.

Thomas took a slice, shoved it in his mouth, made slapping noises as he chewed.

Daniel went to the fridge and closed it. 'You can't just take stuff.'

Thomas held the packet out to Ciaran. The younger brother took a slice, folded it, and nibbled at the corners. Like he wasn't really hungry and only ate because he was told to. Thomas showed Daniel the packet.

'You want some?'

'No. You can't just take stuff without asking. I won't tell Mum this time. She might not notice. But if you do it again, I'll — '

When he thought about it later, Daniel couldn't remember Thomas moving across the room towards him. Only that he had been by the table, the packet of ham in one hand, then that same hand had been at Daniel's throat, squeezing it tight. Thomas kicked at Daniel's heels, took his legs from under him.

The tiled floor slammed into his shoulders, cracked against the back of his skull. Black circles danced across his vision, a galaxy of dark stars. Thomas grinning through them, his weight on Daniel's chest.

Ciaran stood over them both, his face without expression. Not amusement, not anger, not fear. A blankness that still woke Daniel in the night.

Thomas reached out his hand, the one that didn't have a hold of Daniel's throat. He felt around for something that Daniel couldn't see. Daniel heard plastic slide on tile, and something wet. Thomas's hand came back, a slice of ham in his fingers, retrieved from the floor where he'd dropped it. Daniel saw hair and grit clinging to the pink flesh.

79

'You sure you don't want some?'

Daniel shook his head.

'Ah, go on,' Thomas said.

Daniel croaked out the word, 'No.'

'Ah, go on.' Thomas grinned. 'Ah, go on, go on, go on, go on . . . '

He repeated the words over and over, like that housekeeper from the old comedy programme Daniel's parents loved.

Daniel opened his mouth to shout something, leave me alone, get off, something, his mind hadn't formed the words yet, but Thomas's fingers rammed between his teeth, along with the ham and the hair and the grit. He gagged as the saltiness cloyed at the back of his throat, felt the hardness of the fingers on his tongue. Through no will of his own, his body bucked, throwing his hips from side to side, but Thomas stayed on him, laughing.

Daniel didn't know how long had passed, how much he had endured, before the idea entered his head to close his teeth together. He hesitated, doubting his desire to do this boy harm in spite of the torment. Then he tightened his jaw. He felt the flesh and the bones through his teeth. Thomas's grin widened, his eyes flashing. He did not pull his hand away.

'Do it,' Thomas said. 'Bite harder.'

A scream trapped in the back of his throat, Daniel increased the pressure.

'Bite them off,' Thomas said. 'I dare you.'

The fingers writhed, the nails scratching his tongue, the insides of his cheeks, the soft floor of his mouth.

No air. Not a breath in the world. Pressure behind his eyes. Fear came in like a torrent of water. Panic, wild and thrashing in his heart. The roaring in his ears drowning out Thomas's laughter.

He felt the heat then, spreading between his legs. And with it, almost instantly, the burning shame. He stopped resisting. His defeat total, his humiliation complete, he let his body go limp.

The fingers withdrew from his mouth, and he coughed up torn meat and bile. Thomas's weight left his chest. He gasped air, coughed it out again, gasped, coughed, tears streaming from his eyes.

When he had recovered enough to breathe without hacking, to open his eyes and see through the tears, he realised Thomas and Ciaran had gone. Probably up to their room. The urine had started to chill. He pulled himself up to a sitting position and battled himself under control.

By the time his mother came home, he had changed his trousers, cleaned his face, and had mopped up most of the liquid. He had poured bleach on the floor to cover the smell.

His mother asked what had happened as she put the shopping bags on the counter.

'I spilled a can of Coke,' he said, his shame real, even if the words were a lie.

'Who said you could take a Coke?' she asked.

'No one,' he said. 'I just took it.'

'Well,' she said, looking down at the wet floor, streaked by the mop. 'Serves you right for stealing. You know you're not to take things without asking. You might think it's only a can of Coke, but next thing you know, it'll be money. Or worse. And what'd you use bleach for? Sure, water would've done.'

'I don't know,' he said, his head down, his voice small in his throat. 'I wanted to make it clean.'

'Go on,' she said, taking the mop from his hands. 'I'll sort it out. Go to your room.'

And he did. He went there every time he was alone in the house with the brothers, closed the door behind him. But sometimes the door opened again, and Thomas would come in, sometimes with his brother.

Daniel still occasionally woke from his dreams, kicking and thrashing. Niamh had tolerated his nightmares for the two years they'd been together. She had the bruises to show for it.

A pang of guilt resonated in his chest for the way he'd spoken to her, the way he'd pushed her aside like she didn't matter. He switched off the TV, turned out the lights, and made his way to the flat's sole bedroom.

Niamh didn't acknowledge him as he entered, but he knew she was awake. He lay down on the bed, on top of the covers, put his arm around her shrouded form.

'I'm sorry,' he said.

Silence for a while, then she let out a long sigh. 'It's all right. I know it's hard for you. But I wish you wouldn't dwell on it. There's nothing you can do about it. There's nothing you can change. You have to put it behind you and move on.'

'I know,' Daniel said. 'I'll try.'

He kissed her ear, felt her hair soft against his cheek. She reached from under the duvet and patted his hand.

Within ten minutes, her breathing had deepened and established the rhythm of sleep. He lay awake, still dressed. Sleep came as easy to her as it was elusive to him. He took his phone from his pocket and opened the Notes app.

The car's registration number.

He added the words, 'Nissan Micra, black.'

11

Paula Cunningham swallowed the last of the wine. It left a metallic sweetness at the back of her mouth. The quietness of the house pressed in on her. Even the breathing of her dog Angus on the couch beside her barely cut through the silence. He was a mongrel she and Alex had adopted from the pound. Alex was long gone, but the dog stayed. She hadn't complained when Alex named him after the guitarist from AC/DC. It seemed to suit the scruffy hound anyway. They had wasted many hours trying to name the constituent parts of his breeding, from lurcher to black Labrador. It didn't matter in the end. Not after what Cunningham had done. Alex left, told her she could keep the dog, it was nothing but a scrawny mutt anyway.

She looked at the clock on the wall. Past midnight. The cigarette cravings had been bad tonight. Three weeks in, and she still longed for that heat in her chest, that taste, that sparkling in her brain.

There was a bottle of vodka in the kitchen cupboard. Ice in the freezer, tonic in the fridge, lemons in a bowl on the dining table. Two minutes to make the drink.

'Fuck it,' she said, and went to the kitchen.

Three minutes later she felt the cold prickle of tonic bubbles on her lip, the hot bite of the vodka in her throat. Half the glass gone in two swallows.

Cunningham did not remember falling asleep, only the sickly shock of waking, her mobile phone trilling and vibrating on the coffee table. She reached for it, clumsy fingers knocking it to the floor. After a few more seconds of fumbling she squinted at the display, trying to make sense of the number. She didn't recognise it. She pressed answer.

'Hello?'

Her voice hoarse, the L softened by the alcohol. She swallowed, ran her tongue around her mouth. Don't sound drunk, she told herself, a futile command.

'Hello, Paula?' A man's voice, rattle and bustle in the background.

'Yes. Who's this?'

'Tom Wheatley.' He waited for some sort of acknowledgement as her sleep- and drink-blunted mind tried to catch up. 'From the hostel,' he said eventually, and the Liverpool accent registered.

'Oh,' Cunningham said. 'Oh? What . . . ' She swallowed again. 'What time is it?'

'Coming up to one,' he said, his tone apologetic. 'Sorry to call you this late. Sounds like I woke you. But I thought you'd want to know.'

She turned her mouth away and coughed, then asked, 'Know what?'

'You remember that little spat in the common room earlier? Between Ciaran's brother and the other lad.'

'Yes.'

'Robbie Agnew, a nasty little git, just between you and me. Anyway, he didn't come back for nine tonight. It's not the first time, he's had a few warnings already. But I got a call about eleven from the A&E ward at the Royal. He'd been found just up the road, seven kinds of shit beaten out of him.'

'Jesus,' Cunningham said, clarity creeping in behind her eyes. 'How bad?'

'Bad enough, but he'll be all right. Nothing broken, cuts and bruises, and he's lost a couple of teeth. They'll probably let him out tomorrow. The police took a statement. He said he'd no idea who did it, just some guys jumped him and gave him a hiding for no reason.'

'Do you believe him?'

'Not for a second,' Wheatley said. 'I asked him flat out if it was the Devine brothers. He just went quiet for a second, then he said no, it wasn't them, he didn't know who it was. Then he clammed up. Thing is, this Agnew lad, he can handle himself. I certainly wouldn't tackle him. Whoever did this to him, the Devines or not, has some balls.'

'Did you say anything to the police?' Cunningham asked.

'No, not much point. A bit of suspicion from me isn't really grounds for them to lift Ciaran or Thomas. Anyway, I thought I'd better let you know. Ciaran seems like a decent enough young fella. It'd be a shame for him to land back inside over a toe-rag like Robbie Agnew.'

'Yeah, thank you,' Cunningham said. 'I've a

meeting with Ciaran in the morning. I'll see if I can get anything out of him.'

Wheatley apologised once again for waking her and hung up. Cunningham dropped her phone to the couch beside her. Angus sighed and pushed at her thigh with his paws. She reached across and scratched his belly as his tail thumped against the cushions.

One-fifteen now. She should go to bed, even if it was cold and empty, and get some proper sleep.

Bubbles still rose in the glass on the coffee table, the ice not yet melted.

Cunningham reached for it.

12

Daniel Rolston had worked at the call centre for six months, the only real job he'd ever had. He hated it. The centre took up the entire eleventh floor of a tower block overlooking the River Lagan. If Daniel walked from his portioned-off workstation to the windows, he'd be able to look down on the Waterfront Hall, and across to the crystal dome of the Victoria Square shopping mall. Further in the distance, the high rise of the Divis Tower to the west of the city, the mountains beyond.

But he did not look out of the windows. Instead, his attention remained fixed on his monitor.

Another notification popped up on the display: a name, telephone number, a link to open the customer's details. Someone who had only a few moments before supplied their personal information to a website that provided car insurance quotes. If he clicked on the link, the person's details would appear on his screen and he would hear a ringtone in the earpiece of his headset as the system called the customer, and he would ask them if the quotes they'd received had met their expectations, and could he clarify any of the deals, perhaps see if he could better any of them?

As often as not, the customer would be annoyed at the intrusion, tell him firmly but politely that they had only wanted a price and hadn't expected to be bothered with a phone call. Sometimes the customer would swear and hang up. But occasionally, enough times to make the exercise worthwhile, the customer would feel pressured into agreeing to a purchase and he would take the long number on the face of their debit card, please, thank you, I'll get that organised for you right now if you'll hold for just a moment.

But Daniel did not click the link. After a few seconds, the notification would disappear and reappear on another member of staff's screen. He was well ahead of his calls-per-hour quota so he could afford to ignore a few sales leads for the moment.

He entered the car's registration number into the form and waited while the circle spun in front of his eyes, telling him the system was working, digging for the information he had requested.

There.

Name: Paula Jessica Cunningham.

Daniel checked the date of birth, counted in his head. She'd turned thirty-six four months ago.

Single. No other drivers named on her policy; she'd removed an Alexandra Stephanie Pierson when she'd last renewed. Claimed for a windscreen replacement two years ago. Three points for a speeding offence that were about to expire. Clean apart from that.

Profession: Civil servant. Probation officer. Daniel had guessed that much as he lay awake thinking about her the night before.

Two telephone numbers, a landline and a mobile. He checked her address. East of the city, Sydenham, the warren of two-up-two-down terraced houses that stood beneath the airport's flight path. He imagined the glasses rattling in her cupboards as jets descended overhead.

Daniel grabbed his notebook from the backpack that sat tucked under his desk, began scribbling down the information. He could have sent the page to the printer at the far side of the office, but the risk was too great. Taking data off the premises meant instant dismissal.

Next, he opened the credit history page, copied and pasted her name and address across. A few seconds of processing, and he had her financial life laid out before him.

Two credit cards, three store cards, accounts at two different banks, and a mortgage at a third. A year ago she'd allowed her cards to ride close to their limits, then a late payment on her mortgage, before she'd got it under control and began chipping away at the balances. Nothing unusual. Almost every credit report he looked at showed something similar. Certainly not enough to prevent her getting a monthly payment plan for her car insurance, which she had.

A new notification appeared on his screen. Not a sales lead this time, but a note from the company's internal messaging system. He clicked the link to open the message.

Melanie Sherry, the Human Resources manager, asking if he could pop into her office when he had a free minute.

Daniel said, 'Shit.'

He took off his headset, packed his notebook away, and changed his system status to say he was away from his desk. Melanie's office lay on the corner nearest the river. He knocked her door and entered.

'Hiya,' she said, her tone as bright as it had been the day she'd interviewed him for the job, and every bit as artificial. 'Have a wee seat.'

She was one of those cheery people who described everything as wee. Have a wee cup of tea. Sign this wee company contract. Blow your wee fucking head off with a wee shotgun if you have one to hand. He blinked the image out of his mind and sat down facing her across the glass desk.

'How's things, Daniel?' she asked, her lips stretched into a mile-wide smile.

'All right,' he said.

'You feeling okay?'

'Yeah, fine.'

'You went home early yesterday. And you were late in this morning. What did you say, a bad tummy?'

'That's right.' He gave her a smile. 'It's cleared up now.'

'Good.' Her smile broadened in response to his. 'How are you feeling in general?'

He shrugged. 'All right.'

'No wee problems at home or anything?'

'No. Why?'

Melanie's smile dimmed a fraction as she turned over the sheet of paper that had been lying face down on her desk. 'It's just I've had a

91

wee bit of feedback. I'm afraid it's not entirely positive.'

Sweat moistened the small of Daniel's back. 'Oh?'

Her smile remained fixed in place, but a crease appeared between her eyebrows, a tone of parental concern in her voice. 'Did you have a wee confrontation with Chris Greely a couple of days ago?'

'No,' Daniel said, though he had no idea why. She clearly had a report from Greely in front of her. 'Yes. I mean, I'm not sure. Depends what you mean by 'confrontation', I suppose.'

Still, that smile. 'What I mean is, you had a wee argument with Chris outside the kitchen. He says you gave him a wee shove.' She mimed the gesture with her hand. 'Do you remember that?'

Daniel remembered it all right. Greely had been in charge of Daniel's team that week. He tackled Daniel about his numbers, why they were down on previous weeks. He wouldn't leave it alone, kept cornering him, nagging him about it. Daniel had thought about doing much worse to Greely than a shove.

As a kid, he had always been on the receiving end of the casual violence that young boys mete out to each other. The strong and the weak claiming their places. A spotty, pudgy kid like him never stood a chance. But now he was grown, now he was big enough, and recently the urge to do harm had come upon him more often. That urge had become action for the first time when Greely came at him once too often. He regretted it instantly, yet there remained a warm satisfaction in seeing the fright on Greely's face.

Then he remembered pushing Niamh last night, another urge unchecked, and any warmth drained away.

Daniel swallowed and shook his head. 'No, I don't remember pushing anyone. We did have a few words, but nothing serious. At least, I didn't think so, anyway.'

'Chris doesn't see it like that, I'm afraid. He was a wee bit upset about the whole thing. You know, I should really be talking to you about a termination of your contract.' Her smile tightened and broadened until he thought her lower jaw might fall off onto the desk. 'But your performance here has been excellent ever since you started. It's just the last couple of weeks haven't been so good.' She leaned forward. 'Now, here's what I want you to do. I want you to take a wee break. Take the rest of today off and we'll see you Monday week. How's that sound?'

'I'd rather not. I'm saving my leave.'

'Take them as unpaid days. They won't count towards your leave.'

'Do I have a choice in this?'

'Not really, no.'

Daniel returned to his desk and packed away his things. Paula Cunningham's information still showed on his screen. He stared at the fragments of her life for a few seconds. Then he hit the print button on both pages.

When he crossed to the Xerox machine, his backpack slung over his shoulder, Chris Greely stood reading the pages as they emerged from the printer's mouth.

'What's that?' he asked.

'None of your business,' Daniel said as he folded the pages and tucked them into his jacket pocket.

'You're not supposed to take customer data out of here.'

Daniel laughed. 'What are you going to do? Tell on me?'

Greely pointed at Daniel's pocket. 'You'll get sacked for that.'

'Maybe.' Daniel moved close enough to smell Greely's coffee breath. 'And then I'll have no real reason not to come back here and beat the living shit out of you, will I?'

He left Greely at the printer, staring after him.

13

Reception called up to tell Cunningham that Ciaran had arrived almost five minutes before he was due, but she already knew that. She'd seen him approach along North Street as she looked for the hundredth time out of the window nearest her desk. All morning, through the sluggish tides of her hangover, she'd been stealing glances instead of concentrating on her paperwork.

It wasn't Ciaran she was looking for. Rather, it was another young man, one she seemed to remember from the day before when she'd taken Ciaran to the shopping centre across from the hostel. He had watched them pass, and Ciaran had stared back. It had barely registered with Cunningham at the time, but this morning, when she had called in to the shop down the street for a coffee and a packet of mints on her way to the office, she had noticed him at the magazine shelves. She had not seen him look directly at her, only his head turning away as she glimpsed him in her peripheral vision. But still, his attention had been on her. She was certain of it.

Cunningham made Ciaran wait until his allotted time before she took the stairs down to collect him. He stood when he saw her come through the secure door.

'Have you signed in?' she asked. 'Good. Follow me.'

She went back to the door, keyed in her security code, and held it open for Ciaran. She caught a scent as he walked by, one of those shower gel and deodorant brands that target young men. She pictured him choosing it in the supermarket aisle, driven by television ads that showed girls throwing themselves at boys who used the right products.

He didn't say a word on the way to the interview room. Even when she asked if he wanted a tea or coffee, he simply shook his head.

Ciaran sat down when she asked him to, joined his hands on the tabletop, and didn't lift his gaze from them as she took the seat opposite. She opened her notebook, placed it on top of his file, and readied her pen.

'So what did you do yesterday evening?' she asked.

'Nothing,' he said.

She kept her voice friendly, a soft smile fixed to her mouth. 'Well, you did something. I saw you go off with your brother. Where'd you go?'

'His flat.'

'And what did you do there?'

'Just talked.'

'What about?'

'Just stuff.'

'Sounds interesting.' She hadn't meant to sound sarcastic. If he noticed, he didn't show it. 'And you got back before nine, didn't you?'

Ciaran nodded.

'Good,' she said. 'Did Thomas tell you about his job?'

Ciaran said, 'Yeah.'

'It's good to have a job,' Cunningham said. 'It gives you something to do every day. A reason to get out of bed in the morning. And you'll have your own money. You can spend it on whatever you like. Maybe driving lessons. You could get a car too, like Thomas has.'

Ciaran shrugged.

'I tried to get you an interview at the hotel Thomas works at, but they didn't have any spaces. But I've something else you might like. I'm told you were good at gardening when you were at Hydebank.'

She waited for some response, anything, but none came.

'Well, I know a company that does commercial gardening. Landscaping, laying out lawns, flower beds, that kind of thing. They do it for housing associations, and companies that have grounds they want to keep tidy. They're based just out of the city, but they'd send a van every day to pick you up. A few of the boys from your hostel work there. You could all go together. How does that sound?'

She studied the tufts of dirty-blond hair on top of his head, waiting for an answer.

'Ciaran, I asked you a question. Would you like to work for a gardening company?'

He shifted in his seat. 'S'pose.'

'Good,' she said, and handed a card across the table. 'Go and see Mr McClintock at four o'clock this afternoon. That'll give you time to get back to the hostel and smarten up. Mr Wheatley at the hostel will give you money for a taxi. All right?'

Ciaran nodded.

Cunningham had a rising urge to shake the boy, tell him to open his mouth, say something, engage her with more than shrugs and nods. She took a breath before she spoke again.

'Ciaran, before you came back to the hostel last night, did anything happen?'

He looked up from his hands. Such blue eyes.

'No,' he said. Barely a whisper.

'Are you sure?'

'Yeah.'

'Do you remember Thomas had a few words with another boy in the common room?'

A swallow. A shrug.

'That boy, his name's Robbie. Somebody attacked him last night. He had to go to hospital. He'll be okay, but it was a pretty serious assault.'

Ciaran's breathing deepened, his shoulders rising and falling. He chewed at his nail until Cunningham saw a tiny glisten of red on his lips.

'Ciaran, do you know anything about that?'

The rasp of his breathing resonated between the walls of the interview room. His foot tapped on the floor, a jittering rhythm.

'Ciaran?'

He looked to the window.

'Ciaran, answer me. Do you know anything about what happened to that boy?'

He looked back to his lap.

'Ciaran, please answer me.'

Cunningham watched as the walls went up around him, as he closed her out. She knew she might as well have been a ghost as far as he was concerned. There, across the table from her, an empty space.

An impulse hit her, too strong to be ignored. Even though she knew it wasn't allowed, even though it went against every moment of her training, even though Edward Hughes would berate her for it, she acted on the impulse anyway.

Cunningham stood, reached across the table, took Ciaran's hand, pulled it away from his mouth, and squeezed.

No response.

She squeezed harder. Then harder still, applying more and more pressure until Ciaran had no choice but to look up. His eyes locked with hers, froze her in place. She did not know how long passed, did not break the lock he had on her until the sound of her own sharp breathing cut through to her consciousness.

Still he stared back.

'Ciaran, listen to me. Are you listening?'

'Yes,' he said, clearer than any word he'd spoken since he entered this room.

'I am not a police officer. I couldn't make you tell me what happened to Robbie Agnew even if you knew. That's not the point. The point is: if you get in trouble, you'll have to go back inside. Do you understand? If you or your brother hurt that boy, there'd be no choice. You'd have to go away again. Do you understand me?'

'Yes,' he said.

'And if your brother committed an assault, if he was tried and found guilty, he'd have to go to prison. Not Hydebank. A real prison. You wouldn't be able to see him. Do you understand?'

Ciaran remained still and silent. His gaze boring into her. She eased the pressure of her hand on his, but kept hold of his fingers.

'That boy says he doesn't know who attacked him. So long as he doesn't change his mind, this doesn't have to go any further. But if anything like this happens again, you know the consequences.'

Cunningham released his hand. He let it hang there, as if suspended by a puppeteer's string.

'Can I go now?' he asked.

14

Flanagan barely tasted the sandwich she ate in her car. Sunlight had crept over the station walls and swamped the car park, warming the interior of her Volkswagen Golf. Quiet here, the radio a low babble, it almost felt peaceful. Her only regret was buying a supermarket sandwich instead of something decent. She could have gone to the station canteen, but yesterday's experience with DCI Thompson over at Ladas Drive had put her off the notion. Silence was better. Over recent months, she'd come to appreciate the peace of being alone. The calmness of it, no one's needs to address but her own.

Selfish, perhaps. But Flanagan felt she owed herself a little self-absorption.

Her memory had been flitting through the days before her children were born, when she and Alistair had only each other and the world. A weekend trip to Ghent in Belgium, both of them drunk as lords, staggering from bar to bar, stopping on a bridge across a canal, watching the reflection of the town's lights glimmer on the water. A smile might have been on her lips when the words from the radio snagged her conscious mind and made her reach for the volume control.

' . . . found by a family member who heard what she believed to be a gunshot in the early hours. Police and ambulance services were called to the scene, but the as yet unnamed couple were pronounced dead this morning. A police spokeswoman said that while the investigation is at a very early stage, they are currently seeking no one else in connection with the deaths.'

The street name. It was the street name that had caught Flanagan's ear. She held her breath as she listened, telling herself she had misheard, willing the newsreader to repeat some other address.

'Neighbours on Mill Street said the dead couple had lived there for many years, and were well known and liked in the area.'

'Oh no,' Flanagan said.

The remains of the sandwich scattered in the footwell as she jammed her key into the ignition.

* * *

Flanagan had to abandon her car at the end of the narrow street, blocking in another vehicle. From here, she couldn't quite tell which of the row of terraced houses was sealed off, which had men and women in white forensic overalls clustering in its garden.

For a moment, as she drew closer, half jogging, she thought it was another home, not the one she feared. But then she moved out into the road, got a better angle, and saw that it was. She stopped, let out a shuddering sigh.

'Oh, Penny, no,' she said.

No one paid attention as Flanagan approached the police line. She waved to a young uniformed constable on the other side. 'What happened?'

He walked to the tape, saying, 'Sorry, you'll have to move along.'

Flanagan produced her warrant card.

The constable blushed. 'Sorry, ma'am. I don't really know anything, I've been stuck here since I arrived.'

Flanagan lifted the tape, went to duck beneath it, felt the constable's hand on her shoulder. He called to someone beyond her vision. 'Sir? Sir!'

DCI Brian Conn appeared from behind a marked van.

'You can't come in . . . ' He slowed his step as recognition broke on his face. 'Serena? What are you doing here?'

'They're friends of mine,' she said, her voice quivering as she held back her emotions.

'I see,' Conn said. He looked to the constable, signalled him to leave them alone. 'I'm sorry. Even so, you shouldn't be here.'

'Tell me what happened.'

'The daughter says she was woken around two a.m. by what she thought was a gunshot from the next bedroom, her parents' room. She got up, went in, found the mother lying on the bed, a pillow over her face, and the father sitting in a chair with the rifle in his hands — a .22, he had a licence for it. That's exactly how the first uniform crew on the scene found them. There were sleeping pills on the bedside locker. No signs of a struggle, so it looks like the wife knocked herself out with some pills, he smothered her with the pillow, then turned the rifle on himself.'

Flanagan looked towards the house, a happy home into which she'd been welcomed many times over the last few months. 'I just saw Penny last night,' she said. 'She'd had bad news, but she was strong. I didn't expect anything like this. Not her.'

'The daughter says the husband was worried about how he'd cope without his wife,' Conn said. 'He didn't know if he could look after himself. I'm guessing he didn't want to find out.'

Flanagan gave a dry laugh. 'He was learning to cook. For Christ's sake, Ronnie, you could have tried.'

Conn put a hand on her shoulder. 'Listen, I'm sorry about your friends. But I need to get on here, and you've no reason to be on this side of the tape. So . . . '

Flanagan nodded, turned to walk away, but stopped. 'Wait, is Julie — the daughter — is she here?'

Conn pointed to a marked police minibus in the gateway to the small business park across the road. Flanagan saw moving forms through the tinted windows. 'Her boyfriend's with her.'

'Can I speak with her?' Flanagan asked.

Conn shoved his hands down into his pockets, exhaled through loose lips. 'All right, go on. But don't be long, okay?'

'Thank you,' Flanagan said, and walked towards the minibus. She went to the far side and found the sliding door open. Inside, Julie Walker, early-thirties, still in her nightclothes, a coat over her shoulders. A slender woman, not quite pretty. Beside her, a man of around forty, wearing thick-rimmed glasses and a shabby suit.

'Julie, I'm Serena Flanagan. We've met once or twice. I don't know if you remember. I'm a friend of your mother's.'

Julie looked back at Flanagan, her eyes red and wet, a vacant expression on her face. 'I'm sorry, I don't . . .'

'Don't worry,' Flanagan said. She pointed to the seat opposite the couple. 'May I?'

Julie nodded, and Flanagan climbed into the van.

'Barry Timmons,' the man said. He put an arm around Julie's shoulders.

Flanagan smiled and nodded.

'Wait,' Julie said, studying Flanagan's face. 'You're the policewoman. From that support group Mum went to.'

'That's right,' Flanagan said. 'I'm not here officially. I heard a report on the news, and I knew it was Penny and Ronnie. I saw your mother last night. She told me the cancer had spread.'

'Yes.' Julie nodded. 'She told me last week. She didn't say anything to Dad until yesterday afternoon. I was at work. He had locked himself away in his study by the time I got home. I could hear his music playing. That old jazz he listened to. I knocked the door after Mum went to her meeting, asked if he wanted me to make him a bit of toast or anything, but he told me to . . . go away. I mean, he swore at me. He'd never done that before.'

'I'm so sorry,' Flanagan said. 'Your mother seemed so at peace with things last night.'

105

'I thought the same,' Julie said, her gaze on the tissue in her hands. 'We had a talk when she came home from the meeting. About how she wanted things handled, when the time came. The funeral, all that. I asked her about Dad. She just said not to worry about him, he'd be fine.'

She looked up at Flanagan. 'I think they planned this. I think they knew when there was nothing more to be done for Mum, they would just make it easier for themselves.'

'Maybe,' Flanagan said. 'I suppose we'll never know. It's funny, Penny told me she'd booked a cottage up in Portstewart for the weekend. She and your father were going to have one last trip together.'

Something moved behind Julie Walker's eyes before she looked away. Flanagan felt a cold finger on her heart and said no more.

They sat quiet for a time, only the whisper of Barry's hand making circles on Julie's back. He stared out through the window to the street beyond.

'Well,' Flanagan said, 'I just wanted you to know I'm here if there's anything you need. Anything at all. I'm sorry for your loss.'

She reached out and stroked Julie's hand, then climbed out of the van. As she walked back towards the tape, the tears came. Grief driving them first, then something else. It had started as an itch in her mind the moment she got into the van, then had grown in those few minutes to a quiet rage, the source of which she could not identify.

DI Conn was talking to the constable who had

stopped her when she arrived. Flanagan approached. The constable had the good sense to walk away. Conn's expression turned from impatience to concern when he saw Flanagan's tears. She wiped at her cheeks and sniffed.

'You all right?' he asked.

'Yeah,' Flanagan said. 'It's just . . . '

Conn stared at her for a moment, then said, 'What?'

'I don't know,' Flanagan said, truthfully.

She turned away, ducked under the tape, ignoring Conn's calls as she walked back to her car, that senseless fury burning in her all the way.

15

Ciaran walks into the hotel lobby. People everywhere. It's all modern, all stone and glass, a fake fireplace, leather couches and armchairs, books on shelves that no one has ever read. The city outside, rumbling and screeching. Noise upon noise.

He crosses to the desk, a wall of dark polished wood. A pretty woman behind it smiles as he approaches. He stops a few feet from her. She keeps looking at him, her eyebrows raised. Her name tag says 'Sarah'. He wants to run.

After a while, Sarah asks, 'Can I help you, sir?'

'I want to see Thomas,' Ciaran says.

Her smile flickers off and on again. 'I'm sorry, Thomas . . . '

'Thomas Devine,' Ciaran says. 'My brother.'

'Is he a guest?' Sarah asks.

'No,' Ciaran says. 'He works in the kitchen.'

Sarah's smile goes away. 'Just a moment,' she says before moving along the desk. She lifts a phone, stabs at a few numbers, and waits. Ciaran can't hear what she says. She puts the phone down and points to the couches by the fake fireplace, tells him to wait.

Ciaran does as he's told, like a good boy.

It takes a long time for Thomas to come. He wears a white top, a chequered hat on his head, black trousers. He looks strange to Ciaran. And angry.

Thomas doesn't say anything, just takes Ciaran's arm and leads him to the exit. Outside, Thomas walks towards the side street beside the hotel, dragging Ciaran behind, his fingers squeezing tight through Ciaran's sleeve. Ciaran knows he's done a bad thing, but he isn't sure what. Thomas finds a deep doorway, shoves Ciaran into a metal shutter so that they're hidden from the street. Ciaran wants to cry.

'What are you doing?' Thomas asks.

'I wanted to — '

Thomas slaps Ciaran's forehead with his palm, knocks his head against the shutter.

'Why'd you come here? Why'd you come to my work?'

Another slap. The shutter rattles off the back of Ciaran's head again.

'I wanted to see you,' Ciaran says.

His eyes are hot. He wants to go to the toilet. Thomas's teeth flash. It's been so long since Ciaran felt them on his skin. He doesn't want to feel them now.

'You could've called my mobile,' Thomas says.

'You didn't answer,' Ciaran says. His bladder aches.

'Then you could've left a message.'

'But I wanted to see you.'

Thomas pushes Ciaran back, grabs a handful of his hair, closes his teeth on Ciaran's neck. Pressure there, the heat of his breath, and wet. They stay like that for a while, Ciaran frozen, Thomas ready to bite. Then Thomas moves his mouth away.

He cups Ciaran's face in his hands, comes

close, his lips against Ciaran's cheek.

'Listen to me,' Thomas says. 'You don't come to my work. They don't allow people to just call in. Do you understand? It's okay, I'm not angry. You didn't know. Just don't do it again. All right?'

'All right,' Ciaran says.

'Good boy. Now what's wrong?'

'Paula. The probation woman.'

'What about her?'

'I had to go and see her. She asked about that boy. The one from yesterday.'

Thomas wets his lips with his tongue. 'What's he got to do with us?'

'She said I could go back to Hydebank. She said you could go to prison. She said we wouldn't be able to see each other.'

Ciaran feels a hot, fat tear roll down his cheek. Thomas wipes it away.

'That's not going to happen,' Thomas says. 'Listen to me. That is not going to happen. I won't let it happen. Ever.'

'But she said — '

Thomas pulls Ciaran close, embraces him, arms tight like a trap around Ciaran's body. Lips against his ear.

'I love you,' Thomas says. 'And you love me. They will not separate us again. Never. I promise you. Do you believe me?'

Ciaran nods. Thomas's arms relax and slip away.

'Say it.'

'I believe you.'

'Good,' Thomas says. 'Has she got you a job lined up?'

'I have to go somewhere today,' Ciaran says. 'A gardening place. She gave me a card.'

'All right,' Thomas says. 'You go there, you talk to them, you be polite and friendly. Tell them you'll work hard. You need a job so they'll know you're being good. All right? It's important for them to think you're being good. I've been good these last two years while I've waited for you. And you're a good boy, aren't you?'

'Yeah,' Ciaran says.

'All right. I'm on the evening shift tomorrow, so I don't have to be in till six. We'll go for a spin in the morning. Maybe go to the seaside. What do you think?'

'Okay,' Ciaran says.

Thomas hugs him, kisses his cheek, leaves him there.

Alone, Ciaran allows the tears to come. Just a few, then he wipes his face clean. His groin aches from holding on. He had feared he might wet himself there on the street. Then Thomas would have surely used his teeth. But Ciaran held it in. Now he turns in the doorway, opens his fly, and lets it go, shame burning in him.

★   ★   ★

The man at the gardening place isn't friendly, but he isn't angry either. He tells Ciaran he can start on Monday, to be ready for the van at seven every weekday morning. Three other boys from the hostel work for him. They'll all go together. It'll be hard work, he says. Ciaran says that's all right, he wants to work hard. The man seems

111

pleased. He wants Ciaran's National Insurance number. Ciaran doesn't know what that is. The man says never mind, he'll get it from Mr Wheatley at the hostel.

The taxi ride back into the city takes a long time. Rush hour, the driver says. He curses at the traffic and punches the face of the steering wheel, making the horn blare.

Ciaran stops noticing the buildings and the pedestrians as they creep past. He thinks about his mother. He remembers her as a shadow, a scent, a disturbance of light. There used to be a photograph of her. A young, thin, dark-haired woman, sitting outside a tent in a field full of tents. She wore a red checked shirt, muddy jeans, Wellington boots. A cigarette held between her fingers.

The last time he saw it, Ciaran had been sitting alone on the bed in the room he and Thomas shared. He couldn't quite remember who the foster carer was. An older couple, he thought, but it was hard to see from all these years away.

He had the photograph in one hand, the fingertips of the other tracing her outline, touching her face, trying to remember what her voice sounded like. Music, Ciaran thought. Probably like music, the gentle kind.

How old was he then? Maybe seven. He remembered the dirt beneath his nails and the smudges his fingers left on the photograph's gloss.

Then Thomas walked in. One of the foster carers had taken him away a few minutes earlier, said she needed a word with him. Ciaran didn't

112

know how long he was gone, but when he came back, Thomas's face told him to be afraid. Anger there, and hate, black beneath his skin. Ciaran could almost feel the teeth already.

Thomas sat down on the bed opposite, his hands balled into fists on his knees, breathing hard. His nostrils flared.

Ciaran stayed very still, waiting. His throat dried, but he was afraid to swallow.

Eventually, Thomas reached his hand across the space between them. Ciaran knew not to pull away. That would only make it worse. Thomas gripped the photograph between his forefinger and thumb, took it from Ciaran's hand. He turned it towards himself, studied the image of their mother. The tent, the checked shirt, the hair dark as his own. Ciaran could see the words written in pen on the back: 'Trip to Tipp 93'. He did not know what they meant.

'She's fucking dead,' Thomas said.

A bad word. Thomas almost never said bad words. Ciaran began to shake.

'A heart attack or something. Because of the drugs. Fucking stupid bitch.'

Thomas took the photograph in both hands. Tore it down the middle. Placed one piece on top of the other and tore again. And again and again. So many pieces scattered on the floor.

'So that's that,' Thomas said. 'Do you want to go to the park? Mr Breen said we could.'

Yes, Mr and Mrs Breen, Ciaran remembered now. He had liked them, but Thomas had said he shouldn't. He said they were all the same, people like them.

They went to the park. In a far corner, high up in a tangle of overgrown bushes, they found a nest. Two adult birds circled overhead, crying out in alarm. A clutch of chicks inside the nest, blind and chirping, their beaks open.

Ciaran watched Thomas kill them all.

★ ★ ★

Mr Wheatley is waiting at his office door when Ciaran gets back.

'How'd it go?' he asks.

'Okay,' Ciaran says.

'Just okay? Did he give you a job?'

'Yeah,' Ciaran says.

'Good,' Mr Wheatley says. 'Well done. Work hard and make the most of it.'

'Yeah.'

Ciaran stands there in the hall, Mr Wheatley in his office doorway, each of them looking at the other. Ciaran doesn't know what to do next. Perhaps he should say something, but he can't think of a single word.

Mr Wheatley nods, says, 'All right, then. See you later.'

Ciaran walks up the stairs towards his room. On the second landing he sees that boy, Robbie Agnew, coming out of the bathroom. His face bruised and cut. Swelling over one eye. Ciaran hears the sound of a cistern filling beyond the door.

Robbie stares at Ciaran for a moment, frozen there, his mouth open. Then he drops his gaze to the floor. He's shaking. He opens the bathroom

114

door and steps back inside.

Ciaran goes to his room, closes the door behind him, sits on his bed.

He thinks of Thomas and the baby birds crushed beneath his feet.

16

Flanagan sat at her desk, the telephone's handset in one hand, the fingers of the other hovering over the keypad. Don't do it, her better mind said.

The anger that had sparked into flame while she spoke with Julie Walker had not abated through the afternoon. It smouldered in her like a hot coal. None of it made sense. The only logical answer she had could bear no logic whatsoever. But still it lingered in her mind.

Flanagan closed her eyes, gave a silent curse, and hit the key.

'Ladas Drive, please,' she said. When the call was answered, she asked if DCI Conn had returned from the scene. The duty officer put her through to his office.

Conn spoke with the distracted tone of someone interrupted in his work. 'What can I do for you?' he asked.

Flanagan swallowed and said, 'I wondered how you were getting on with the Walker case.'

'Okay, I suppose. It's mostly paperwork. Once the coroner's report is in, it's just a matter of pushing forms at the PPS.'

'Have you spoken with Julie Walker? Or the boyfriend?'

'I've scheduled statements for tomorrow afternoon,' Conn said.

Flanagan swallowed again. Pressed her finger-tips against her forehead. 'I mean, an interview.'

'What, as a suspect?'

'Well, maybe not as such, but . . . '

'But what?'

'Some things don't add up.'

'Like?'

'Well, for one thing, why would Penny and Ronnie arrange a weekend away if they planned to do this?'

'I suppose we'll never know,' Conn said, the edge of his voice sharpening. 'Is that it?'

'I mentioned it to Julie, and she seemed . . . thrown by it.'

'Thrown by it,' he echoed.

'It was just a feeling I had,' she said, hating the words as she spoke them.

'Just a feeling.'

'Surely it's worth following up on.'

Flanagan listened to the hiss in the earpiece, waiting.

Eventually, Conn said, 'First of all, I'm not going to question a grieving young woman on the strength of a feeling. Second, I don't much appreciate you sticking your nose into my case. I know they were friends of yours, but that's no excuse.'

'I'm sorry, I just thought — '

'Next time, keep your thoughts to yourself. Goodbye.'

A distorted rattle and click in the earpiece as he hung up.

Flanagan returned the handset to the cradle and stared at it. Only a matter of time before the call came.

Less than half an hour passed before the phone rang.

Flanagan went to DSI Purdy's office as soon as she was summoned. She could feel his rage from the doorway.

'Sit down,' he said through thin lips.

He made her wait while he typed an email. Long enough for her to know she was in trouble.

When he'd finished, Purdy said, 'Four days back. Only four days. And already you've pissed off two fellow DCIs.'

'I have that knack,' Flanagan said, hoping levity might ease things. She was wrong.

'DCI Thompson went straight to the ACC, said you were accusing him of negligence.'

'I accused him of no such thing,' Flanagan said. 'I only asked if he'd explored every avenue with those witnesses.'

'You're lucky he didn't call his Federation rep. Jesus, imagine the shit that'd be falling on our heads right now.'

'I was hoping he'd give me some pointers on this mess he's leaving behind.'

Purdy shook his head. 'Bad idea. Thompson's a lazy git, and a miserable shite too, he always has been. You might as well have asked that wall for help.'

'All right,' Flanagan said. 'I'll not trouble him again.'

'Good. But that was only the first call I got from the ACC today.'

Flanagan braced herself.

'Detective Chief Inspector Brian Conn,' Purdy said. 'Do you think he's incompetent?'

'No, sir.'

'Do you think he's lazy?'

'No, sir.'

'Do you think he's a frigging idiot?'

'No, sir.'

Purdy leaned forward. 'Then why in the name of Christ did you walk onto his crime scene? Why did you call him up and tell him how to do his job?'

Flanagan took a breath as she chose her words. 'You're quite right, I should have approached it — '

'You shouldn't have approached anything,' Purdy said, his voice rising. 'You had no business getting involved in the first place.'

'The victims were friends of mine.'

'There was only one victim there, one victim and a suicide. And it doesn't matter two shites if they were friends of yours or not. You didn't just walk into this job yesterday. You know better than to barge into someone else's case like that. And you sure as hell don't go throwing around those kinds of accusations while you're at it.'

Flanagan met Purdy's hard stare. 'I didn't make any accusations. I just asked DCI Conn if he might consider questioning Julie Walker. But I acknowledge that I let my personal feelings get the better of me. I apologise. I will call DCI Conn in the morning and apologise to him too. And the ACC, if you think it's necessary.'

Purdy sat back in his chair, his expression softening. 'Okay, you do that.'

'But . . . '

Purdy took off his glasses and rubbed his eyes. 'But what?'

'But I strongly recommend that DCI Conn question Julie Walker and her boyfriend, look for any inconsistencies in their stories.'

'That'll be DCI Conn's choice, and no such suggestion will come from you. Understood?'

'But it doesn't add up,' Flanagan said. 'That they'd do this. It doesn't make sense.'

He tossed his glasses onto the desk. 'In all your career, have you ever seen a single murder — or a suicide, for that matter — that made sense?'

'No,' Flanagan said. 'But Penny Walker told me she'd booked a weekend away only that morning. If they were planning this, why would she book a cottage by the seaside?'

'You're reaching,' Purdy said.

'But surely if they wanted to end things like this, they'd at least do it while they were alone at the cottage, not at home with their daughter sleeping in the next room.'

'Reaching.'

'But — '

'Go home,' Purdy said. 'Make your apologies in the morning, then that's the end of it.'

Flanagan swallowed her growing anger and said, 'Yes, sir.'

She left Purdy's office, went back to her own, gathered her things, and left the building. She went to her car, got in, locked the doors, and cried for her friend Penny Walker.

17

Paula Cunningham read the wine bottle's label.

No, not tonight, she thought, and put the bottle back in the fridge. The hangover had dragged on her all day, coating each of her senses, dulling them all. Part of her knew that at some point later in the evening she'd open the fridge again, open the bottle, and pour a glass. But for now, she could pretend that wouldn't happen.

The microwave pinged as Cunningham poured herself a pint glass full of water. Angus followed her from the kitchen to the living room, tail wagging, staring in hope at the plate in her hand. She flicked through TV channels as she ate, seeking out the most brainless trash she could find. Alex had always given her a hard time about her taste in television, never seeming to understand how badly she needed the vacuous pleasure of these programmes after the days she had. Maybe after a day selling newspaper ad space Alex desired something more cerebral, but having spent hours in the company of violent offenders, Cunningham needed shows about competitive brides and amateur cooks.

She scolded herself for letting her mind wander back to her former partner. More than a year, and there was Alex, still interrupting her simple joys of microwaved curry and trashy television.

'Get out of my fucking head,' she said aloud.

Angus looked up from his spot by her feet.

'What?' she said. 'Are you judging me?'

Sixty minutes had passed, and a whole recorded episode of *The Only Way is Essex*, when the doorbell rang. Angus had pre-empted the chime, sitting up, ears erect at a sound she hadn't heard. Then a furious peal of barking, his nails scrabbling on the once-glossy floorboards as he tried to sprint to the hall.

Cunningham followed him out, saw the shape of a man through the frosted glass of her door. She pointed back to the living room. 'Angus, in.'

Angus put his paws up on the glass, his barks ringing through the hall.

'For Christ's sake, Angus, come on, in, now.'

The dog ignored her. She grabbed his collar, hauled him back to the living room, closed him inside. His barking rose in intensity, the door rattling in its frame as he scratched at it.

Cunningham went back to the front door, opened it, trapped a breath in her chest as she recognised the young man on her step.

'Paula Cunningham,' he said.

The same young man who had watched her buying coffee that morning.

'My name's Daniel Rolston,' he said.

She stared at him for seconds on end before she thought to ask, 'What do you want?'

He cleared his throat. His hands shook. Fear radiated from him, the kind of fear that turns to anger. Cunningham eased the door a few inches closer to its frame.

'My parents were Jenny and David Rolston.

Ciaran Devine was convicted of killing my father. Thomas was convicted as an accessory.'

'Okay,' Cunningham said, adrenalin charging through her system. 'Again, what do you want?'

Angus's barking had not abated. His nails still scratched at the door. Cunningham silently wished she had not closed him in, had held him here by the collar, let him growl and show his teeth to this visitor.

'I want to talk to you,' Daniel Rolston said.

'I don't think we have anything to talk about,' Cunningham said, hoping the tremor was not audible in her voice.

'We do,' Daniel said. He gave her a smile that he probably intended to be friendly. 'I'm sorry, I know this is a bit out of the blue, me calling like this.'

'How did you get my address?' she asked.

'Through work,' Daniel said. His eyes widened as soon as he spoke, a clear realisation that he'd said too much.

'Your work?' Cunningham asked. 'Where do you work?'

'Doesn't matter,' he said. 'Look, I just need to — '

'Daniel, I think you should go now. If you want to talk about Ciaran Devine's case, call the Probation Board and they'll set up an appointment for you. Then you can sit down with me and my department head, and you can ask us anything you want.'

Daniel's smile faltered. 'But I want to talk to you now. It won't take long, honestly.'

'Daniel, I'm going to close the door now. If

you don't leave, then I'm going to call the police. Do you understand?'

'Please don't,' he said, putting his hands up.

'I'm closing the door now, Daniel. Please leave.'

'It wasn't Ciaran,' he said.

Cunningham pushed the door, but Daniel blocked it with his hand.

'All this time, everyone thought it was Ciaran. Right from the start. But they were wrong.'

'Please move your hand,' Cunningham said.

Trembling now, but she kept it hidden. The barking from the other end of the hall had reached a level of hysteria, Angus sensing her distress from the other side of the wood.

'Listen to me,' Daniel said. 'Please just give me five minutes.'

She put her shoulder to the door, shoved it closed, locked it.

From outside, his voice. 'It was Thomas. I tried to tell them at the time, the police, everybody, but nobody would listen to me. They wouldn't even let me say it in court. It wasn't Ciaran. It was never Ciaran.'

'Daniel, I'm calling the police.'

Her mobile was on the coffee table in the living room. She opened the door, and Angus bolted past her, charged along the hall. Through the glass, she saw Daniel step back. But still he talked — no — shouted now.

'You ask him. You get the truth out of him. He confessed for his brother. They destroyed my family, the two of them. They destroyed my life. And they've lied all this time.'

Cunningham took her phone from the table, dialled the emergency number, said, 'Police, please.'

By the time the marked car pulled up outside, Daniel had gone.

18

Daniel was still shaking by the time he got home. He knew it was a mistake before he did it, but he had gone to the probation woman's house anyway. In his mind, two hours ago, it seemed better to talk to her at home than tackle her on the street. He had told himself she would feel less threatened that way.

The mistake became clear as soon as she opened her door. He had walked for more than an hour after he left her front garden, the dog barking inside the house. Up one street, down the next, cutting through alleyways. Each street looked much like the next, the same small houses, the same bedraggled Union flags hanging from the lamp posts.

He realised he'd lost his bearings when he recognised a mural that he'd passed fifteen minutes before. Where was he? He stopped on a corner and turned in a circle, looking all around. His mobile couldn't pick up a 3G signal, so the map feature would do him no good. A roar in the darkening sky drew his attention and he saw lights descending towards the airport.

That way was north. The railway line he'd used to get here was also in that direction. A light drizzle began to fall as he walked. Five minutes brought him to the platform and the small shelter. Twenty minutes before a city-bound train arrived.

Daniel watched the glittering buildings through the window, Belfast looking like a proper city from here. If he searched, he'd find the building he worked in. He remembered telling the probation woman how he'd found her. No point in worrying now, he thought.

He exited Great Victoria Street station, walked through the arcade that cut beneath the Europa Hotel, past the sculptures of the Monument to the Unknown Woman Worker, the figures of two stout women in bronze. Someone had draped strings of beads around their necks. The noise of the street jarred his senses, the traffic, the hordes of people. The string of bars across the road called to him, even if they were jammed with tourists and drunks, but he kept his head down and walked south-east. Close to twenty minutes later, he reached his apartment building with its view over building sites and car parks.

Niamh met him in the hall, already in her pyjamas.

'Where've you been?' she asked, her voice carrying a mix of anger and concern.

'I had a few things to do,' he said.

'I called your work. They said you left before lunch.'

Daniel stepped past her into the kitchen. He opened the fridge, asked, 'Is there anything to eat?'

Niamh stood in the doorway, arms folded. 'What have you been doing all day?'

'Just some messages,' he said. 'I'd a few things I needed to get in town. That's all.'

The buzzer in the hall rang.

Niamh went to lift the telephone handset by the door.

'No,' Daniel said, rushing after her. 'I'll get it.'

She lifted the handset, saying, 'It's all right, I've got it.'

He tried to snatch the handset from her, but she wouldn't let go. They tussled over it for a second or two until he pushed her back, harder than he'd intended. She stumbled against the wall, hit the side of her head against the plaster. He couldn't meet her gaze when she stared back at him.

Daniel brought the handset to his ear, and Niamh punched his arm as she passed him on the way to the living room. He felt the rush of displaced air as she slammed the door.

'Hello?' he said, knowing already who it was.

★   ★   ★

Niamh lingered in the kitchen doorway, her face expressionless, as Daniel spoke with the police officers around the small dining table. A sergeant and a constable, both tall men, dark green uniforms. He noticed the pistols at their belts. They smelled of fried food. He pictured them in their patrol car, parked up in some side street, eating fish and chips.

The sergeant did most of the talking. He said there would be no further action, they just wanted a quick chat. No harm done. But don't go back.

'I won't,' Daniel said. 'I shouldn't have gone in the first place. Please pass on my apologies.'

'Miss Cunningham believes you were following her this morning,' the sergeant said. 'And that you'd followed her and a client yesterday. Is that correct?'

Daniel cleared his throat. 'That client confessed to killing my father.'

'That's as may be,' the sergeant said, 'but Miss Cunningham is just doing her job, and you've no call to be harassing her. If you have an issue with how the Probation Board has handled things, then there are ways of raising your concerns with them. You don't go doorstepping people. Now, I believe you got Miss Cunningham's address through your workplace. Where's that, exactly?'

The sergeant wrote on his notepad as Daniel told him. 'Hang on, you're not going to tell them what happened, are you?'

'I'm not,' the sergeant said. 'But if Miss Cunningham wants to make a complaint about how you used her information, then I think she's entitled, don't you?'

Daniel said nothing. Over the sergeant's shoulder, he saw Niamh close her eyes and shake her head. Her lips so thin they almost disappeared.

'Anyway, I think you've got the message.' The sergeant got to his feet. 'I don't want to be hearing any more about this. Understood?'

'Yes,' Daniel said.

The policemen saw themselves out. They did not speak to Niamh as they passed. She came to the table, sat down opposite Daniel. He kept his gaze on the grain of the oak tabletop.

After a while, she said, 'Well?'

Daniel swallowed. 'Can we talk about it tomorrow?'

'No, we can talk about it now.'

'What do you want me to say?'

'You could start with telling me why.'

He looked up, met her gaze, saw the anger there. 'I thought if I could just talk to her, get her to ask Ciaran the right questions, maybe she could get the truth out of him.'

'But what good would it do now? They served their sentences. Even if the wrong one was convicted, they both did time. What could you possibly gain from this?'

'I could clear my father's name. They said he was abusing Thomas. The things they said my father did. That never went away. Even though nothing was ever proved, what they said followed me and my mother around. You know what happened to Mum, what those lies did to her.'

A little of the anger faded from Niamh's eyes. 'Yes, I know. But you can't help her now. You can't change anything.'

'I can't help her, but what about me? I can help myself. What's so wrong with that?'

She reached for his hand, held it tight. 'Look, I understand how angry you are. I know how important all this is to you. But if we're going to stay together, you have to promise me you'll let it go. Maybe get some counselling. Maybe we could go away for a couple of weeks. Whatever it takes to help you get past this.'

Daniel shook his head. 'If you really understood how I felt, you'd know there isn't any getting past this.'

Tears formed in her eyes. 'Then where does that leave us?'

'I don't know,' he said.

Niamh slept on her own in the bedroom while Daniel took the couch in the living room. Sleep came and went in slow waves, bringing memories and dreams, the real and the unreal overlapping. He recalled his mother's long decline, how she had crumbled from the inside out. The pills from the doctor dulling her edges but not flushing out the rot that had taken hold of her mind. He had gone to live with his aunt and uncle, their children viewing him with the same distrust as he had viewed the foster kids that had invaded his own home over the years.

He remembered his aunt taking him to see his mother — still in the old house, in spite of everything — the weekend before the news of her suicide came. She had seemed better, more alert, more positive. Changes, she had said. She was going to make changes, make things better, so Daniel could come back home.

Then, three days later, she had driven for miles along the Ards Peninsula and found a small, isolated beach. There, she had undressed at the edge of the water, and walked naked into the surf. Her body washed up two days later. The coroner had said the cold probably killed her before she drowned.

Daniel did not cry at his mother's funeral. He would not allow himself.

The next morning, Niamh left for work without speaking to him.

A text message from Melanie Sherry at 8:37 a.m. asked him to call in to her office at ten-thirty. Daniel showered, dressed in fresh clothes, and went to catch the bus.

19

Weariness dried Flanagan's eyes as she stepped from the shower and towelled herself. She went to the mirror over the hand basin, watched her reflection as she ran a brush through her wet hair.

She did not look down.

With no conscious effort, she had developed a knack for avoiding seeing her body. She had only become aware of the habit of aversion in recent weeks and quickly decided she could forgive herself for this foible. Now, she made herself look.

It wasn't that bad. It really wasn't. Other women had it so much worse, their bodies devastated, but she had needed no reconstruction. In truth, it was only a bit of scarring, just like she'd said to Alistair two nights ago. It had only been a lumpectomy, after all. She examined the shiny pink disturbance of flesh on her breast.

No, it wasn't that bad.

But it was bad enough.

Of course, her body had changed over the years: she was far from the pert girl she had been twenty-five years ago. Age and childbearing had taken their toll, and the Tamoxifen she now had to take daily had caused her to gain a little weight, but she'd done her best to keep in shape.

Now this, this mark that she would carry for the rest of her days. Her body was no longer her

133

own. It belonged to the cancer now. No wonder Alistair couldn't bring himself to touch her, not if she could barely stand to look at herself.

Flanagan cursed and turned away from the mirror, feeling guilt for considering her husband so shallow, and for her own self-pity. Poor-me wallowing, and she'd be damned if she'd indulge in it.

She had slept badly the night before. Alistair had lain on the bed beside her, listening attentively, a serious expression on his face, while she recounted what had happened to Penny and Ronnie Walker. He passed no comment on her suspicion of Julie Walker's account of events.

'Well, argue with me,' she had said, 'tell me I'm wrong, whatever, just say something, for Christ's sake.'

'What do you want me to say?' he asked. 'Should I tell you you're crazy? Or should I tell you you've nailed it?'

'Just tell me what you think.'

'I think you've got nothing solid to base this on,' he said. 'All you've really got is a feeling. Is that enough to accuse this woman of killing her parents?'

'It's not enough to arrest her, but surely it's enough to take a second look, to ask some questions.'

'Don't you think this other DCI — Conn, wasn't it? — don't you think he's capable of sorting through this case for himself?'

'Of course I do,' Flanagan said, hearing the hard edge of defensiveness in her own voice. 'But he doesn't know the victims like I do.'

Alistair turned on to his side, facing away from her, pulled the duvet up to his chin. 'Get some sleep,' he said. 'Worrying about this isn't going to do you or them any good.'

But she slept little, turning it over and over in her mind, trying to see every angle. Yes, the events appeared to have flowed in exactly the way Julie Walker described them. A suicide pact between a couple unable to face their own future. Ronnie Walker putting that pillow over his wife's face, bearing his weight down on her even as her body fought to live. When Flanagan tried to picture such an act, she simply could not. Not dear shambling Ronnie who no more had the will to take a human life than he had the power to walk on water.

And Penny. She would not ask such a thing of her husband, even if she had no desire to let the disease take its agonising course.

But Julie Walker — could she do this? Could she take two lives, snuff out her parents as if they were lame horses? Was it to spare them the pain of separation? Or was it that she couldn't face caring for her father in his dwindling years?

These questions kept Flanagan from sleep through much of the night, and now her mind felt weighted by them.

A little after ten o'clock, Flanagan sat at her desk, rereading the notes from the Milligan case, fighting the weight of her fatigue as her head nodded forward again and again. The ring of the telephone cut like a light through the fog inside her head, and she was glad of the disturbance as she reached for the handset.

'I've got a Paula Cunningham from the Probation Board,' the duty officer said. 'Shall I put her through?'

'Yes,' Flanagan said, curious.

'Sorry to disturb you again,' Cunningham said. 'I wondered if we could have another talk about Ciaran Devine.'

'Go on.'

'In person.'

Flanagan hesitated for a moment, then said, 'All right. Where?'

A coffee shop on the Lisburn Road, on the southern edge of Belfast. Noon, they agreed, and ended the conversation.

Flanagan had given little thought to Ciaran Devine, or his brother, in the day or two since his release. He was grown now, had served his time, and had nothing to do with Flanagan any more. Now she remembered the boy, so young, so still and quiet on the other side of the interview room desk. She thought of the family he and his brother had destroyed, the devastation they'd left behind.

MONDAY 26TH MARCH 2007

Flanagan sat on an armchair in the Rolstons' living room, Mrs Rolston on the couch, a tissue pressed to her mouth, her eyes red. Beside her, Daniel Rolston, a pimply boy, still carrying puppy fat. The kind of boy who got bullied at school, who was picked last for sports. He had been staying with an aunt and uncle since yesterday. They had driven him over and now waited in the kitchen.

Only two days since Flanagan had last been in this room. It had seemed darker, smaller then. Now the sun shone through the window, glinting off china and picture frames. But the sunlight did not touch the Rolstons, as if averting its gaze in shame.

'Have you charged them yet?' Mrs Rolston asked.

'No,' Flanagan said. 'We have the confession from Ciaran, but we can't take it at face value. Confessions from children are always treated with caution. A child in custody will say almost anything to get out. We have to be certain before the charge is made.'

Daniel spoke, then. 'It wasn't Ciaran,' he said. 'It was Thomas.'

Flanagan paused, then asked, 'Why do you think that, Daniel?'

'Because Ciaran's my friend. Thomas is the mean one.'

Mrs Rolston took Daniel's hand. 'Ciaran hasn't got a school placement yet,' she said. 'Thomas has to take a bus across town for his school, so there were about forty minutes or so on school days when Ciaran and Daniel were alone together. They got to be pals, sort of, as much as anyone can be friends with a boy like Ciaran.' She looked directly at Flanagan, lowered her voice as if her son wasn't sitting right beside her. 'Daniel doesn't have many friends.'

'Thomas used to hurt me,' Daniel said. 'I told Mum and Dad, but Mum didn't believe me.'

Mrs Rolston squeezed his fingers between hers. 'I thought it was just boys being boys. You know how rough they play. David gave the boys a talking-to, all three of them, told them to go easy.'

Daniel pulled his hand away. 'You should've believed me.'

Mrs Rolston seemed to retreat into herself as she dropped her gaze to the crumpled tissue in her lap. 'It was David wanted to foster children, not me,' she said. 'I couldn't have any more after Daniel, so David wanted to take in the ones who needed help, as he put it. He was an orphan himself, you see. He thought he was doing good. They were decent kids at heart, he said, they just needed a bit of care. He was trying to help Thomas with his schoolwork, telling him he could make something of himself. And look what that got him.'

When she was sure Mrs Rolston had finished,

Flanagan leafed through her notes and said, 'I have a difficult question to put to you. I have to warn you both, you'll find this upsetting.'

Mrs Rolston looked up from her tissue. Daniel kept his stare fixed on the wall somewhere over Flanagan's shoulder.

'The Devine brothers have made an accusation against Mr Rolston.'

'What kind of accusation?'

Flanagan swallowed. 'They have alleged that Mr Rolston sexually abused Thomas Devine repeatedly over the three months leading up to the killing.'

Fresh tears welled in Mrs Rolston's eyes before rolling down her pale cheeks. 'The bastards,' she said, her voice quivering in her chest. 'Those evil little bastards.'

Her hands began to shake.

'I'm sorry, Mrs Rolston, I understand how difficult this is, but I have to ask. Had you any knowledge or suspicion that your husband might have abused Thomas?'

Mrs Rolston shook her head. 'How can you say that?'

'I have to ask the question, however hard it is.'

'I'd like you to leave now.'

Flanagan turned to the boy. 'Daniel, have you ever seen or heard anything like this? Had your father ever behaved inappropriately towards you?'

'Get out,' Mrs Rolston said as she stood.

'Daniel?'

Daniel stared straight ahead.

'Get out of my house,' Mrs Rolston said, her

139

voice rising in pitch and volume with each word, her finger pointing to the door.

'Please, Mrs Rolston, I have no choice but to follow this line — '

'Get the fuck out of my house!'

The force of Mrs Rolston's cry jangled in Flanagan's ears.

Footsteps in the hall, then the door opened, and the uncle looked through. 'Everything all right?' he asked.

'Get this bitch out of my house,' Mrs Rolston shouted, her voice shrill and piercing. 'Get her out of my fucking house right now!'

'It's all right,' Flanagan said, packing away her notebook and pen. 'We can do this another time. Thank you.'

She looked no one in the eye as she left the room, hurried along the hall, and exited the house. Once inside her car, she closed her eyes and willed herself to be calm.

★ ★ ★

The social worker — a different one from yesterday and the day before — looked bored as she sat beside Ciaran in the interview room. She had contributed almost nothing to the interview save for the occasional nudge or whisper in the boy's ear.

Flanagan had stacked up hour after hour in this room. She'd worked Ciaran all day yesterday, and more today. The vague questions narrowing down until they reached the specifics of the act. Nothing changed. Not a single

140

variation in the answers. It bothered her that neither he nor Thomas had misremembered a single detail the way most people would under pressure.

It was too good.

'I spoke with Mrs Rolston and her son earlier today,' Flanagan said. 'Mrs Rolston denied any knowledge or suspicion of her husband ever abusing your brother. Do you have anything to say to that, Ciaran?'

He shook his head.

'For the record, the detained person responded in the negative. Ciaran, I also spoke by telephone with three boys the Rolstons fostered over the years. They're grown-ups now. I asked all of them if Mr Rolston had ever sexually abused them. All of them said no. In fact, all three of them were very shocked at the suggestion. They all said Mr Rolston had been very kind to them. I'm going to speak with as many boys the Rolstons fostered as I can. I have to tell you, I expect their responses to be similar. Do you have any comment to make?'

Again, Ciaran shook his head.

'The detained person has responded in the negative. Ciaran, please think very carefully about what you're accusing Mr Rolston of. You have to think about how much more hurt this is going to cause his family. Remember we talked about the truth? The truth is the best thing for everybody — for you, for Thomas, for Daniel, for Mrs Rolston. If Mr Rolston did those things to Thomas, then that's what you have to tell me, and the court when it comes to trial. But if he didn't, Ciaran, please don't lie about it.'

'He did do it to Thomas,' Ciaran said. 'I heard him. That's why I had to kill him. To make it stop.'

'Why didn't you tell anyone before that? You could've told your case worker. A teacher at school. The police. Anyone.'

'No one would believe us,' Ciaran said.

'They might have,' Flanagan said. 'Then you wouldn't have had to hurt Mr Rolston. You wouldn't be here now.'

'I had to kill him,' Ciaran said, staring hard at Flanagan. 'For Thomas.'

★   ★   ★

'So?' Flanagan asked as DCI Purdy shut off the video.

DI Mark Speers studied his own notes across the table. He had logged hours of interviews with Thomas Devine, he and Flanagan reporting back to Purdy. Newspapers lay scattered over the surface of the table, the Sunday rags, and Monday dailies. And not just the local Belfast papers. There was the *Sun*, the *Mirror*, the *Daily Mail*. Glaring headlines about the barbaric killing of a decent man by the children in his care. The Devine brothers hadn't been named, though the reporters surely knew who was in custody, and Flanagan hoped that would remain the case.

'Apart from what the Rolston boy told you,' Purdy said, 'we've nothing to contradict Ciaran's confession. You've both compared notes. Their

142

stories match up. Every last detail. Tell me what you're thinking.'

Flanagan sat back in her chair and exhaled. She brought her fingertips to her temples, massaged them, as if the pressure would solidify her thoughts into a cogent argument.

'I'm just not sure,' she said. 'The time I've spent with Ciaran. He doesn't seem like the kind of boy who could do this. Thomas, on the other hand . . .'

Speers looked up from his notepad. A few years older than Flanagan, a clear and handsome face. He enjoyed being a cop, acted as if he was constantly on camera in some TV drama.

'Thomas is a cold one, all right,' he said. 'But he hasn't put a foot wrong since he was brought in, from the First Account on. I've used the cognitive method throughout, narrowing it right down, the information funnel, just like you and me were trained to do. Thomas has been rock solid all the way. From what you've reported, so has Ciaran. The events, as far as we can ascertain, run like this: Ciaran goes upstairs to the master bedroom, finds Thomas cornered there by Mr Rolston. Ciaran grabs the bookend, sets about Mr Rolston with it. Thomas tries to stop him, but Ciaran's too far gone, he's lost control. The only person who's saying different is a kid who was miles away when it happened. I don't know how else to come at it. Do you?'

'If I can keep working with Ciaran,' Flanagan said, 'see if I can get him to open up. I don't mean on record, we don't need the social worker there. I mean talk to him alone, as a friend, see if

143

I can get him to — '

Purdy interrupted. 'We've had them coming up on forty-eight hours without a charge. That's pushing things as it is. It may be a murder case, but they're still children. If I go to the superintendent and ask for another extension, you know damn well he's going to tell me to shit or get off the pot.'

'But, sir, you can try,' Flanagan said. 'I know another twenty-four hours is a lot to ask for when we're dealing with kids, but Christ, if we get this wrong, it's the rest of their lives we're talking about.'

Purdy leaned forward, rested his chin on his palm. 'All right, fuck it. I'll give it a go.'

'Thank you.'

'But I'll tell you now,' Purdy said. 'You're wrong on this one. Ciaran Devine is the killer.'

20

Ciaran has been waiting outside the hostel for ten minutes already. His stomach is all fluttery inside. Nerves and joy, joy and nerves. As the minutes grind past, the nerves turn to fear. Has Thomas forgotten? Ciaran chews his thumbnail. Of course Thomas hasn't forgotten. Thomas never forgets anything.

Almost another five minutes go by before the red car pulls in from the main road. Ciaran feels the grin break on his face, a laugh rising up all bubbly from his belly. He lifts a hand and waves. Thomas does not wave back. He's too busy turning the car.

Ciaran opens the passenger door and lowers himself into the seat. Thomas leans across, puts a hand around Ciaran's neck, draws him closer and plants a kiss on his cheek.

'Newcastle,' Thomas says. 'Will that do?'

'Yeah,' Ciaran says. He can't keep the laughter from his voice.

Newcastle, not far from where they lived in those last good days. County Down, he thinks. Ciaran hasn't been back since. He knows there's a place in England with the same name, but Newcastle here is different with its long beach and rolling waves.

'It's a bit of a drive, but we've got all day.'

Thomas puts the car in gear and sets off. Soon they are heading out of the city, going south,

145

buildings left behind, all around.

Ciaran notices the torn skin on Thomas's knuckles.

He says nothing.

21

Daniel arrived at the office five minutes late. Melanie stood at her door, waiting for him, the smile on her lips looking like it had been fixed there since the previous morning. She stood back and allowed him to enter.

Beside the desk sat Andrew Hanna, the regional manager. Daniel recognised him from his picture in the company newsletter. Hanna stood and extended a hand. Daniel shook it.

'Take a wee seat,' Melanie said.

Daniel did so, waited for her to do the same.

When everyone was in place, Melanie said, 'So.'

She looked towards Hanna, who looked at Daniel.

Hanna said, 'Daniel, we're letting you go.'

Just like that. No preamble. No soft landing.

Daniel cleared his throat, said, 'Okay.'

'I assume you know why,' Hanna said. 'But I'll explain anyway. We received a complaint early this morning that you had, for whatever reason, used our network and databases to find personal information on someone and then harass them.'

'I didn't harass anybody,' Daniel said. 'I just knocked on her door to — '

Melanie spoke now, that smile still on her lips. 'And one of your colleagues tells me you printed out this information here in the office, then took it home with you. By the terms of your wee contract, that's an immediate dismissal. Do you have anything to say for yourself?'

'Just one thing,' Daniel said. 'Please, for the love of God, stop smiling.'

She did, for a moment.

'And stop calling everything wee. It's not a wee contract. It's fifteen pages, for Christ's sake.'

Hanna pushed an envelope across the desk. 'Here you go. You'll be paid up to the end of the month, which I'm sure you'll agree is more than fair under the circumstances. Now, if you've no more questions . . . '

Daniel stood and left the office without lifting the envelope. At the Xerox machine he saw Chris Greely, a paper cup full of water in his hand, waiting for a printout. Greely saw him approach, smiled, said, 'You off, then?'

Daniel slapped the cup from Greely's hand, sent water splashing across the copier. He felt a surge of pleasure as he seized Greely's throat, pushed him back against the wall, forced his knuckles in under his chin, squeezing the windpipe. Greely's eyes bulged, his mouth opening and closing. Gasps around the office. A hand on Daniel's shoulder. He turned his head to see Hanna. Whatever Hanna saw in Daniel's eyes was enough to convince him to take his hand away.

He turned back to Greely. 'I'll be back for you,' Daniel said. 'Might be here, might be somewhere else. Might be today, might be some other day. But I promise I'll get you.'

Daniel let go and Greely fell to the floor. Colleagues rushed to help him, giving Daniel

148

fearful glances. Daniel supposed he should have felt ashamed, embarrassed, possibly regretful. Instead, he felt taller than he ever had.

He took the lift down to the ground floor, exited the building, and walked the hundred yards or so to the bus stop. When the police car rounded the corner he knew they were coming for him, and he was glad.

22

Flanagan found Paula Cunningham in the far corner of the coffee shop. Early lunchtime chatter all around, the smell of cooking food and sweet things. Her stomach rumbled, and she remembered she'd skipped breakfast that morning.

Cunningham stood as Flanagan approached, extended her hand. She already had a half-empty coffee cup on the table. Flanagan ordered a tea from a passing waitress. Cunningham declined another cup.

'So, you needed more on Ciaran Devine,' Flanagan said as she took a seat.

'That's right,' Cunningham said. 'Him and his brother.'

'I'm not sure I can tell you anything that isn't already on record.'

'I've read everything I could get my hands on,' Cunningham said. 'But I wondered how you felt about him and his brother, personally. Setting the confession aside, did you have Ciaran for this?'

The hunger left Flanagan's belly, her appetite frozen out by a sudden chill there. She hoped it didn't show on her face. 'It didn't matter much what I thought personally. It wasn't my case, remember, I just worked on it. It was the coordinating DCI who called the shots. In the end, all that mattered was the confession, and

150

what the Public Prosecution Service could do with it.'

'I understand that,' Cunningham said. 'I know these things are never black and white, this case more than most, but it's your gut feeling I'm interested in.'

A pot of tea arrived. Flanagan left it to brew. 'Has Ciaran said something?'

'No, not directly. Do you remember the Rolstons' son?'

'Yes,' Flanagan said. 'Daniel. I only spoke with him once. He was a bright boy. But very mixed up.'

'He called at my house last night.'

'What, just out of the blue?'

'Yes. He was angry, and frightened, I think. I had to call the police. He'd gone by the time they came, but they tracked him down, gave him a warning.'

'What did he want?' Flanagan asked.

'To tell me the police and the court had got it all wrong. That Ciaran hadn't killed his father. It was Thomas. I suppose he thinks I can get something out of Ciaran, something the police couldn't, but I don't know why. Did Daniel say anything at the time of the investigation?'

'Not on record. His statement barely came into things, the case seemed so clear cut, particularly with the confession. He didn't have to give evidence during the trial. Everyone felt it would be too hard on him; it wouldn't have made enough of a difference to justify putting him through that.'

'Not on record, you said. What about off the record?'

Flanagan poured tea into her cup, followed by milk, watched the swirling clouds, and her own glinting reflection on the surface.

Cunningham waited.

No avoiding it, Flanagan spoke. 'Yes, Daniel told me he believed Thomas had killed his father. He said Ciaran and he had become friends. That Thomas had been hurting him. I put that to Ciaran, of course, but his story never changed.'

'You spent a lot of time with Ciaran,' Cunningham said.

Flanagan shifted in her seat and reached for the cup. 'That's right.'

'A lot more than most investigating officers would spend with a suspect.'

Steam rose from the cup and warmed Flanagan's lips.

'It took a long time for him to open up,' she said. 'Even with the confession, we needed to understand what exactly happened in that house. I spent hours and hours working with him. I needed to get his trust. Remember, he and his brother had been from institution to foster home and back again for most of their lives. I'm not sure how well Ciaran really knew his mother. A situation like that, the bond between siblings becomes incredibly strong. They build a wall around themselves. It becomes them against the world. I had to try to break through that.'

'It looked like you managed,' Cunningham said.

'Eventually.' Flanagan took a sip of tea. Stinging hot in her throat.

'Tell me about it,' Cunningham said. 'Please.'

MONDAY 26TH MARCH 2007

While Purdy talked to the Superintendent, Flanagan and Ciaran sat opposite each other in the interview room waiting for another social worker. She'd brought him two slices of buttered toast and a cup of milky tea. She watched as he picked the crusts off the bread.

'I'll cut them off next time,' she said.

Ciaran didn't answer. He licked melted butter off his fingers. The same fingers that had been slickened red only two days before.

Flanagan looked at her wristwatch, then up at the clock on the wall. The social worker was approaching ten minutes late.

'What's your favourite thing to eat?' she asked.

Ciaran shrugged, took a bite of toast.

'There must be something,' Flanagan said.

He shrugged again, chewed.

'What about burgers? Sausages? Crisps?'

Ciaran took a breath. Flanagan held hers. He did not speak.

'Tell me,' she said.

'I like chip butties.'

'Ah.' Flanagan nodded respectfully. 'Red or brown sauce?'

'No sauce,' Ciaran said. 'Just salt and vinegar.'

'I like red sauce on mine. Do you know what my husband likes on his?'

'What?' Ciaran asked.

'Mayonnaise.'

Ciaran's nose wrinkled in distaste.

'I know,' Flanagan said.

Ciaran smiled. Flanagan's heart floated in her chest. A knock on the door, and she went to it. Purdy waited on the other side.

Flanagan stepped through, pulled the door closed behind her. 'Well?'

'He gave us another twelve hours, starting at five-thirty,' Purdy said. 'Unless you turn up something remarkable, those boys will be charged before dawn tomorrow morning.'

Flanagan shook her head. 'That's not enough time.'

'It's all you've got,' Purdy said, walking away. 'Make the most of it.'

The social worker dashed along the corridor, apologising as she approached. Flanagan brought her into the interview room. Once the audio recorder was running, as soon as Ciaran was cautioned, the child whose smile had thrilled her so had vanished. Instead, here was this boy who repeated the same answers to the same questions until Flanagan wanted to shake him.

She ended the interview after forty-five minutes, sent the social worker on her way, and signed Ciaran back into the custody suite.

Outside in the car park, Flanagan called Alistair from her mobile.

'I'm sorry,' she said, 'it's looking like an all-nighter here.'

'You can't,' Alistair said. 'Not in your condition. What about the baby?'

154

'I'll be fine. And so will the baby.'

Her hand went to her stomach. This thing in her belly, not much bigger than a peanut.

'Just you worry about Ruth,' she said. 'Give her a kiss for me.'

'All right. But take it easy.'

'You too,' she said. 'Love you.'

'Love you too.'

Warmed by those last words, Flanagan walked from the station to the chippie one street over. She ordered two chip butties, one with red sauce, the other with salt and vinegar, along with a can each of Coke and Fanta, and brought them back to Ciaran's cell. She sat beside him on the mattress, the cell door open, and handed the plain buttie to him. He took it from her fingers, breathed in the aroma of fried potato and malt vinegar.

'Did you get Thomas one?' he asked.

'No,' Flanagan said. 'Just you and me.'

Ciaran held the bread roll in his thin fingers, chips squeezing out from within. He hesitated, then took a bite, big enough to puff his cheeks out. Flanagan did the same. They sat side by side in the cell and ate in silence until every bite was gone.

Only when she'd drained the last swallow of cola from the can did Flanagan realise that Ciaran was leaning against her, shoulder to shoulder. She suppressed the urge to put an arm around him, to gather him in. But nor did she move away.

He took a breath, held it in his chest. A word unspoken.

'What?' Flanagan asked.

'What's it like in jail?' he asked, the fear rippling beneath his voice.

'It won't be a proper jail,' she said. 'It's a young offenders centre. Hydebank. It'll be tough, but it won't be prison. It's probably not that different from places you and Thomas have stayed before.'

'Will I be there for the rest of my life?'

Flanagan closed her eyes against the ache his question caused. If his confession was real, he didn't deserve her pity, child or not. But it was there, regardless.

'There's no fixed sentence for a child,' Flanagan said. 'It'll be years, but if you're good, you'll be out before you're twenty. You'll still have your life ahead of you.'

'Will Thomas be there too?'

'Yes,' Flanagan said. 'But he'll get out before you do.'

She felt him tense against her arm. 'So I'll be on my own?'

'He'll be able to visit you.'

He began to shake, and now Flanagan did put her arm around him. He leaned in to her, chewed on his thumbnail.

'Thomas is nearly fifteen, isn't he?'

'Yeah,' Ciaran said.

'You know, if Thomas had done this, it'd be very different. He'd go to Hydebank, just like you, but he'd be held longer. Very probably, he'd move to a real prison, to Maghaberry, when he turned twenty-one. But if you took the blame for him, because you're younger, the judge would go easier on you. And even lighter still on Thomas.'

Ciaran became still and silent, not even a breath.

'You'd do anything Thomas asked you to, wouldn't you?'

He seemed to shrink in her embrace, as if retreating from the world. She ran her fingertips over his short-cropped hair.

'You'd say you killed someone if he asked you to, wouldn't you?'

He turned his face downward and away so she couldn't see him. His shoulders hitched.

Flanagan let the air out her lungs in a weary exhalation. 'Oh, sweetheart, it's going to be a long night.'

23

A chilled breeze comes in off the sea as Ciaran sits on the bench beside Thomas, eating the chip buttie his brother bought for him. Thomas eats nothing. Sunlight reflects off the water, a sheet of solid grey, like storm clouds stretching away from them. Ciaran had forgotten the smell of salt on the air, the sound of waves on sand. He savours them now.

They had arrived late morning and walked the length of the beach twice before seeking food. Once they'd found the nearest chip shop, they came back to the waterfront and settled on a bench beneath the grand buildings and sloping gardens of the Slieve Donard hotel. Elderly couples walk arm in arm along the sand, dogs and their owners play, a few children shout and run through the foaming edge of the tide.

Ciaran should feel happy, but Thomas is thoughtful. Thomas never spends thought on good things. He is restless, his fingers tapping on his thighs, the soles of his shoes grinding on the fine layer of sand that coats the concrete under their feet.

'When your supervision's up,' Thomas says, 'we'll go away somewhere. Maybe to England. Somewhere decent, somewhere nobody knows us.'

Ciaran is too busy eating to think of a reply.

'Where would you want to go?' Thomas asks.

'Dunno,' Ciaran says. 'America, maybe.'

'You can't just go to America to live,' Thomas says. 'You need a visa or a green card or something. We don't even have passports. If we get passports, we can go somewhere in Europe. Germany or France. Maybe even Spain. They've nice beaches there. Would you like that?'

'I can't speak foreign,' Ciaran says.

'Me neither,' Thomas says. 'It'll have to be England, then. Maybe Scotland. Not Wales, though.'

Ciaran doesn't ask why. Thomas looks back out to sea.

'Mum's old house is near here,' Ciaran says.

Thomas turns to him again. 'Yeah. Just up the coast a bit.'

'Can we go there?'

'No,' Thomas says.

'Why not?'

'Because I don't want to. Besides, it's not ours any more. Not since I sold it. It was a dump anyway. Its all fenced off now. I suppose they'll knock it down soon. I'm surprised you even remember that place.'

Ciaran remembers. The only clear memories he has of his mother are located in that house. He can't recall his father: his first memory is the funeral. The weeping carried on the breeze through the graveyard. They lived in another house then, but it had to be sold, and the two boys and their mother moved to the old farmhouse by the sea. It had belonged to her parents, and Ciaran remembered her telling him how she and his father had planned to fix it up,

159

to make it a holiday home for them all.

How happy they would have been, she said. And then it was all gone, stolen from them by a teenager in a hijacked car.

The land surrounding the house was sold off acre by acre to keep them going, until it stood alone behind its walls, cold and damp, the air seeming to creep through the rooms and hallways in ghostly currents. They would huddle around the fire in the kitchen every evening, sometimes sharing a blanket. Teresa staring into the flames, her soul drifting farther and farther away.

At first, she would hug her boys and tell them everything was going to be all right. But that lasted only a few months. After a while, she barely spoke to them at all. She kept them fed, made sure they had clothes to wear. But if Thomas didn't want to go to school, she wouldn't argue. And if Thomas stayed home, then so would Ciaran. The brothers would leave her in the house and walk the quarter-mile to the beach. Running through the fields and grass-capped dunes, they would laugh and chase each other until they were too cold or too hungry to stay out any longer. Then their laughter would die in their throats as they headed back to the house.

The social workers started to call. Asking after the boys. Why had they missed so much school? How was their health? Were they eating properly?

Teresa would make tearful apologies and promise to do better, to make them go to school, to be a better mother.

A man came twice or three times a week. A small man with dead eyes. Sometimes he would go no further than the doorstep, other times he would follow Teresa to her bedroom. But he always left a small package behind.

'Mummy's medicine,' she said, when Ciaran asked.

One morning Ciaran and Thomas woke late in the room they shared. They walked downstairs together and found Teresa slumped over the kitchen table, her eyes half closed and glassy, drool pooling on the wood.

The needle still in her arm.

They stood and watched their mother for a time, listening to the shallow wheezes from her chest. She smelled of urine and excrement. Her bare feet rested in a puddle.

Eventually, Thomas said, 'I should get a doctor.'

They had no telephone, no car. Ciaran had to wait half an hour before Thomas came back with a neighbour who had called an ambulance. In that time, he sat opposite his mother, counting the puncture marks on her skin.

They spent the night in a shelter, and Ciaran never entered the house again.

He wonders if the table is still there, and the syringe sitting on top of it.

'The other night,' Thomas says, 'why were you looking up that woman cop on my computer?'

Ciaran stops chewing for a moment, feels something fold in on itself low down in his stomach.

'Well?'

Ciaran swallows. Takes another bite. Thomas takes the buttie from his fingers and tosses it away onto the sand. Seagulls swoop and feast. Ciaran wipes his empty hands on his jeans.

'Answer me,' Thomas says.

'I don't know,' Ciaran says, his voice very small. 'I wanted to know if she was still in the police. Maybe if she'd been in the news for anything. Something. I don't know.'

'She was a bitch,' Thomas says.

Ciaran forces his hands down into the pockets of his hoodie to keep them still.

'She's probably still a bitch,' Thomas says. 'She tried to get between us. To break us apart. And you almost let her. I told you a million times, you can't trust people like that. Not cops, not probation officers, not social workers, not foster carers. They're all the same. They'll make out they're on your side, that they're only trying to help you. But all they care about is putting you away. That woman cop, she let you think she was your friend, didn't she?'

Ciaran looks out to sea, picks out the hazy shape of a freighter on the horizon.

'Didn't she?'

'Yeah,' Ciaran says.

'And what did she do in the end? She made sure you went away for seven years. What kind of friend does that? So why were you looking her up?'

'Just because,' Ciaran says. Anger has sharpened his voice.

Thomas's hand where Ciaran's neck meets his shoulder, squeezing tight. 'Don't get thick with

162

me. We're only talking. Right?'

'Right,' Ciaran says, breathing the anger out.

'What would you do if you found her?'

The question sends Ciaran's mind into a spin. He couldn't speak the answer even if he knew it. Thomas's hand moves to the back of his neck. Slow, soothing motions, like he knows the chaos he's caused.

'Would you talk to her?' Thomas asks.

'Dunno.'

'Would you hurt her?'

'No.'

'Would you try to kiss her?'

'No!' A shout, carried away from them on the breeze. Ciaran pulls away from his brother's hand.

Thomas grins. 'She's married. She has kids. What would she want with you?'

Ciaran wants to tell Thomas to shut his fucking mouth, but he doesn't dare. Instead, he bites his knuckle, hopes the pain will chase the anger out of him.

The grin slides away from Thomas's face. 'You know, if you ever went near her, she'd put you back inside. No question. She'd go to that probation woman, and they'd say you were a risk. You'd be back inside, and I don't know if I could wait for you like I did these last few years.'

Ciaran's eyes are hot, but he will not cry. He will not.

Thomas leans in close, his warm damp hand wrapped around the back of Ciaran's neck, his lips against Ciaran's ear. 'Do you want to hear a secret?'

Ciaran closes his eyes.

'I know where she lives.'

Thomas stands and walks away across the sand.

24

Cunningham listened as Flanagan spoke, picturing the child Ciaran Devine had once been. The child he still was, really.

'I suppose that's the thing that struck me most,' Flanagan said. 'He was at that age when boys change. I could see the man he might have been, if he'd had a chance, and the little boy he was leaving behind.'

'That's the saddest part of kids that age being locked up,' Cunningham said. 'Ciaran went away a twelve-year-old, and he came out seven years later, still a twelve-year-old. All that growing up he's missed. How anyone expects him to cope, I don't know.'

'I guess that's your job,' Flanagan said.

'My job is risk management. To do my best to make sure he doesn't hurt himself or anyone else. I can take him shopping, I can help him get a job, but I can't show him how to live among ordinary people, how to cope without the structures forced on him when he was inside. Whether or not he's mentally fit enough to look after himself is neither here nor there. I don't get to make that decision.'

Flanagan gave a sad smile. 'That's the problem with jobs like ours, isn't it? The gap between what we wish we could achieve and what we can actually do.'

Cunningham nodded. 'True.'

She wondered what it would be like to know Flanagan outside of her work. Cunningham had lost more friends than she'd gained over the years. Since she and Alex had split, she had often found herself wondering about the people around her. Were they all lonely too? Were their lives more complete than hers? The trilling of her mobile phone brought her back to the present, away from this self-indulgent wallowing.

She took the phone from her bag, saw the number. 'I'd better take this.'

Flanagan nodded.

'Miss Cunningham? This is Sergeant Peter McMurray.'

'Yes,' Cunningham said. 'What can I do for you?'

'I just thought you should know, Daniel Rolston was arrested this morning following a disturbance at his workplace. He was fired. Seems he didn't take it too well.'

'Is he in a lot of trouble?' Cunningham asked.

Flanagan looked at her across the table.

'The management at the call centre don't want to make a fuss about it,' McMurray said. 'He'll be let go with a caution. I just thought I should let you know. If he comes anywhere near you, if you see him at all, call 999 immediately. I'm guessing he'll just lie low now, but it does no harm to be careful.'

'Okay,' Cunningham said, 'thank you.'

She returned the phone to her bag and repeated what she'd been told to Flanagan.

The policewoman gave her a smile that was probably meant to reassure. 'Like the sergeant

166

said, he'll lie low. I'm sure there's nothing to worry about.'

'It's not me I'm worried about,' Cunningham said. 'What if he goes after the Devines?'

Flanagan shrugged. 'If it happens, it happens. There's nothing you can do about that.'

Cunningham pushed that thought aside and asked, 'So what went wrong?'

'Excuse me?'

'You said you'd got through to Ciaran. Got him to open up to you. But he wound up getting charged anyway. He didn't withdraw the confession.'

Flanagan's eyes focused on the street outside. 'No, he didn't.'

'Why not?'

'It was complicated. A lot of factors. Things I didn't . . . '

The words trailed off, and Cunningham considered pressing harder, but she sensed Flanagan's discomfort. She held her silence, waited to see if the policewoman would find a way to say what she wanted to say.

Eventually Flanagan said, 'The last interview didn't go so well. Let's just leave it at that.'

Cunningham had known enough police officers to understand the trauma they endured in the course of their work, and that often they found it hard to revisit those ugly moments.

'All right,' she said. 'When you feel like you can talk about it, I'll be ready to listen.'

Flanagan looked back to the window, wading in some dark memory.

MONDAY 26TH–TUESDAY 27TH MARCH 2007

They talked almost to eleven. About superheroes, about *Star Wars*, about football, about family, about love, about death. She told him secrets, and he told her lies. Curled there, held beneath her arm. Ciaran talked about Thomas, how his brother always had looked after him and always would. They talked about the future, the years ahead of him.

When she asked him to imagine a life without his brother, he froze, as if the watch on her wrist had stopped, along with every other clock in the building.

'You can live without him,' she said. 'You haven't seen him for nearly three days. You're still alive, aren't you?'

Silence until, eventually, he said, 'I'm tired.'

'I'll let you sleep, then. But it's an early start in the morning. Unless something changes, you're going to be charged at five-thirty a.m. Then I won't be able to talk to you again.'

As if it was the most natural thing in the world, as if there was no line to be crossed, he lowered his head into her lap.

Flanagan lifted her hands away. They hung above him, suspended by uncertainty. She looked up at the camera in the corner, held her palms up and out. Not touching. Her mouth

168

opened, ready to ask him to move, when he spoke.

'I want to tell the truth,' he said.

Flanagan lowered her hands. She touched her fingertips to his cheek. 'Okay. But not now. It has to be on record or what you say doesn't count. I'll arrange an interview for the morning, before the deadline. All right?'

He nodded and closed his eyes. Soon his breathing settled, his shoulders rising and falling as he slept. His breath warmed her thigh. As gently as she could, she lifted his head, slipped from under him, and left the cell. He did not wake.

As Flanagan left the block, Sergeant Richie approached, ready to lock up after her. His gaze fixed on her, eyes hard. She did not look away.

'Everything all right in there?' he asked.

'Fine,' she said.

'You were a long time. I was watching on the monitor.'

She stopped, challenged him with her posture. 'And?'

'You were getting awful friendly with him,' the custody sergeant said. 'I was close to coming in to see what was going on.'

Flanagan took a step closer. 'And what exactly do you think was going on?'

He seemed to lose an inch in height under her stare. 'Nothing. But I'm responsible for that kid while he's in here. I won't have any . . . '

'Any what?'

The custody sergeant backed away. 'It's late. I think it's best you leave the block now.'

Flanagan walked to the car park and called DCI Purdy. He grumbled at his sleep being disturbed, and even more when she told him she wanted to set up an interview for four-thirty a.m. But he agreed. One more call secured yet another out-of-hours social worker.

She re-entered the building and found a stained and weathered couch to sleep on.

She dreamed of small, bloodied hands on her body and woke up gasping.

★ ★ ★

Flanagan brought tea and toast to Ciaran's cell at four a.m., along with a fresh set of clothes. She left him to eat and dress before signing him out of the custody suite and taking him to the interview room. Checking her watch, she saw they had five or six minutes before the social worker was due. She slouched at the table, Ciaran on the chair beside her. Weariness made her head heavy and dried her eyes.

'What do you want to be when you're older?' Flanagan asked.

Ciaran leaned his chin on his forearms. 'I wanted to write comics. Do you have to go to university to do that?'

She studied him beneath the room's hard fluorescent lighting. A handsome young boy. She wondered what he'd look like as a grown man. Then she felt a pang of sadness for the future he'd thrown away.

'I don't know,' she said. 'I don't think there's a particular qualification you need. But having a

170

degree is good, no matter what you want to do.'

He traced imaginary shapes on the desktop with his forefinger. 'I'll never go to university now.'

'There's no reason why not,' Flanagan said. 'You'll be in the Young Offenders Centre for a few years, there's no getting away from that. But it doesn't mean your life's over. You can still get an education and do your exams. GCSEs, A levels even. There's nothing to stop you going to university when you get out. Not if you work hard enough and keep out of trouble.'

Ciaran stayed quiet, staring across the room.

'What?' Flanagan asked. 'Tell me what you're thinking.'

Ciaran sniffed, rubbed his nose on the back of his hand. 'Thomas won't let me go to university.'

'Well, that's not really up to Thomas, is it?'

He rested his forehead on his arms, his nose touching the desktop. Flanagan watched the rise and fall of his back, his ribcage expanding and contracting.

'Is it?' she asked again.

'Everything's up to Thomas.'

Flanagan placed her hand on his back, between his shoulder blades, felt the bones of him through the sweatshirt. 'I know you love him,' she said. 'But he doesn't own you. You're your own person. No one can tell you how to live but you.'

His shoulders quivered. A sharp inhalation, then a watery exhalation. Tears pooled on the desktop. She moved her hand in a circle, then down his spine, back up again.

'I wish it hadn't happened,' he said, the words choked between sobs. 'I wish I could take it back. I don't want to go to jail. I don't want Mr Rolston to be dead. I want . . . '

The words were lost, drowned by weeping.

'C'mere,' Flanagan said. She gathered him up like a bundle of rags, took him in her arms, held him close. Rocked him as he cried his heart out once more.

She didn't know how much time had passed as the sobbing died away, his cheek hot against hers, his lips against her neck. Only that she became aware of the movement of his hand beneath the hem of her skirt. She inhaled, her mind suddenly paralysed.

His hand, so warm there.

Flanagan put her hands on his upper arms, eased his body away from hers. She reached down, moved his hand back to his own lap. His eyes, still red with tears, remained fixed on hers.

'Ciaran, you can't touch me like that.'

His hand crossed the space between them, went to her breast, his fingers spreading, cupping. His eyes so blue.

She slapped him once, hard, rocking his head to the side. The sting of it hot on her palm. She stood, left the room, closed the door, leaned her back against it. Trembling all over, heart galloping.

From the other side, the noise of thrown furniture, screaming rage, animal fury.

'Fuck,' she said.

25

They let Daniel go at six that evening. No further action so long as he accepted the caution. They'd taken him to the police station on Victoria Street, by the shopping mall in the city centre. He'd spent most of the day in a cell, had been calm and compliant all along, even when they stopped in the street to arrest him. The other two people at the bus stop had tried to look uninterested in what was happening, looking anywhere but at Daniel. But they could have looked all they wanted. He didn't care.

The policemen had been polite and friendly. Daniel had watched many reality shows on television following the police on traffic patrols and drug raids. The criminals on the television always fought, always wound up face down on the ground, their hands bound behind their backs, sometimes their legs strapped together to stop them kicking. Sometimes they were even pepper-sprayed, leaving them screaming in agony and fury as their eyes streamed and snot bubbled from their noses. Daniel didn't understand why. It wasn't that bad being arrested.

At five minutes past six, Daniel left the station and crossed the road to the bright yellow ornamental fountain at the shopping mall's eastern entrance. The pub beside it had already filled with workers from the surrounding office buildings having a drink to celebrate the end of their week's labour. After a moment's thought, he decided to join them.

Three and a half hours later, pleasingly drunk, Daniel let himself in to the flat. He found Niamh in the bedroom stowing a last few items into their biggest suitcase.

'What are you doing?' he asked from the doorway.

'I'm going to Mum and Dad's for the weekend.'

'All the way to Strabane? At this time?' He looked at his wrist, realised he wasn't wearing his watch.

'If there's a late bus, I can be there by midnight,' she said, zipping the case closed. 'If there's not, I'll stay in a hotel and go in the morning.'

He wiped his hand across his mouth, wondering what there was to drink in the flat. 'But you'll be back on Sunday, won't you?'

'I don't know,' she said. 'Probably not.'

'So when?'

'Maybe never.' She would not look at him. 'Probably never.'

'But I need you.'

Niamh sniffed, covered her eyes with one hand as if shielding them from the light. 'I'm not what you need. What you need is counselling. You need to talk to someone who can help you move on. That's not me. I can't live like this. I can't live in fear of you.'

'Fear?'

'The way you've been. That side of you.'

'What do you mean?'

'You've gotten physical. You've pushed me. How do I know you won't go further next time?'

'I'd never hurt you,' he said. 'Never. You know that.'

'But I *don't* know that. I really don't.'

She hoisted the suitcase off the bed and crossed the room to him. He did not move.

'I want to get past,' she said. 'I've ordered a taxi to the bus station. It'll be waiting.'

Daniel felt numb from his chest to his stomach. 'Please,' he said. 'Not now.'

She did not make eye contact. 'Let me past.'

'You're killing me.' The words felt thick in his throat. 'Do you know that? You're killing me.'

'I'll ask you one more time,' she said. 'Please let me past.'

'No, love, please don't — '

Daniel saw the flash of the keys in her hand, felt the hard pain in his cheek as she stabbed at him. He fell back into the hall, clutching at the wet heat on his face. Niamh staggered past, the suitcase thudding against her thigh. Before he could recover, she was gone, the apartment door slamming closed behind her. He called her name once, then dropped to the floor, his back against the wall. Blood streamed through his fingers, onto his shirt, red streaks down his chest towards his belly.

'Shit,' he said.

He pushed himself onto his hands and knees and crawled to the bathroom at the far end of the hall, leaving a trail of penny-sized red dots on the laminate wood flooring. At the sink, he pulled himself up onto his feet and saw his bloodied face in the mirror. He turned the tap and scooped handfuls of water up to his face, washed the red smears away. A quarter-inch rip beneath his right eye, the skin around pink and puffy. His eyelid flickered of its own accord. Not as bad as it felt. He wondered if he should go to the hospital, see if it needed a stitch.

'No,' he said aloud.

He grabbed a facecloth from the top of the radiator, soaked it beneath the tap, wrung it out, then pressed it against his cheek. As he held the cloth there with his left hand, red seeping from beneath it, he studied his reflection in the mirror. He formed his right hand into a fist, drew it back, felt the strength gather in his arm and shoulder.

'No,' he said again.

Daniel Rolston had better things to do with his anger.

★ ★ ★

Early light woke him as it crept between the open blinds of the bedroom. A grinding ache pulsed inside his head, keeping time with the throb in his cheek. He'd drunk most of a bottle of wine after he'd left the bathroom and had no recollection of climbing onto the bed. Stains covered the pillowcase and duvet cover, deep red to dark brown. His vision in that eye seemed diminished, smaller, as if the swelling had constricted not only the flesh but also the light allowed to find his retina.

Daniel was already on his way to the bathroom

when he felt the first tightening of his stomach, the first loosening in his throat. He retched over the toilet bowl until his sides ached and his nostrils stung, his belly emptied.

It took another thirty minutes to clean himself up, change, and head out. The other passengers on the bus stole glances at the cut and the swelling. Probably assumed he'd been in some bar fight. Didn't look the type, they probably thought. Not a clean-cut young man like him. He smiled at the idea.

The bus stopped at the shopping centre opposite the hostel. As Daniel stepped off the bus, he checked the time on his mobile. Just after nine. Still early.

Time to wait. Time to watch.

26

Ciaran counts the money out onto the bed. Fourteen pounds and eighty-seven pence. Thomas gave him some yesterday. Told him he could buy anything he wanted.

Ciaran wants a bacon sandwich.

The shopping centre is just across the road. Two minutes' walk. Ciaran can do that. There's a café at the Marks & Spencer store. He can get a cup of milky tea and a bacon sandwich. Or he could stay here, hungry and alone. Thomas is working all day, so he can't come and take Ciaran out in his car. Ciaran sits on the bed beside the money and looks around the room. Can he sit here all day? If he has to, then yes.

But he doesn't have to. Ciaran can do what he wants.

That idea is so shiny bright in his mind he should say it out loud.

'I can do what I want.'

A whisper, really, but true all the same.

Ciaran doesn't know how much a bacon sandwich and a cup of milky tea costs, but he thinks fourteen pounds will be enough. He stands, gathers the money up, and stuffs it into his pocket. Downstairs, he sees Mr Wheatley at his office door.

'You going out?' he asks.

'Yeah,' Ciaran says.

'Anywhere interesting?'

Ciaran points. 'Across the road. To buy food.'

'I see.' Mr Wheatley nods. 'Are you okay on your own? I can come with you, if you like.'

'I can go on my own,' Ciaran says. He goes to leave, then thinks of something important to say to Mr Wheatley. He turns back. 'I can do what I want.'

Mr Wheatley smiles. 'That's right. Within reason.'

Ciaran remembers what to do at the crossings. Press the button, wait for the green man. Soon the chitter-chatter racket of the shopping centre is all around him. Parents and children. Whole families, and people on their own. Just like him.

Ciaran is terrified. There's too much noisy noise. Too many people, too close to him. His hands shake so he keeps them in his pockets. His legs feel like they can't hold him upright. He keeps walking just to keep from falling over. Paula told him the Marks & Spencer was at the far end. Not far at all if he just keeps moving.

There, the café is an island in front of the store, tables and chairs surrounding a counter. Like the canteen at Hydebank. Ciaran knows how to do this. He goes to the counter, takes a tray, puts a plate on it. The bacon sandwiches are already made, wrapped in plastic. He brings it to the lady at the till. She takes the sandwich, says she's going to heat it for him. With a quiver in his voice that he can't hide, he asks her for a cup of tea. Lots of milk. She looks at him strangely. She knows he doesn't belong here. He swallows. Remembers he can be here, can buy this food, if he so chooses.

'I can do what I want,' he says.

The lady looks at him for a moment, then smiles an uncertain smile. Ciaran realises she's afraid of him. He doesn't like how that feels.

The sandwich and the tea cost much less than fourteen pounds. The lady gives Ciaran his change, and he finds a free table. It feels like all the other people are watching him. He knows it isn't true, but he feels it anyway. His hands are shaking so much he almost drops the sandwich as he brings it to his mouth. It tastes good. Tea spills over the rim as he lifts the cup. The cup rattles in the saucer when he puts it back down.

A man across the way, a man Ciaran doesn't know at all, asks, 'Rough night, was it?'

The man winks. Ciaran doesn't know why this man is talking to him. He does not reply, turns his gaze away. He hears the man say something about bloody foreigners to the lady beside him.

Ciaran chews and sips, the fear subsiding a little, until someone sits down in the chair across the table.

'Hello Ciaran,' Daniel Rolston says.

Ciaran stops chewing, a wad of bread and bacon on his tongue. Every part of him jingly-jangles, like he wants to run or hit out or cry. Daniel has a cut beneath his right eye. The flesh is red and swollen. The cut glistens with new blood. Some of it is smeared around Daniel's cheek.

'Are you looking at this?' Daniel asks.

Ciaran looks away.

'My girlfriend did it. My own fault, if I'm honest. I've been really shitty to her this last

180

while. She was right to leave me. Go on and eat your breakfast.'

Ciaran swallows the food in his mouth. He doesn't want any more.

'Where's your brother?' Daniel asks. 'I was watching for the both of you from the car park across the road. I didn't think you'd have the nerve to come out on your own. But here you are.'

Ciaran wonders if he could get up and leave. But maybe Daniel would start shouting. Then Ciaran would have to run. He stays in his seat.

'I asked you a question, Ciaran. Where's your brother?'

'At work,' Ciaran says.

'I see. I got fired from my job yesterday. It's been a pretty fucking awful week all round. Pretty fucking shitty. And how have you been?'

Daniel's eyes glisten, teardrops ready to fall from them. Ciaran feels like he should answer, but he doesn't know what to say.

'You were never very chatty, were you? Even when we got to be friends. Do you remember? You used to come to my room without Thomas, before he got home from school, and we'd hang out. Just you and me. You didn't say much, but you never hurt me. Not like Thomas did.'

Ciaran remembers. Thomas was going to a different school, and he had to take two buses to get back to the Rolstons' house. They were still trying to find a space for Ciaran, so he had to stay at home. Forty-five minutes of every weekday, it was just Daniel and Ciaran. Daniel let Ciaran use his PlayStation, though he wasn't very good at it. Daniel helped him.

When Ciaran asked Thomas not to hurt Daniel any more, Thomas bit him hard. He didn't ask again.

'You know,' Daniel says, 'I think that's why it happened. I think Thomas saw you and me were getting to be friends, and he couldn't stand it. He thought I'd take you away from him. So he had to do something.'

Ciaran wants to go. He gathers things onto his tray, starts to rise. Daniel takes his wrist. His hand is harder and stronger than Ciaran thought it would be.

'Sit down, Ciaran.'

'I want to go back to the hostel,' Ciaran says.

'Sit down, now, or I will beat the shit out of you right here in front of these people.'

'I can do what I want,' Ciaran says.

Daniel pulls Ciaran's arm, takes his balance, making him stumble into the table. Tea slops over the rim of the cup.

'Sit. The fuck. Down.'

Ciaran does as he's told. Like a good boy.

'Now, where was I?' Daniel keeps hold of Ciaran's wrist. 'Oh yes. It was the bit about you killing my father. Except you didn't, did you? It was Thomas. Then the both of you cooked up this story about my father abusing your brother. He talked you into saying you did it. You took the blame for him so he wouldn't have to spend so long inside. Isn't that right?'

'No,' Ciaran says, his voice a wet whisper in his throat.

'That's what happened. Don't lie to me. Not

now. Not after all this time. Tell me Thomas did it.' He squeezes Ciaran's wrist. 'Tell me.'

'No.'

Daniel squeezes harder, hurting now. Tears rolling. 'It was never you. It was always him. And my dad never touched him. You know my mum killed herself?'

'My mum died too,' Ciaran says, his gaze fixed on Daniel's hand.

Daniel's fingers relax as he weeps. Tears drop fat and heavy on the table. His shoulders judder. He whines, a high desperate sound that comes from somewhere down inside him.

People look. Ciaran's face burns.

'You destroyed us, you and your brother. My whole family. Thomas might as well have killed all three of us.'

'It wasn't Thomas,' Ciaran says.

'Stop it!' Daniel slaps the table. Cutlery rattles. More tea spills. 'Just fucking stop it. The one thing in the world you could do to help me is tell the truth, and you won't even give me that, will you? Just the fucking truth.'

Ciaran wants to tell Daniel so many things, but he doesn't know how.

'I'm sorry,' Ciaran says.

'Are you? Then tell me the truth.'

Ciaran goes to speak, but he hears someone say his name. He looks around.

Thomas, alone in the crowd, staring at him from across the barrier that separates the café from the rest of the shopping centre.

'What's going on?' Thomas asks.

27

Daniel turned his head and saw him through the tears.

Thomas Devine, big as life. Just standing there as if he had every right to live and breathe among human beings. Daniel let go of Ciaran's wrist. Saw the fear on the younger man's face.

Daniel stood, the chair scraping back and rattling into the others behind.

'Ciaran, come with me,' Thomas said.

Ciaran didn't hesitate. At his brother's word, he left the table, followed the barrier to the gap, and went to Thomas's side. Thomas took his arm and led him away.

'Wait,' Daniel said. They didn't. 'Wait.'

He followed them as Thomas quickened his pace, pulling Ciaran behind him.

'Stop,' Daniel called. 'Fucking stop.'

He reached out, took Ciaran's free arm, planted his feet on the tiled floor. Stretched Ciaran between them. Thomas halted, turned, said, 'Let go.'

'No,' Daniel said. 'You can't run away from me.'

'Let go of my brother. Now. Please.'

Daniel jerked Ciaran's arm, pulling him away from Thomas. He noticed the security guard's attention on him, saw the uniformed man lift a walkie-talkie to his mouth.

Thomas stood quite still, glaring back at

Daniel. 'I'll ask you one more time. Let him go.'

'Not until you — '

Thomas was quick, covering the ground between them in a blink, his hand on Daniel's, prising the fingers loose. Almost eye to eye. So close Daniel could smell him. And, oh, he remembered that smell.

Daniel could recall little of it later on when his mind had cleared. Only the first impulse to swing, the deep savage pleasure of his fist connecting with Thomas's cheek. He pieced it together eventually, pulling fragments of memory from the confusion.

The first blow sent Thomas staggering, then Daniel was swinging at air, one fist following the other in meaningless arcs. Ciaran called something, Daniel couldn't tell what through the rushing in his ears. Another punch landed and put Thomas on the floor, his lip bleeding. Daniel saw Thomas shake his head, signalling something to Ciaran.

His hands outstretched, his teeth bared, a howl escaping his mouth, Daniel was about to fall on Thomas when the security guards rushed him, one at each arm, dragging him away. Ciaran went to Thomas's side, helped him to his feet. Daniel saw the hate in Thomas's eyes as the brothers marched towards the exit.

'You can't run away from me for ever,' Daniel called after them. 'I'll be back. I'll get the truth from you. I swear on my father's grave I will.'

One of the guards talked into his radio handset, something about the police.

Daniel threw his weight to one side, then the

other. The guard who'd asked for the police tripped over his own feet, tumbled onto his back. The other guard put his arm up to shield himself from the swing of Daniel's free hand, then Daniel was spinning in clear air.

He regained his balance and ran, blindly through the crowd at first, then towards the far exit. The guards called from behind but Daniel kept going, the people parting before him.

He kept running until the shopping centre was lost around the bend in the road, until his lungs ached, until his legs could carry him no further. Then he staggered to the nearest wall, leaned against it as he vomited up the last watery contents of his stomach.

28

Ciaran knows Thomas is angry with him even though it isn't his fault. He glows with it, like the anger is burning up his insides. His breathing is hard, a ragged sound trapped in the car with them. As Thomas presses a tissue to his bleeding lip he keeps looking out through the windows, around the car park, as if searching for Daniel. All jerky and fidgety, hands ready to lash out.

'What happened?' Thomas asks.

'I was having breakfast,' Ciaran says. 'You said you were working, and I didn't want to sit in the hostel all day.'

'I don't start till eleven. I called at the hostel and that manager told me you were over here. What was Daniel doing there?'

'I don't know. He just sat down in front of me.'

'What did he say?'

'He talked about us. About what happened to Mr Rolston.'

Thomas's voice is quiet and brittle, words like broken glass. 'What about it?'

'He wanted me to say I didn't do it.'

'And?'

'I told him it was me.'

'Good boy.' Thomas reaches across and squeezes Ciaran's shoulder. His fingers are hard and sharp like needles. 'Good boy.'

'He said his mum killed herself. Just like our mum.'

'The drugs killed our mum. Anyway, that's nothing to do with us.'

'I told him I was sorry,' Ciaran says, expecting more anger from Thomas, but there is none. 'I don't think he noticed, but I said it.'

'There's some things you can't apologise for.'

Ciaran already knows that. Doesn't mean he can't try, but he keeps that thought to himself.

'I never really thought about it before,' Ciaran says. 'Not while we were inside. Not until now.'

'Thought about what?' Thomas asks.

'About the ones we left behind. Daniel. Mrs Rolston. What we did to Mr Rolston, we did it to them too. Just because we left them behind, it doesn't mean we didn't hurt them too.'

Ciaran feels a sudden terror for what Thomas will do.

He closes his eyes and waits for teeth on his skin.

Instead, Thomas squeezes Ciaran's shoulder once more. 'It's all right. No real harm done. But here's the question.'

Ciaran opens his eyes, swallows, and asks, 'What?'

'What do we do about Daniel?' Thomas asks.

29

Flanagan found DCI Conn in his office at Ladas Drive station. Alistair had wanted the family to go out together, maybe to the zoo, or a drive to Bangor, but she had told him she had paperwork to catch up on. Guilt at the lie had felt like needles in her skin, but she told it anyway.

Conn looked up from his computer keyboard. Anger flashed on his face for a moment before he caught it, masked it.

'Serena,' he said. 'What brings you here on a Saturday morning?'

She lingered in the doorway. 'I just wondered how the Walker case was going.'

'It's more or less wrapped up,' he said, looking at his computer monitor. 'Just waiting for the coroner to put a bow on it, then I'm all done.'

'Did you talk to Julie?'

Conn exhaled through his nose. 'We took a statement, yes.'

'I mean, did you interview her?'

'We took a statement,' Conn repeated, his voice hardening.

Flanagan felt the building anger radiate from him. She spoke slowly, keeping her tone light and respectful. 'What about the boyfriend?'

'We also took a brief statement from him, even though it wasn't really necessary.'

She stepped into the room, approached his desk. 'Could I take a look at them?'

'Why?'

'Just to satisfy my curiosity.'

Conn sat back, the muscles in his jaw bunching as he thought. Eventually, he opened the file on his desk, removed four printed A4 pages, and passed them across. Flanagan took them, said thank you, and began to read.

Three pages for Julie's statement. Less than half a page for Barry Timmons. More or less what she'd already heard. Julie Walker woken by the single shot, finding her mother and father dead, calling 999. Barry Timmons woken in the early hours by a phone call from his distressed girlfriend. Flanagan handed the pages back.

'Thanks,' she said. 'Listen, would you mind if I had a chat with them?'

He looked up from the pages. 'Yes, I would bloody mind.'

'I'd make it quick. Treat it as a follow-up to the statements, nothing more.'

Conn got to his feet, rested his knuckles on the desk as he leaned towards her. 'Let me make this very clear. You will not talk to Julie Walker or Barry Timmons. If you do, I'll have the ACC on you so fast your head will spin.' His expression softened a fraction. 'Look, I know the Walkers were friends of yours, and you're upset at what happened, but you can't let that push you into making an accusation with nothing to back it up.'

Flanagan nodded, smiled, and left the office.

By the time she got to her car, she had made her decision.

* * *

Barry Timmons was a lecturer at Queen's University and rented a house nearby. Flanagan guessed Julie would stay with him while her home remained a crime scene. She parked her Golf opposite the Queen's Film Theatre, in the shadow of the Lanyon building, and walked the short distance to University Street with its rows of terraced houses. Most of them bore To Let signs, waiting for the influx of students that would come with the new academic year. The area felt ghostly quiet without the bustle of students, as if an evacuation had taken place.

She found Barry's house close to the University Road end, tidier than the other properties along this street, the front door and window frames newly painted, wooden Venetian blinds behind the glass. A leafy green pot plant on the sill of the living room window.

Flanagan knocked and waited.

She was not here officially, she thought, but as a friend. If she wanted to show her support for the orphaned daughter of a couple she had grown close to, then DCI Conn could have nothing to say about it.

No answer. She knocked again.

A sickly relief accompanied the realisation that no one was home. What was she doing here? What good could she do? Conn would be furious, as would the Assistant Chief Constable, not to mention DSI Purdy. Flanagan imagined being called into his office on Monday morning, the bollocking he would give her.

'All right,' she said, and turned away from the door, heading back to University Road. Maybe if she got back home to Moira in time, the day wouldn't be wasted. She and Alistair could still get out somewhere with the kids.

Across University Road, through the stream of traffic headed for the city centre, she saw Julie Walker and Barry Timmons seated at the window of a café. Flanagan stood still on the pavement and watched for a few moments. Deep in conversation, their heads close together.

Leave them be, Flanagan thought. Go home to your family.

Then she thought of Penny Walker and a pillow held tight to her face.

Flanagan went to the pedestrian crossing, waited for the green man, keeping the couple in her sight. She crossed the road, walked towards the café. Julie and Barry were oblivious to anything but whatever it was they discussed. Flanagan stood no more than six feet away, only a pane of glass between her and them. They did not notice her attention as they talked.

Or rather, Julie talked.

Her forefinger extended, punctuating her words, stabbing the air inches from Barry's face. He wept, Flanagan saw, his cheeks wet with tears. Rocking back and forth slightly, a gentle self-comforting motion. Contained rage on Julie's face.

Barry went to say something, but Julie's finger prodded at his chest, her anger reaching a new height. She must have spoken too loudly, because now she lifted her head, looked around the café to make sure no one heard, then glanced out of the window.

She saw Flanagan, and the fury drained from her face, replaced by fear. Barry turned his tearful gaze towards the window, saw what had silenced his girlfriend. He sniffed, removed his glasses, and wiped at his eyes and cheeks with the heel of his hand.

Flanagan entered the café and approached their table, keeping her expression friendly. She indicated one of the unoccupied leather-bound tub chairs and asked, 'May I?'

Barry turned his face away. Julie nodded.

Flanagan sat down. 'I called over at your house, but no one was home. Lucky I saw you through the window.'

'What can we do for you?' Julie asked.

'I'd like to ask a few questions, if you don't mind.'

Julie looked to Barry, who looked at his lap. She turned back to Flanagan. 'I didn't think you were working on my parents' case.'

'I'm not,' Flanagan said. 'It's just for my own curiosity, completely off the record.'

'Now isn't the best time,' Julie said. 'If it's not official, I'd rather not — '

'It'll only take a few minutes. A couple of questions and I'll be out of your way.'

Julie sat quiet for a moment, then said, 'All right. So long as you're quick.'

'You know I saw your mother the evening she died,' Flanagan said.

'Yes.'

'She told me that she and your father were

planning a weekend away. She'd booked a cottage that morning. If they hadn't died, your parents would be in Portstewart right now.'

'But they did die,' Julie said, her face expressionless. 'So they're not.'

'What strikes me as odd,' Flanagan said, 'is why your mother would book a cottage that she never intended to use. If she and your father planned to die that night, why make plans for the weekend?'

'Maybe they didn't plan it. Maybe it was spur of the moment. They just did it without thinking it through.'

'Maybe,' Flanagan said. 'You know, I liked your father. Ronnie was a good man. The Alzheimer's diagnosis must have been a blow. For your parents, of course, but you too. He would've become quite a burden, wouldn't he? How do you think he would have managed without your mother?'

'Not well,' Julie said. 'That's why he did it, I suppose.'

'Put a pillow over his wife's face and smothered her.'

Julie paled. Barry's eyes brimmed.

'That's right,' Julie said.

'It's not easy to kill a human being,' Flanagan said. 'Even if they're unconscious from sleeping pills. Even if they can't struggle too much. It's a very difficult line to cross. Most of us can't do it. We just aren't wired that way. Only a very few can end another's life, and fewer still can suffer the guilt. Mr Timmons.'

Barry looked up, shame on his face, as if she

194

had caught him in some unspeakable act.

'You said in your statement that you were at home alone all Wednesday evening.'

He wiped his eyes and cleared his throat. 'That's right.'

'And you got a phone call from Julie some time after two in the morning.'

'Yes. Then I drove straight over.'

'And you found the bodies of Mr and Mrs Walker in their bedroom.'

'Yes.'

'How long do you think it took for Penny Walker to die?'

He shook his head, confusion on his face. 'What?'

'How long would a man have to hold a pillow over an unconscious woman's face until she suffocated?'

'I don't understand.'

'How much pressure would he have to apply to make sure she couldn't breathe?'

'Stop it,' Julie said.

'I wonder if she moved,' Flanagan said, keeping her gaze hard on Barry. 'Even unconscious, did her body fight to live? When that man put his weight on the pillow, maybe he thought she would lie there like a doll.'

'Please stop it,' Julie said.

'Maybe he didn't expect her to resist. How would he know what it's like to kill someone?'

For a moment, no more, Flanagan saw a pleading in Barry's eyes. As if begging for release. Then he looked away, and she knew for certain.

'Please leave us alone,' Julie said, a tremor in her voice.

'All right,' Flanagan said. 'Thank you for your time.' She stood, put a hand on Barry's shoulder. 'Remember, when it comes right down to it, the truth is all you have left.'

'Go,' Julie said. 'Please.'

Flanagan left them there, fear of the consequences already growing in her.

30

Daniel Rolston had been drinking since the morning. He had jumped onto the first bus that stopped and found himself in the city centre. Not long after eleven, he wandered into a bar on Chichester Street and ordered a pint of lager. It was gone in minutes, and he asked for another. The barman looked at the cut beneath his eye and asked if he was all right. Daniel did not answer the question, repeated his request for another drink. The barman obliged.

As lunchtime clientele began to fill the bar, Daniel neared the end of his fourth pint. Lifted the glass to get the barman's attention, relishing the buzz in his head.

'Maybe you should have something to eat,' the barman said. 'A glass of water, too.'

'No,' Daniel said. 'Just give me another.'

'I'll get you a sandwich. On the house.'

'No. Another pint. Please.'

'All right,' the barman said. 'One more, but after that, I want you out the door.'

Daniel nodded and handed over his money.

As he left the bar, the noise of the city rushed in on him, the cars, the people, the undying clamour of it all. He marched past the front of the City Hall, hating the kids who gathered there, mouthy little bastards all of them. He bumped shoulders with some tracksuit-wearing knuckle-dragger who shouted after him to watch where he was going. Daniel spun to the angry voice, saw the confidence drain from the boy's face at the sight of him. He kept walking, headed south, around the City Hall, past the upmarket restaurants and fashionable bars, out of the city centre, towards Shaftesbury Square and beyond, until he made his way to the northern end of Botanic Avenue. If he kept walking, he'd come to Botanic Gardens, the trees and the grass there, the flowers. As the sun warmed him, that seemed a wonderful place to be.

Daniel stopped at an off-licence and bought a bottle of cheap vodka, paid the extra few pence for a plastic bag to conceal it. The purchase left him with less than ten pounds on his person. He had less than a hundred in his current account. Not that he cared much.

A few minutes' walk took Daniel to the park, its open lawns, tree-shaded paths, the Palm House as its centrepiece. He found a bench with a view of a green where a gathering of people threw balls and sticks while their dogs chased and gambolled.

Happy people, he thought, every reason to enjoy a Saturday afternoon in the park. He would never be one of them, Daniel knew that: a normal contented life was lost to him long ago.

He twisted the bottle cap, breaking the seal, and took a deep swallow of vodka. His stomach threatened to expel the liquid, and he doubled over, coughing and spitting, but kept the vodka inside. The second mouthful went down a little more easily. The third easier still. He did not remember the fourth.

A hard hand shook Daniel from a dream of mangled flesh and bone, of horrors upon horrors, death walking among the living, cutting them down as it went.

He opened his eyes, blinking at the sun, now low in the sky. His mind scrambled and tripped, trying to piece the real world together from the scattered fragments of his drunken sleep. He swallowed, his mouth dry and sour-tasting, then a wet burp forced him to cough.

'Come on, son,' someone said. 'Wakey, wakey.'

Daniel blinked, said, 'What?'

Another voice. 'Time to go home, young fella. Up you get.'

A hand taking his arm, pulling him upright. A policeman, and another.

'Can you stay on your feet?' one of them asked.

Daniel wasn't sure. He tried and flopped back down onto the bench. His trousers clung to his thighs, and he felt a spear of humiliation knowing that he had wet himself.

The policemen each took an arm, hoisted him up again.

'Right,' the older of them said, 'I'm giving you one chance to stay on your feet and walk away. If you can't, then I have to place you under arrest. You'll have to spend the night in a cell to sleep it off. Do you understand?'

Daniel laughed. He wanted to say he'd seen enough of police cells to do him for a good long time, but somehow he couldn't make the words come out in the right order.

'Now, start walking,' the policeman said, nudging him in the direction of the park's southern exit.

The policeman emptied the remainder of the vodka onto the grass and tossed the bottle into a bin. 'Get yourself a taxi, if you can find one who'll take you in that state.'

Time stretched and bent as Daniel walked, clinging to fences and walls as he went. A car horn blared as he staggered into the road. He fell onto its bonnet, was carried a few yards, but somehow managed to slide off and onto his feet without slamming into the ground. The driver got out of the car, called after him as he lurched away.

The sun had sunk lower, barely showing above the rooftops, and Daniel felt suddenly cold. He looked around, realised he had no idea where he was. Just another street of redbrick two-up two-downs of which there were hundreds, probably thousands, in Belfast. Not even a flag on a lamp post to tell him what kind of area it was. But it couldn't be far from the park, he thought, maybe Stranmillis.

He felt his stomach tighten. His mouth opened through no will of his own, and he doubled over, leaning on a garden wall. The sound of a knuckle rapping on glass. He looked up, saw an elderly woman open her living room window and lean out.

'Don't you be boaking in front of my house. I'm not clearing that up. Go on and do it somewhere else.'

Daniel stumbled on, one hand on his stomach,

the other on the garden walls and fences to keep him on his feet. At the end of the block he turned the corner, found the alleyway that ran between one terrace and the next. He walked into the cool shadows, deeper, until he couldn't hold back any more. The force of it doubled him over, spraying vodka on the ground. He collapsed against a yard wall, supporting himself with his shoulder as he retched again and again.

As a sliver of sobriety crept in, it brought with it a clarity Daniel did not welcome. The reality of it, how low he had fallen in less than a week. As he coughed and spat, he thought of Niamh and what she would think if she saw him now, puking his guts out in an alley, covered in his own vomit and piss. Through the heaving of his stomach, he began to cry, helpless child tears, for that's what he was: a child lost in the world of adults. He had only been playing a grown-up for all these years. He knew he remained the child he had been when his mother and he sat in the big McDonald's in town, a special treat for him because he'd been doing well at school despite all the distraction at home, and she had brought him there and told him he could order anything he wanted.

Almost fifteen, then, he should have been going into town with his own friends, should have been embarrassed to be seen out and about with his mother. But he didn't care; he simply enjoyed having her to himself for a couple of hours, leaving the Devine brothers at home with his father. Not that she was an affectionate woman, far from it, but he still longed for her attention. He had been eating an ice cream sundae when she took a phone call. He still remembered how her face transitioned from that of his mother to a cold hollow woman unknown to him.

That was the moment his life was broken, and the first step on his seven-year journey to this alley, now complete.

Daniel straightened, gasping for air, dizzy more from the exertion of vomiting than the alcohol still in his system. He wiped his mouth on his sleeve, leaned his forehead against the wall, his skin sensing every grain of texture on the concrete rendering.

A movement behind him.

He turned his head, saw only the vaguest shape before the searing pain in his side, something sharp and fiery hot between his ribs. He went to cry out, but a hand slammed into his head, rammed his skull against the wall. His legs disappeared from beneath him, then he was sprawling in his own foulness.

Someone, on his lower back, pinning him down. And that piercing pain again, higher, between his shoulders. And another, his neck now, his cheek, his arm, more and more, coming faster and faster.

The weight left his back, a tugging at his pockets, footsteps running away.

Then he was alone, the last of him draining away onto the cement and weeds.

And then Daniel was walking into the roaring sea with his mother, hand in hand, to stay there with her for ever and ever.

31

Ciaran can't sleep.

Close to midnight, he is wide awake and very alone. He can hear voices from the other rooms, music somewhere, and someone watching a television.

Thomas had promised to come and see him tomorrow, take him shopping for boots before he goes to work at the hotel. They'll get lunch together, he said. A proper one, not a sandwich outside a supermarket.

Ciaran imagines sitting opposite Thomas as they eat. He can't think of what they'll say to each other. Not with what Ciaran knows.

For the first time in his life, Ciaran wonders if he really wants Thomas to be his brother.

He immediately scolds himself for such a wicked idea.

Thomas is all he has. All he's ever had, all he ever *will* have.

When Ciaran was very small, Thomas told him God wasn't real. Just a made-up story to make people behave themselves. But Ciaran wishes God was real so that he could say a prayer, ask God to let him go back to the start, to be a baby once more, with all these nineteen years to try again.

Ciaran says the prayer anyway, a whisper trapped between the walls.

32

Flanagan paced her kitchen, back and forth, mobile pressed to her ear as Alistair cooked bacon and sausages for the children.

'I want this case,' she said.

Purdy said, 'It's not mine to give you. It's B District. Why would it go to you?'

'You can ask the ACC for me,' she said, sidestepping her husband as he moved from the cooker to the table, a plate stacked with toast in his hand. 'Who've they got in B District now? They can hardly give it to Thompson, can they? And Conn's still working on the Walker case.'

'Oh yes, about DCI Conn and the Walkers — '

'You can tear me to pieces for that tomorrow,' Flanagan said. 'Right now, I want the Daniel Rolston case. Just talk to the ACC.'

'Maybe I'm forgetting. Who's the higher ranking officer here, you or me?'

'If you won't talk to him, I bloody will.'

Alistair scolded her with his eyes for the language.

'All right,' Purdy said. 'You talk to him if you want. I'd sooner he tells you to fuck off than me.'

'Why would he? It makes sense. The Devine brothers have to be the first suspects, and I know them both, Ciaran in particular. I know how to talk to him. I know their history. Come on, it's the logical thing to do. Talk to the ACC.'

'Oh, Christ, all right. One condition, though.'

'Name it.'

'You keep your neb out of the Walker case. Conn's spitting bullets at you trampling all over his feet. Promise me you'll drop it, and I'll talk to the ACC.'

Flanagan leaned against the sink, screwed her eyes shut, cursed silently to herself. Eventually, she said, 'All right.'

'Okay,' Purdy said. 'I'll get back to you.'

'Thank you,' she said.

As she ended the call, the phone vibrated in her hand: a voicemail from Paula Cunningham. Flanagan didn't bother listening, just called her straight back.

Alistair asked if she was going to sit down and eat. Flanagan waved him away as she listened to the dial tone.

'I saw the news,' Cunningham said. 'They named him, but they just said he'd been stabbed.'

'He'd been drinking,' Flanagan said. 'Two uniforms saw him in the park yesterday evening, told him to go home. They took an almost empty bottle of vodka off him. He already had a cut on his face, they said. I've requested that I be given the case.'

'And will you?' Cunningham asked.

'I'd bloody better. I begged hard enough.'

'So what happens next?'

'Unless something presents itself, physical evidence or a witness to actually link either of the Devines to the killing, I've no grounds to interview them under caution.'

'But they have to be involved,' Cunningham

said. 'It's too big a coincidence.'

'Knowing that and proving it are two different things. But there's nothing to stop me having a word. See what I can shake out of them.'

'Do you think Ciaran will talk to you?'

'I don't know,' Flanagan said. 'But I have to try.'

'Okay. You'll keep me informed, won't you?'

'Of course.'

When she hung up, Alistair asked, 'Will you come and eat now? It's getting cold.'

'You have it,' she said, reaching for her car keys.

As she kissed each of the children, telling them she was sorry she had to go, Alistair grumbled under his breath and shovelled food from her plate onto his.

33

'I can tie them myself,' Ciaran says.

Thomas kneels at his feet, pulling the laces of the work boots tight. He sets about securing them with double knots.

'I can do it,' Ciaran says.

Thomas doesn't look up, keeps pulling and tying. 'How's that?' he asks.

'S'okay,' Ciaran says, flexing his toes beneath the steel cap and black leather.

Thomas has been strange today. All quick movements, jittery fingers, lickety lips.

Ciaran is afraid of him today. He thinks Thomas might be broken, that he might be coming apart. He seemed fine on Wednesday, but now it's Sunday, and each day a little more of him has cracked open.

Thomas stands. 'Get up and walk about a bit.'

Ciaran does as he's told. He walks back and forth past the display of work boots. Children and mothers chatter in other parts of the shoe shop. Fathers stand around looking bored and impatient.

The sales girl steps over. 'How do those feel on you?'

Without thinking, Ciaran looks to Thomas for permission to answer. When Thomas lifts his chin in agreement, Ciaran feels an unfamiliar emotion. Not hate, but something like it. Resentment, maybe? No matter. He turns to the girl.

'They're all right,' he says.

'You sure?' Thomas asks. 'Not too tight?'

'They're fine.'

'We'll take them,' Thomas says to the sales girl.

'Do you want to wear them now, or will I box them for you?'

Again, Ciaran looks to Thomas. Again, he feels that same bitter anger.

'He'll wear them now,' Thomas says. 'They need breaking in.'

The sales girl packs Ciaran's trainers into the box and leads them back to the till. Once Thomas has paid, and they've exited the store into the swarming tide of Sunday shoppers on Royal Avenue, Ciaran opens his mouth. Nothing comes out. He's afraid to say it.

Thomas notices. He hands Ciaran the box with the trainers in it. He asks, 'What?'

Ciaran opens his mouth again. Closes it. Shakes his head.

'Come on, say what you're thinking.'

'I can talk for myself,' Ciaran says.

'How do you mean?'

'You always talk for me. When people ask me things, I have to look at you first before I can answer. It was always like that. But I can talk for myself.'

Thomas watches him as passing shoppers nudge them both, making them sway like wind-worn trees. After a while, he says, 'All right. Let's get something to eat.'

They walk to the McDonald's at the top of the street, join the queue at the row of tills.

The boy at the other side of the counter asks if he can take their orders, please.

Thomas orders a Big Mac meal. He stands aside to let Ciaran order.

Ciaran stares up at the board. His mind freezes.

Thomas says, 'He'll have a McChicken Sandwich meal, large, with Coke.'

They find a table upstairs. Ciaran eats in silence. The food is tainted by the small defeat he has just suffered. Just ordering a burger at McDonald's. It shouldn't be difficult. He hates himself. He hates Thomas.

No.

He banishes that thought from his mind, chases it away. Ciaran does not hate his brother. Thomas looks after him. He can't hate Thomas. But even so, he can talk for himself. And now he does so.

'Will the police come today?' Ciaran asks.

Thomas doesn't answer. He looks around the room.

'That security guard,' Ciaran says. 'If he sees Daniel's picture on — '

Thomas reaches across the table, seizes Ciaran's wrist. 'Maybe talk about it later.'

'If he sees his picture on the news, he'll recognise him.'

Thomas squeezes. His eyes flash. 'We'll talk about it later.'

'He'll call the police. He'll describe us.'

'Ciaran, stop talking.'

'Daniel told me his mum killed herself,' Ciaran says. 'His mum and dad are both dead, just like ours.'

'Ciaran, shut your mouth.'

'Now they're all dead. The whole family.'

Thomas stands, takes Ciaran's arm. 'Do you need the toilet? Let's go to the toilet.'

He pulls hard. Ciaran gets to his feet, allows Thomas to guide him towards the stairs leading to the men's and ladies' rooms. The fingers digging hard into Ciaran's flesh.

'My trainers,' Ciaran says, looking back at the box on the table.

'Leave them.'

At the top of the stairs, Thomas hits the door so hard it slams into the wall. It bounces back, hits Ciaran's shoulder as Thomas drags him through, and on into the men's room. Thomas looks around. No one at the urinals. The two stalls open and empty. Thomas pushes Ciaran inside the far one, crowds in behind him, locks the door.

Ciaran backs into the space between the bowl and the wall, as far into the corner as he can go. He didn't need the toilet before, but he does now.

'I told you to stop talking,' Thomas says. 'And you kept talking.'

'Daniel didn't deserve it.'

Ciaran's head rocks to the side with the force of Thomas's palm. The sting hot and fierce. He closes his eyes, ready for another. It doesn't come.

'He was causing trouble,' Thomas says. 'He was mouthing off. If he kept on, they might have started paying attention. We can't have that. We won't stand for it.'

Ciaran opens his eyes. 'But he didn't have to die.'

Now it comes, Thomas's palm. A ringing in Ciaran's ear as the pain blooms there.

'Listen to me,' Thomas says. 'Are you listening to me?'

Ciaran nods. He wants to cry, but he holds it back.

'Do you love me?' Thomas asks.

'Yes.'

'Then say it.'

Ciaran keeps his gaze downward. 'I love you.'

'Do you trust me?'

'Yes.'

'Then say it. Look at me and say it.'

Ciaran raises his eyes to meet Thomas's. 'I trust you.'

'Good,' Thomas says. 'Daniel Rolston had to go away. He brought it on himself. If he'd stayed out of it, he'd have been fine. But he didn't. That was his choice. Not yours. Not mine. You've nothing to feel bad about. Neither of us has. Do you understand?'

Ciaran nods.

'Say it.'

'I understand.'

'All right,' Thomas says. 'Now give me your arm.'

Ciaran's eyes are hot now. He feels the tremors in his fingers. He shakes his head and says, 'No.'

'Give me your arm,' Thomas says. He reaches out his hand.

'Please, no,' Ciaran says. The tears come then.

Sudden and shocking hot. 'I'll be good. I promise.'

Thomas takes a breath. His voice is flat, the demand final. 'Ciaran, give me your arm.'

Ciaran does as he's told. Like a good boy.

Thomas rolls back Ciaran's sleeve, reveals the smooth freckled flesh of his forearm. Old scars there, faded pink. One hand holding the wrist tight, Thomas's mouth opens. Ciaran sees the wet sheen of his teeth. Feels them on his skin, then the pain, fiery hot.

Ciaran knows he should be quiet, a good boy should always be quiet and take his punishment, but it's been so long and the pain is so fresh and new. He opens his mouth, lets out a high whine that wishes it were a scream. Thomas leans his body in close, clamps his free hand over Ciaran's mouth, presses his head back into the corner of the stall.

Outside, the men's room door opens. Through the thunder in Ciaran's head he hears someone enter, a zip opening, water splashing, taps flowing, then a hand-dryer roaring. All the time, Ciaran is locked there, still, only the movement of Thomas's mouth and tongue, seeking unmarked skin. The wetness, the hardness, the pressure.

At last, whoever is outside goes, and Thomas releases Ciaran, steps back, wipes his mouth. Ciaran crouches down in the corner, leaning on the toilet bowl, cradles his arm, weeps like a baby.

'All right,' Thomas says. He unspools a fistful of toilet paper, hands it to Ciaran. 'Pull yourself together.'

Ciaran wipes at his face, soaking up the wetness from his cheeks, the snot from his nose and chin. Thomas reaches down and pulls him to his feet. When his brother's arms snake around him, Ciaran wants to push him away. But he knows he can't. Instead, he stands very still in Thomas's embrace, even when Thomas's lips press against his cheek.

They leave the bathroom together, lift Ciaran's trainers from the table where he'd left them, then downstairs, out onto the street.

Ciaran does not touch his forearm or look at the marks on his skin until he's back at the hostel. Then he draws the blind, lies on his bed, and cries until he has nothing left.

34

Flanagan waited at the hotel's reception desk with DS Ballantine. She had briefed Ballantine on the background on the drive over, told her to keep her mouth shut, just watch and listen, notepad and pen at the ready.

They had spent an hour and a half at the scene of Daniel Rolston's death, the body still *in situ* when they arrived. Flanagan had watched Ballantine, making sure she could handle it, which she did. Even when they examined his corpse, counting the wounds, with the smell trapped in the alley, coating everything.

Flanagan suggested they get something to eat on the way to the hotel, but Ballantine declined. The aroma of food wafting from the restaurant beyond reception made Flanagan's stomach growl.

'Ma'am, is it that obvious we're cops?' Ballantine asked, noting how the hotel's clientele and staff reacted to their presence. As if they knew these two women did not belong here. The guests gave them glances as they headed out into the darkening evening, off to enjoy a night in one of Belfast's bars.

'You get used to it,' Flanagan said. 'The way people look at you. Particularly if you're a woman. They're probably trying to figure out which one of us is Cagney and which one's Lacey.'

Ballantine smiled and visibly relaxed.

The hotel's assistant manager appeared from the door behind the reception desk. The tag on his suit jacket said his name was Brolly.

'If you'll follow me, officers, I have a meeting room free.'

He led them past the elevator bank, along a corridor, to a closed door. Brolly unlocked it with a keycard and stepped aside to let them through. Inside was a long desk surrounded by chairs, a whiteboard on an easel, and a projection screen on the far wall.

'Thank you, this is fine,' Flanagan said.

'I'll have Thomas with you in just a minute,' Brolly said, and left them alone.

Ballantine pulled out a chair and sat down. When she saw that Flanagan remained on her feet she coughed, stood, and pushed the chair back, her face reddening. They waited in silence until the door reopened and Thomas Devine stepped through dressed in the uniform of a kitchen worker.

He froze when he saw Flanagan.

'Hello, Thomas,' she said. 'How've you been?'

'Okay.'

'Sit down.' Flanagan pointed to a seat. 'Just a quick chat. It shouldn't take long.'

Thomas lowered himself onto the chair. His back stiff, the chair out from the table as if he was ready to run. At Flanagan's signal, Ballantine sat down opposite Thomas, opened her notepad, clicked her pen.

Flanagan moved close to Thomas, perched on the table beside him. He inched his chair away.

215

'You didn't have to come to my work,' he said. 'Dinner service is just over. I'm supposed to be washing dishes. Chef's going to give me grief for this. You could've talked to me at home.'

'True, but let's just say time was a factor.'

'All right,' he said. 'What do you want?'

'Have you seen the news today?' Flanagan asked. 'Listened to the radio, maybe?'

'No.'

'Then presumably you haven't heard about a fatal stabbing in the Stranmillis area last night.'

'No.'

'A young man, stabbed repeatedly in an alley, found at seven this morning. His wallet was missing, his pockets were emptied, so it looked like a robbery. But they missed a Translink travel card, so he was quickly identified.'

Thomas folded his arms. 'I'm sorry to hear that. But what's it got to do with me?'

'The victim was an old acquaintance of yours.'

Thomas said nothing.

'Daniel Rolston.'

Silence.

'I should think you'd remember him. You and your brother were convicted for killing his father, after all.'

Thomas looked up at her. 'I was convicted as an accessory, even though I'd nothing to do with it. It was Ciaran who killed him. It was Ciaran who was convicted for it.'

'Oh yes,' Flanagan said. 'Forgive me, I should have chosen my words a little more carefully. Tell me, when was the last time you or Ciaran saw Daniel Rolston?'

'Not since back then.'

'Back then? You mean, since you and your brother were involved in his father's death?'

'You know what I mean.'

'So you're telling me you haven't seen Daniel Rolston for more than seven years.'

'That's right.'

'Well, let Detective Sergeant Ballantine here tell you what happened just before we came over to see you.'

Ballantine's face flashed with startlement for a moment before she gathered herself, leafed through the pages of her notepad, and spoke.

'We got a call from a security guard at the Forestside shopping centre about thirty minutes ago. He recognised Daniel Rolston's photograph when it was shown on the news. He said a young man who looked very like him had been involved in an incident at the shopping centre yesterday morning. It involved two other young men. There was some shouting, apparently, and punches were thrown.'

Thomas remained quiet for a few seconds, then said, 'So?'

Flanagan asked, 'How did you get that cut on your lip, Thomas?'

'I fell. I had to call in sick yesterday because of it.'

'Ah, I see. Forestside is right next to Ciaran's hostel, isn't it?'

'Yes. So?'

'Well, that security guard is going to give us a full statement tomorrow, with descriptions of all three involved in the incident. I'll interview him myself. We should have the centre's CCTV footage by tomorrow evening. Do you think the two young men involved in that incident with Daniel might look a bit like you and Ciaran?'

'How would I know?'

'If those two young men look like you and your brother — and something tells me they will — I'll have you both brought in and questioned under caution. You could save me a lot of trouble and just tell me what happened yesterday.'

Thomas looked from Flanagan to Ballantine and back again. 'Have you talked to Ciaran yet?'

'No,' Flanagan said. 'But we will.'

'And I'm not under caution.'

'Just a friendly chat, that's all,' Flanagan said.

'So there's nothing to stop me just getting up and going back to my work.'

'Not a thing in the world.'

Thomas stood, walked to the door.

'One thing,' Flanagan called after him.

He stopped, the door open, his fingers on the handle.

'Three nights ago, Daniel called at the home of Ciaran's probation officer. He made some pretty serious claims.'

Thomas remained quiet and still, staring back at her.

'Daniel said Ciaran was wrongly convicted. He reckoned you killed his father and made Ciaran take the blame.'

Thomas turned and left the room.

Flanagan turned to Ballantine. 'You got all that?'

'Yes, not that there was much of it. Can I ask,

if we haven't got enough to interview them under caution yet, why talk to them at all?'

'To rattle them,' Flanagan said. 'And to get the measure of them. We know Thomas will be evasive when he's interviewed, try to shut us out. No comment all the way. So I can work on grinding him down. Ciaran, on the other hand . . .'

She thought of the child she had known, felt a sudden terror at the idea of seeing him again. Ballantine said something, but Flanagan didn't hear.

TUESDAY 27TH MARCH 2007

At five-twenty a.m., Flanagan watched from behind the bars as DCI Purdy brought Ciaran in front of the custody sergeant. Their shoes scuffed and squeaked on the linoleum floor. Purdy with his hand on the boy's shoulder, Ciaran weeping with terror, one step from hysteria. The social worker following behind.

God help him, Flanagan thought.

God help me.

She still felt the heat on her palm from slapping him. His cheek still red.

Like watching an execution, she thought. This boy's life being taken, every other possible future gone. She put her hand over her mouth to smother a quivering inhalation.

Ciaran heard. He turned his head, saw her there. A hollowness in his eyes.

There's nothing I can do for you now, she wanted to say. But it was too late.

He turned back to the small window and the custody sergeant on the other side.

As the charges were read, Ciaran sank to the floor as if his spirit had departed his body, leaving only the shell of a boy.

Flanagan could watch no more. She left the building, left him behind, certain he hadn't beaten David Rolston to death.

Later that morning, while Flanagan showered with the intention of going straight to bed, the first cramps doubled her over, almost took her legs from under her. Then she began to bleed. The miscarriage was confirmed at the Royal Victoria Hospital's maternity unit that afternoon.

In the days that followed, Flanagan couldn't think of Ciaran Devine without seeing swirls of red circle a drain. Soon, she did not think of him at all.

35

Ciaran is sitting alone in his room, letting the dark gather around him, when Mr Wheatley knocks on the door.

'Phone call for you,' he says.

Ciaran follows him down the stairs to the payphone in the entrance hall. He lifts the handset and says, 'Hello?'

'It's me,' Thomas says. 'The cops are coming to talk to you.'

'When?'

'Right now. They'll be there any minute. Listen to me. You don't have to say anything to them. You can refuse to talk to them if you want to. You don't have to do or say anything if they don't arrest you. Do you understand?'

'Yeah,' Ciaran says.

'Daniel Rolston went to see your probation officer,' Thomas says. 'They told me. He went to her house. Now she's mouthing off top. She's going to try to put you away again. But don't worry about that.'

'Why?' Ciaran asks.

'Don't worry about it, I said. There's one more thing. One of the cops who came to me. It was that woman cop. Flanagan.'

Ciaran feels a chill on his forehead and back as sweat breaks on his skin. His knees weaken. He leans against the wall.

'You still there?'

Ciaran swallows, says, 'Yeah.'

'All right,' Thomas says. 'Just stay calm. You'll be all right. I'll call you back later.'

Ciaran hangs up. He sees Mr Wheatley standing in his office doorway.

'Everything all right?' Mr Wheatley asks.

Ciaran nods. Mr Wheatley doesn't go away. Ciaran wonders if he ever goes home. Even on a Sunday night, there he is.

'You all ready for work in the morning?'

'Yeah,' Ciaran says.

'You'll have to be up early. The van picks you and the other lads up at seven.'

'Yeah,' Ciaran says. He wishes Mr Wheatley would just go back into his office, leave him alone.

'Maybe you should head on up to bed, get some sleep.'

'Yeah,' Ciaran says. But he doesn't go anywhere.

Mr Wheatley stands and watches Ciaran fidget.

'You sure nothing's wrong?' Mr Wheatley asks.

'Yeah.'

Ciaran can hardly stand it. It's almost a relief when the door buzzer sounds. Mr Wheatley goes into his office to answer it. Ciaran hears his voice from inside, but he can't make out the words. He can guess, though. When Mr Wheatley comes back out he gives Ciaran a hard look before going to the door and opening it.

Two women enter, but Ciaran only really sees one of them.

Dizzy, dizzy, dizzy. His head so light his body

seems to dangle from it like a string from a balloon.

'Hello, Ciaran,' Serena Flanagan says.

★   ★   ★

Mr Wheatley lets them use his office. Ciaran sits on a hard plastic chair in the corner. He feels as if tiny spiders are crawling all over his skin, tingling from the top of his head to the soles of his feet. He tries not to stare too hard at the policewoman as she sits on Mr Wheatley's chair, but he can't look away either. His gaze darts from her to the floor and back again, over and over, until he feels like he might faint. He lingers on her body, and she notices. Heat spreads on his cheeks.

The other policewoman, the younger one, stands by the door, leaning on the frame. She holds a pen and notebook.

'It's been a long time,' Serena says. She'd always told him to call her by her first name. 'How've you been?'

Ciaran can't speak. He tries, but his throat only makes a wet clicky noise.

'I bet you're glad to be out,' she says.

He tries again. 'Yeah.'

'Miss Cunningham, your probation officer, she told me you were very good when you were at Hydebank. You had hardly any trouble there at all.'

Ciaran nods.

'Do you know why we're here?'

Ciaran shakes his head.

'Daniel Rolston was found dead in an alley in the Stranmillis area this morning. He'd been stabbed multiple times.'

Ciaran stays very still. He watches Flanagan's mouth move, the curve of her lips. He remembers how it felt that time she held him close as he cried against the warmth of her neck. He has thought of that often over the years. When he was alone in his room at Hydebank, in the dark, he played it over in his mind again and again. Like a movie. Sometimes, in the version that unravelled in his mind, she did not pull away. She did not slap him when he touched her. And he would reach for himself, there under the covers, the rest of the world fading away to nothing, his entire existence focused on that one point of pressure, building and building until it exploded, the heat spilling out of him.

Sometimes he would bundle the pillow, sheets and blankets into a form that stretched along his bed. He would hold it through the night, imagining it was her, hearing her heart beat next to his. The smooth weave of the sheets becoming her skin beneath his fingertips. Sometimes — not often, but sometimes — he whispered that he loved her. Alone in the dark where no one could possibly hear.

'Ciaran, are you listening?'

He falls back into the office from wherever he's been. 'What?' he asks.

'I said Daniel was seen yesterday morning having a confrontation with two other young men. At Forestside, the shopping centre just across the road from here. Do you know anything about that?'

Ciaran shakes his head. Everything moves slowly. The air feels thick and warm around him.

'Some time tomorrow, we're going to get CCTV footage from the centre. We'll see it was you and Thomas. When that happens, you're going to be arrested and questioned under caution. Do you understand, Ciaran?'

Ciaran says nothing.

'And we're going to trace Daniel's steps from when he left the shopping centre to Botanic Gardens and on to where he was killed. We're going to pull together all the CCTV recordings from that route. There are cameras everywhere. If we see you or Thomas were in the area, if you were following Daniel at any point, then you'll be in a lot of trouble, Do you understand?'

'Yeah,' Ciaran says.

She stands, moves her chair closer to him, sits down again. So close he can almost feel her through the space between them. Like the air conducts currents of electricity, sparks and flashes of it.

'Ciaran, you don't have to protect your brother. You don't need to do what he tells you. You're your own person.'

'I can do what I want,' Ciaran says.

Flanagan smiles. 'That's right. Now please listen very carefully to me.'

She reaches out and takes his hands in hers. He feels his heart swelling inside him, pushing against his ribs, like it might split him open. He tries to shallow his breathing, but he can't. Air rips in and out of him.

'I think you and Thomas know what happened to Daniel Rolston last night. I believe one of you might have killed him. If I'm right, and you were involved, you will go to prison for a very long time. It won't be only a few years, and it won't be like Hydebank. A real prison, Ciaran. Probably a life sentence. Even if you behave yourself inside like you did at Hydebank, you'll be in your thirties before you're allowed out again. What's left of your life will be ruined and thrown away.'

She watches his face for a moment. He doesn't know what she sees there. He doesn't know what he feels himself, so many emotions chasing each other around his soul. So much noise inside him, he can't hear his own mind.

'But it doesn't have to be that way,' she says.

She reaches out and touches his cheek.

He shivers.

He sees the other policewoman straighten.

'Talk to me,' Serena says. 'Tell me exactly what happened. I can make things easier for you.'

Ciaran looks down at his hands. His sleeves have risen. The livid traces of Thomas on his skin have crept beyond his cuff, out where anyone can see them, not hiding like they should. The red and the pink, bruises forming. She notices. Her fingers slip away from his face.

'Jesus, Ciaran,' she says, her voice rippling soft. She takes his wrist, rolls his sleeve up further. 'Are you still hurting yourself?'

He studies her face. More lines there now. Small wisps of grey at the roots of her hair. Then he thinks of Thomas, and how hard he can bite.

'I need to go to bed,' Ciaran says. 'I have to go to work in the morning.'

'Or did Thomas do this?' she asks.

He tries to take his hand away, but she holds on. She touches her fingertip to a break in the skin, already scabbing over.

'No,' Ciaran says. 'I want to go.'

Serena releases his wrist and sits back. 'All right. But I have something else to ask you.'

Ciaran pauses.

'Did you really kill Daniel's father?'

Ciaran does not answer.

'Did you lie to me? To all of us? Did you take the blame for your brother?'

Ciaran stands and says, 'I have to go.'

He walks to the door. Serena is still talking, but he doesn't hear her any more. He leaves the office. Mr Wheatley is waiting in the hall, watches Ciaran pass on his way to the stairs. Ciaran climbs them, goes to his room, and sits on the bed.

He knows he will not sleep tonight.

36

Ballantine didn't speak as she drove back towards the motorway. Her silence grated on Flanagan more than a deluge of words would have.

'What?' Flanagan asked.

'Nothing, ma'am,' Ballantine said as she turned from the Malone Road towards Balmoral, and the M1 beyond. Flanagan would've taken the Hillhall Road, but she passed no comment.

'Speak your mind,' Flanagan said. 'I can hear you biting your tongue. You'll chew it off if you're not careful.'

'It's just . . . '

'Just what?'

'He's strange,' Ballantine said.

'You don't know the half of it.'

Ballantine stopped the car at a pedestrian crossing, waiting for the light to change.

'It's not just that he's quiet,' she said. 'He's strange in himself, all right, but . . . '

As the car got moving again, Flanagan said, 'For Christ's sake, just say what you're thinking.'

'What's strange is the way he was with you,' Ballantine said. 'The way he looked at you. Like a schoolboy with a crush. But deeper than that. When you took his hand, it was like he got an electric shock.'

'Well, I guess he hasn't seen many women over

the last few years. It's hardly surprising he gets a little doe-eyed when he comes face to face with one.'

Ballantine stopped again at the junction with the Lisburn Road, the railway bridge at the other side. Flanagan looked down at her hands, saw the red light reflected there.

'It seemed like more than that,' Ballantine said. 'And ma'am, if you don't mind me saying, you didn't seem to discourage him. And the way you touched him . . .'

The red turned to green. The diamond on Flanagan's engagement ring caught the light in its prism.

'I do mind you saying. I mind very fucking much. Move, for Christ's sake, the light's changed.'

As Ballantine accelerated away from the junction, she said, 'Sorry, ma'am.'

Regret bit at Flanagan's heart, and she might have apologised for her harsh words, but her anger won out. Anger at herself or Ballantine, it didn't matter, it was there all the same, like a sore on her skin.

In truth, she had felt it as soon as she entered the hostel and saw Ciaran. Grown up now, handsome in his pale and shadowy way. And the way he looked at her. She had felt his gaze on her like fingertips.

And she did not turn away from it.

There, in that office, it would be a lie to say she found his attention objectionable. Even as she went to take his hands, she knew it was inappropriate. And the charge had coursed

230

between them. They both felt it. Perhaps he was less conscious of it than she, twisted innocent that he was, but it had run from her palms through her arms, her chest, down to her belly, and further yet.

Flanagan felt herself blush as Ballantine climbed the slip road up onto the motorway, and was glad of the dimness in the car.

37

Cunningham lay in bed, the small flatscreen TV lighting the room, some dreadful rom-com playing, the sound muted. Angus lay curled beside her on top of the duvet, his legs twitching as he chased dream-rabbits. Her laptop open on her thighs. Even now, she was still refreshing the BBC Northern Ireland news page every few minutes in case anything had changed. Daniel's story remained the lead item, the rest of the headlines made up of another fuel laundering operation that had been raided, bickering between politicians over the violence that had erupted with tiresome predictability over the summer, all of them rushing to blame each other without offering anything resembling a solution.

From outside she heard the rumble and clatter of the last Bangor-bound train, the line running by the end of her street. That and the proximity of the City Airport were the only reasons she had been able to afford to buy this house.

Cunningham's emotions had tumbled all day, pity for Daniel Rolston and his miserable end turning to anger at him for not leaving the brothers alone, resentment at his coming to her home. The first she felt reasonable, the others unfair, but she had long since stopped looking for logic in her feelings. The irrationality of emotion is what makes us human, a counsellor had once told her. How else to explain why a person might simultaneously love and hate another? Accepting the absence of logic in one's heart is a key step towards happiness. Counsellors and therapists made their living spouting such bullshit, placebos for the mind, designed to soothe their clients. Cunningham had little time for them. But still, that one point rang true for her.

A half-full bottle of white wine sat on the bedside locker, and an almost full glass. She had taken the bottle from the fridge on her way to the stairs, but found her usual thirst lacking. Perhaps she should have been glad of it, but instead she felt a mild disappointment.

Cunningham's eyelids had drooped, her head nodding forward, when Angus stirred. She jolted awake, a sickly feeling as the room aligned itself around her. Angus rose into a sitting position, his ears erect, a low rumble in his chest.

She reached over and scratched his back, weaving her fingers through his coat.

'It's all right, boy, just someone walking past.'

A single bark, high and anxious.

'Settle down,' she said. 'No one's there.'

Then he leapt from the bed, nails scrabbling on the floor, a stream of yelps melding into one. He stood on his hind legs, pawed at the door handle.

'For God's sake, Angus, all right.'

Cunningham set her laptop aside and got out of bed. She tripped over her shoes, stumbling against the wall, and steadied herself as she went to the door. It was barely open a crack before Angus forced his nose through, pushed it open, and bolted onto the landing. She followed as his paws hammered down the stairs.

She caught a glimpse of a piece of paper wedged into the letterbox in the centre of the front door before Angus seized it, shook it in triumph like some prey he'd hunted down.

'Christ,' Cunningham said as she descended the stairs. She cursed whoever had been leafleting at this time of night. A takeaway menu, a bin cleaning service, some religious tract. Or worse, one of many pages she'd had put through her door telling her foreigners weren't welcome and no property on the street should be rented to them.

At the bottom of the stairs she cornered Angus in the darkness, grabbed his collar with one hand, and the page with the other. 'Leave,' she said. Angus huffed and held on. She said it again, more firmly, and this time he obeyed.

Cunningham felt the dampness against her skin, assumed it was from the dog's mouth, then she saw the dark stains on the paper. She reached for the hall light switch. Her mind struggled for a few seconds to make sense of what she held in her hand, Angus whining and pacing a circle, watching the door.

Then she understood. She released the page from her grasp and it fluttered to the floor. Angus sniffed at the paper and she swatted him away, shouted at him to leave. She could still make out the text, printed black on white.

Customer Details:
Name: Paula J. Cunningham
DOB: 26th May 1979

Her address. Her car make, model and registration. Everything Daniel Rolston had needed to find her. Written by hand, blocky capitals in blue ink, across the page: KEEP YOUR NOSE OUT BITCH.

Outside, a car engine revved, tyres screeching. She ran for the door, pulled it open, ran onto the path, ignored the cold sting of the concrete on her bare soles. Lights raced along the faces of the houses, the car hidden by those parked the length of the street. She reached the gate, opened it, out into the road. The red of the car's rear lights disappeared around the corner, no time to identify the vehicle.

Angus followed her onto the tarmac, ran in circles, yelping at the excitement.

'Bastard,' Cunningham said, her anger and adrenalin threatening to turn to tears. 'Fucking bastard.'

38

Ciaran is the first from the hostel to get into the van. As he approaches it, the passenger window whirrs open, revealing the driver and two other men. The driver calls across, 'You the new boy?'

'Yeah,' Ciaran says.

'In the back.'

Ciaran slides open the door on the side. Three other men are inside: one looks only a couple of years older than Ciaran, the other two middle-aged. Their clothes are all worn and dirty. So are their boots. Ciaran climbs in and sits beside the younger man.

'Where's your lunch?' the young man asks.

Ciaran sees the plastic tub in the young man's hands.

'I didn't know I was supposed to bring any.'

The young man laughs, says, 'Eejit. Who do you thinks going to feed you?'

'Dunno,' Ciaran says.

'I'm Emmet,' the young man says.

'Ciaran.'

Emmet grins and says out loud, 'Ah, Jesus, boys, we've got another Fenian. We'll have youse outnumbered soon.'

The rest of the men jeer.

Emmet leans in and nudges Ciaran. 'Don't worry,' he says, 'you'll be all right. These'uns are a good crowd. Even the Prods.'

A group of boys walk out of the hostel gates.

The sun in Ciaran's eyes obscures their faces. The men in the van jeer again.

'Watch out, lads,' the driver shouts, 'here's the bad boys coming.'

'Up your hole,' one of the boys answers.

The men laugh. Ciaran smiles, a strange feeling in his belly.

'Oh fuck me,' the driver says, 'look at the cut of this. Who did that to you, Robbie? Your granny?'

Ciaran feels the smile fade on his face.

Then the boys climb in, the first of them Robbie Agnew. His face still bruised, the cuts scabbed over, but the swelling gone. 'Away and shite,' he says to the driver. Robbie sees Ciaran as he goes to take his seat at the front. He freezes there, staring.

'I hope you at least got a dig in,' the driver says.

Robbie doesn't answer. The two boys behind push him into his seat so they can take theirs. They notice Ciaran too, exchange glances. Robbie turns his gaze to the window.

'Everybody in?' the driver asks. 'Seatbelts on. You too, Emmet. I'm not getting pulled by the peelers again.'

Emmet buckles himself in. So does Ciaran.

Robbie doesn't turn from the window as the driver pulls away from the kerb, the van's engine roaring as it gathers speed.

★   ★   ★

Ciaran works hard through the morning, surprised at how good it feels. The exertion, the

237

purpose, simply digging soil and turning it. Over and over, a square metre at a time, turning a marked-off section of patchy grass and weeds into a sheet of dark brown earth.

They had driven to the yard outside the city and waited while the driver hitched a large trailer to the van. Under Mr McClintock's direction, they loaded up the trailer with tools: shovels, spades, rakes, other things large and small that Ciaran didn't recognise. Another was loaded with pots of shrubs and blooming flowers, then attached to Mr McClintock's big four-by-four.

The two men who'd been sitting beside the driver in the van's cabin did not work. Instead, they smoked cigarettes and made jokes. Everyone laughed. Everyone except Robbie Agnew, who did not look at Ciaran. But his friends glared.

They drove in convoy for half an hour until they reached a sprawling housing estate between Lisburn and Belfast, tricolour flags hanging from lamp posts, murals on the gable walls of houses showing men long dead, their names written in Gaelic script, crude portraits bordered by Celtic knots. A patch of waste ground at the centre of the estate was being turned into a playground with a garden and benches at one end. Another contractor was building the playground, while McClintock's men landscaped the garden.

Mr McClintock unhitched the trailer from his car and left. Before they set to work, the two men who had done none so far conferred with someone from the other company, shaking hands, slapping upper arms. Old friends, it

238

seemed. A big BMW idled beside the site. All three men went to it and talked to the occupants. Some agreement was reached, envelopes were handed over, and with no signal Ciaran was aware of, everyone began their day's toil. All except those three men, who smoked more cigarettes and played cards.

Now Ciaran digs.

Even with the thick gloves he's been given, his palms sting, but he doesn't mind. Nor does he mind the fatigue he feels through his back, shoulders and arms, or the sun in his eyes. Nothing in the world to think about.

Just dig and turn.

Dig and turn.

Dig and turn.

Once a square metre is cleared, Ciaran drops to his knees and pulls weeds from the loosened earth, tosses them onto a pile. After a couple of hours, one of the older men — the foreman, Ciaran thinks — comes and inspects his work.

'Good job, young fella,' he says. 'Come on and get yourself a cup of tea.'

An urn sits on the trailer's tailgate, along with Styrofoam cups and a plastic bottle of milk. Ciaran pours himself a cup, lots of milk. He looks around at the other men sitting cross-legged on the ground. Emmet pats the earth beside him. Ciaran hesitates, then joins him.

'How you getting on?' Emmet asks.

'Okay,' Ciaran says.

Emmet watches him for a moment. 'Fuck me, you're wild crack, aren't you?'

It takes Ciaran a moment to realise he's being

sarcastic. But not mean. Ciaran laughs and looks at the ground.

Emmet tears open the wrapper on a Twix bar. He looks at the twin fingers of chocolate and biscuit, sighs, then hands one to Ciaran.

'Thank you,' Ciaran says, meaning it.

'S'all right,' Emmet says. 'You can have a bit of my lunch later, but bring your own tomorrow, right?'

'Right,' Ciaran says.

They eat and sip in silence. After a while, Ciaran nods towards the men who don't work, and asks, 'Who are they?'

Emmet turns his head to look at them, then quickly turns back. He glances around, makes sure no one is listening.

'The fat one's Sammy Mathers from the Shankill, the baldy one's Paul Hughes from the Falls. UDA and IRA. I don't know who the fella from the other company is, but he'll be one or the other. Probably 'Ra seeing as we're working round here.'

'Why are they here?' Ciaran asks. 'They don't do anything.'

'The boss has to keep them on the payroll or he couldn't do jobs like this.'

'Why not?'

'Most of his work's in housing estates like this one, either republican or loyalist, so he needs an IRA or a UDA man, maybe UVF depending where it is, to smooth things with the local boys. The locals get a few quid for letting us work with no one getting threats for being a Prod or a Taig. Everybody's happy. Well, except the boss, but he's got no choice.'

Ciaran doesn't remember the Troubles, the first ceasefires were before he was born, but he knows which side was which.

'I thought the IRA and the UDA hated each other,' he says.

'They do. Unless there's money to be made, then they're best mates. Look, I didn't say it made sense, it's just the way it is.'

Before the break finishes, Ciaran walks to the portable toilet on the far side of the Portakabin that serves as the site office. He locks himself into the blue plastic cubicle and pees into the empty bowl, the sound of it resonating strangely in the small space. When he's done and washed his hands, he lets himself out.

Robbie Agnew and the other two boys are waiting for him.

Ciaran tries to run, but there's no time. Their hands grab at his clothes, drag him down to the ground. One of them falls on Ciaran's back, crushing the air from him. Ciaran scrabbles on the ground, tries to get his knees under him, but the boy on his back is too heavy. A fist glances off his head, then again, the punches too wild to do any damage. A boot connects with his shoulder. Ciaran pulls his elbows into his sides, his hands covering his face. More kicks to his shoulders, to his thighs. Hard hands grip at his, try to pull them away.

Then a voice, hard and commanding.

'Get the fuck off him.'

The blows stop, but the weight remains on Ciaran's back.

'I said get off him. Now.'

The weight vanishes, the boy on his back hauled away. Ciaran looks up through his fingers. The bald man, the one from the IRA, has Robbie by the hair. He slaps the boy hard across the cheek. Robbie knows not to fight back.

'None of this shite on the site,' he says. 'Any more and I'll have your knees, you wee bastard. You got me?'

Robbie nods. He's close to tears.

The IRA man pushes him away. 'Get back to work, the lot of you.' He looks down at Ciaran. 'You too, you long streak of piss.'

Ciaran walks back to his patch of ground, head down, and starts digging.

Soon he has forgotten Robbie and the other boys, and Thomas, and Daniel Rolston. Even Serena Flanagan burns less brightly in his mind.

All he does is dig and turn.

Dig and turn.

Dig and turn.

39

The sheet of paper sat on the desk, sealed in a clear plastic bag. The handwritten words glaring blue, Daniel Rolston's blood a deep maroon. Punctures from the dog's teeth.

Flanagan studied the weariness on Cunningham's features as she sat opposite. She'd offered to postpone the statement, allow the probation officer to get some sleep, but Cunningham had declined.

Sleep had proved evasive for Flanagan as well. As Alistair had snored and snuffled beside her, she had lain awake, trying not to think about Ciaran Devine or the feel of his hands in hers. All her life she had been a rational person, every action driven by logic above all things. She knew the strange feelings she'd experienced were a reaction to Alistair's fear of her body, and an instinct to care for this wounded young man. That was all, an intersection of emotions resulting in an irrational desire that would never, could never, be fulfilled.

Her higher mind should have been able to compartmentalise that feeling, fence it off from the rest of her consciousness, but somehow it could not. Instead, the desire lingered softly there, like the memory of a bright light trapped behind her eyelids.

Now when Cunningham stifled a yawn, Flanagan had the urge to do the same.

Flanagan pointed to the page. 'I'll get that off to Carrickfergus this morning. The Forensic Service are still working through the materials from Daniel Rolston's death, but they should have the report back before too long. Three or four days, maybe. If Thomas left any traces, they'll find them. They didn't find anything on your letterbox, though.'

'No,' Cunningham said. 'Looks like he's careful.'

'Very. He left nothing of any use at the murder scene. But he'll slip up sooner or later. They always do. You should know I'm going to apply for a Crime Prevention Order, stop Ciaran and Thomas from seeing each other.'

'That's a big step. It'll destabilise Ciaran.'

'He's a suspect in a murder case. How stable do you think he is now?'

'Can't you wait?' Cunningham asked. 'As soon as Ciaran's arrested, put under caution, the notification will come through the Reportable Incidents Desk. Then I'll have grounds to call a Risk Management Meeting. We can push to have his release licence revoked. Have him back in Hydebank where he can be watched. If he's out and free when you separate him from his brother, God knows how he'll react. At least if he's in custody, he can be controlled.'

Flanagan felt a defensive anger rise. She quelled it and said, 'Controlling him isn't the objective. Getting the truth is. I've a better chance of doing that if going back to Hydebank is a threat I can hang over him. If you have his licence revoked, that leverage is lost.'

Cunningham visibly tensed in her seat. 'My primary concern, my job, is to stop Ciaran harming himself or anyone else.'

'Then you've already failed,' Flanagan said.

Cunningham's face first paled then reddened. A tremor in her voice. 'You think I don't know that?'

Flanagan felt a sting of regret, exhaled as she slumped back in her chair. 'That was uncalled for. I apologise. But I've made my decision. I'm making the application.'

'I advise against it.'

'Noted,' Flanagan said. 'But I'll do my job as I see fit.'

'These past seven years,' Cunningham said, 'you've suspected Ciaran was innocent, even though you helped put him away. That's a heavy thing to carry around with you.'

'I've carried worse,' Flanagan said. 'I still do. Look, we had all the evidence in the world to say the brothers were there, that they were both involved to some extent. And then Ciaran confessed, and that was that. Didn't matter what doubts I had, I wasn't in charge of the case. Once the confession was on record, the PPS went for the conviction. I did everything I could to stop it.'

Flanagan paused, wondered if she should say it. She took a breath.

'There's something you should probably know about Ciaran. And me.'

Cunningham tilted her head. 'Oh?'

'You know I spent more time with him than anybody. I got him to come out of his shell, just a little. It was me he confessed to. We actually got to be quite close in those few days. But there was more to it for him.'

'What, you mean he had a crush on you?'

'Something like that. Remember, he was at that age, just hitting puberty. I was the only woman he'd ever spent time with, the only one who'd ever shown any interest in him. At the time, I thought it was a maternal thing. Like I'd become a mother figure to him. I mean, Christ, I was in my late thirties then, it wasn't like I was some young dolly-bird to tempt him. It wasn't until the end I realised it was more than that in Ciaran's mind.'

'Did he say something?' Cunningham asked.

'No, it wasn't what he said . . . '

Flanagan did not finish the thought, and Cunningham did not ask her to elaborate, so she left it unsaid.

'He wrote me a letter after the conviction, before he was sentenced. I suppose you could call it a love letter. But a school-boy's idea of one.'

'What did you do with it?'

'I destroyed it,' Flanagan said. The same lie she had told Purdy. And her husband. 'The thing is, when I went to talk to him last night, when we were face to face. Whatever he felt for me, it was still there.'

'Does that mean you'll have to step away, hand this over to someone else?'

'Possibly,' Flanagan said. 'That, or I use it. See if I can get Ciaran to open up to me again.'

Cunningham stared at her from across the

desk. 'You can't. It's too dangerous.'

Flanagan did not back down from her gaze. 'Yes, it's dangerous, but it might be my only way in. If we can't find anything to link either of the brothers directly to Daniel's killing, something real and solid, then getting Ciaran to talk is all I've got left.'

'But the security guard at Forestside — '

'Saw Daniel in a confrontation with two young men. I've got DS Ballantine going through the CCTV footage right now. Even if it clearly shows the Devines, all that proves is they had some sort of argument on Saturday morning. It doesn't prove anything about what happened that evening.'

Cunningham shook her head. 'He's a very vulnerable young man. You can't manipulate him like that.'

'I can,' Flanagan said, feeling her own features harden. 'And if I have to, I will.'

40

Cunningham steered her car through the estate, past the murals, beneath the flags, deeper until she found the expanse of waste ground at its centre. She parked close to the Portakabin, got out of the car, and looked for Ciaran.

There, at the far end, digging within a rectangle formed by tape suspended between metal posts. She skirted the ground, and the men who worked there, and made her way towards him. The men ignored her until she set foot on the coarse grassy earth, entering their dominion. Then the catcalls started. Whistles, mostly. Nothing too offensive yet.

Ciaran looked up, saw her coming. She watched his face as it went from an almost serene blankness to fear, a flash of what might have been anger, then nothing. He set the spade down, stood up straight and watched her approach.

Jeers from the other men, suggestions about what she might want with Ciaran. Ciaran blushed, dropped his gaze. A foreman shouted at the men to shut their mouths, leave the lad alone. Cunningham might have reminded the foreman that she was the true target of their taunts, but she doubted he would have understood. She realised she should have sought the foreman's permission before disturbing Ciaran's work, but she no longer felt inclined to extend that courtesy.

'Can I have a word?' she asked.

Ciaran ducked under the tape, pulled his gloves off, wiped his hands on his jeans.

'I just wanted to see how you were getting on,' Cunningham said. 'Are you enjoying it?'

'Yeah,' he said. He smiled.

Actually smiled. Cunningham couldn't help but mirror the expression.

'Good,' she said. 'I'm glad to hear it. Shall we take a walk?'

Ciaran looked over her shoulder. She followed his gaze. An older man stood watching: the foreman. He would know the score, know Cunningham was a probation officer checking on her client. The foreman nodded. Cunningham did the same, then looked back to Ciaran.

'Come on,' she said.

Cunningham made it a habit to visit her clients on their first day in a job. Normally, if nowhere was available, she'd speak with them in her car. But the idea of sitting so close to Ciaran, being so confined with him, sent a shiver to her centre. Instead they walked around the perimeter of the square of houses facing the waste ground. Curtains twitched as they passed, residents watching the interlopers.

'It's good to work,' Cunningham said.

Ciaran kept his hands in his pockets. 'Yeah.'

'Have you made any friends?'

Ciaran's face brightened. 'Emmet. He shared his lunch with me.'

'That was kind of him. You'll remember to bring your own tomorrow, won't you?'

'Yeah,' Ciaran said.

Cunningham wondered if there would be any work for Ciaran tomorrow. A young police-woman had knocked Flanagan's door before she left, said she'd found the footage they needed. Said it looked like the Devines. Flanagan would have them both in custody that evening. This might be Cunningham's last chance to talk to Ciaran outside of a cell. At least until he was released for lack of evidence.

'I know about last night,' she said. 'About the police talking to you.'

Ciaran did not reply.

'I want you to think very carefully, Ciaran. Think about where you've been for the last seven years. Where you could be seven years from now. See, there's something I know about you, Ciaran.'

He stopped, looked at her, terror on his face. 'What?'

'People think you're stupid, don't they?'

He looked back to his feet.

'Because you're quiet, because you don't say much, they think maybe you're not that bright. But I've seen the reports. You're a very smart young man. You could be anything you want to be. You could go back to school. Go to night classes, get your GCSEs, maybe even A levels. Who knows, you could go to university if you worked hard enough. But you've always let Thomas do the talking, haven't you?'

Ciaran started walking again. Cunningham caught him up, kept pace beside him.

'You let Thomas do the talking, and you've

always let him do your thinking too. Isn't that right? He's made you believe you can't talk or think for yourself, that you need him to do it for you. But that isn't true. You don't need Thomas to do anything for you. There's nothing he can do that you can't do yourself. I know you love him, but you don't need him.'

'Fucking shut up.'

He stopped, visibly shaken at his own words. He looked away, put his gaze anywhere but on her.

'Ciaran, don't talk to me like that,' Cunningham said.

'Sorry,' he said, barely audible above the sounds of the estate around them.

'Okay. Look, I don't know how things are going to go over the next few days. I do know you could be in a lot of trouble. I mean the worst kind of trouble. So you need to think, Ciaran. Think about how much you want to give Thomas. Do you want to give him the rest of your life? You've got a future now. Are you going to sacrifice yours for his? Whatever happened seven years ago, whatever happened two nights ago, all that matters now is you tell the truth. Even if that means hurting your brother.'

'I should go back to work,' Ciaran said.

'Okay, I need to get back to the office anyway. Off you go.'

He turned and walked back towards the site.

'Ciaran,' she called after him.

He stopped and looked back at her.

'You're your own person. Your brother doesn't own you. Just remember that.'

251

She watched him as he returned to his patch of ground, to his spade, and started digging again.

41

Ciaran sits alone in the interview room.

They were waiting for him at the hostel when the van dropped him and the others off at the end of the day's work. Serena Flanagan wasn't there; instead, it was the younger policewoman, the one who had stood at the door and taken notes the night before. Her and two policemen in uniforms. She said something about rights as one of the policemen bound Ciaran's hands behind his back, the metal of the cuffs digging into his wrists.

Ciaran kept quiet as the other boys watched. Mr Wheatley stood in his office doorway, looking at the floor. Ciaran stayed quiet as he was led away, put in the back of the car, driven to the station in Antrim, the same one they took him to seven years ago. They swapped his clothes for the same navy-blue sweatshirt and bottoms, the same plimsolls, but a better fit now.

They told him DCI Flanagan would be with him presently. Ciaran tingled at the idea.

Now he waits quietly.

The door opens, startling him. He looks up, expecting, hoping, to see her.

It's a man in a suit. Ciaran exhales disappointment along with spent air.

The man sets a file on the table, extends his hand. Ciaran takes it, feels the man's soft grip before releasing it.

'Ciaran, my name's Michael Wells, I'm the solicitor that's been appointed for you. You're going to be interviewed under caution, so I need to be here to advise you. Do you understand?'

Ciaran nods.

Wells sits down. 'Now, I've been looking over the case and what the police have against you. It's very little, just some alleged footage of you and your brother in an altercation with the deceased man. Not enough to charge anyone, so you don't need to worry. They're going to push you hard on this, so your best bet is to just say no comment to everything. All right?'

Ciaran nods again.

'So long as you keep your mouth shut, they've nothing to hold you for. They'll have to let you go within twenty-four hours. They can apply for an extension, but as far as I can see, they've no grounds. Okay. Are you ready?'

'Yeah,' Ciaran says.

Wells gets to his feet, opens the door, says a word to someone outside.

Serena Flanagan and the other policewoman follow him back into the room. Wells sits down beside Ciaran, the two women across the table.

Serena smiles as she organises her notepad and pen. Ciaran can't help but smile back. The other policewoman shows Ciaran and Wells two sealed blank CDs before she opens them and loads them into the audio recorder at the end of the table.

Then they begin.

42

Flanagan had lifted Thomas at the hotel. The manager and reception staff had watched with horror as he was cuffed and read his rights there in front of the guests.

Thomas said nothing until he was in the car. 'You've probably cost me my job. You know that, don't you?'

Flanagan didn't answer. She didn't much care.

They waited in the station car park for a call to say Ciaran had been processed at the custody suite and taken to an interview room. Then Thomas was booked in and brought to a cell.

Not a word in all that time, but Flanagan could feel the rage and hate pulsing from him. Even as the cell door swung closed he stood at its centre, staring back at her until the metal separated them.

Now here was Ciaran, his gaze also fixed on her, but something entirely different behind his eyes. Something that cut into her sharper and deeper than the surgeon's scalpel that had taken the cancer from her breast months before.

'Ciaran, do you know why you're here?' she asked.

'Yeah,' Ciaran said.

Wells, the solicitor, touched his arm, leaned in, and whispered. 'No comment,' Ciaran said.

'You're here because Daniel Rolston was killed the night before last in an alley in Stranmillis.

255

Now, you don't need me to go over your history with Daniel, do you?'

'No comment.'

'How you confessed to killing his father. How his mother committed suicide as a result.'

'Just a minute,' Wells said. 'As far as I'm aware, there was never a direct link proven between the father's killing and the mother's suicide. That's not relevant here.'

Flanagan ignored him. 'Now, we know you and Thomas had an altercation with Daniel on Saturday morning. We have CCTV footage. There's no question. You and your brother can be clearly seen.'

She took the top sheet from the stack on the table, turned it face up. A still image from the footage. Ciaran held between Thomas and Daniel. She turned another page, set it beside the first.

'The video shows Daniel striking Thomas.'

And another.

'Thomas falling to the floor.'

Another.

'You helping Thomas up.'

Another.

'Before Daniel is taken away by the security guards.'

She let Ciaran study the images for a time, watched his eyes move from one to the other. An echo of sadness there. Regret, perhaps?

'Tell me what happened,' Flanagan said.

Ciaran went to speak, but the solicitor touched his arm. The same arm that bore the teeth marks she'd seen the evening before.

'No comment,' Ciaran said.

'Daniel came to see you,' Flanagan said. 'He came looking for you. What did he want?'

'No comment.'

'What did he say to you?'

'No comment.'

'Did he ask you about his father?'

'No comment.'

'Did he say he thinks Thomas killed his father, that you confessed to protect Thomas?'

'That's not true,' Ciaran said. He pulled his arm away from the solicitor. 'I killed Mr Rolston.'

'Daniel didn't think so,' Flanagan said. 'He told your probation officer he thought Thomas did it. Is that why Thomas killed Daniel?'

'He didn't.'

'Let me tell you what I think happened. I think Daniel was getting too close to the truth. I think Thomas was getting scared. And when Daniel tackled you at the shopping centre, that was the last straw, wasn't it? He had to do something. Am I right?'

Ciaran covered his eyes with his hands. 'No comment.'

'Stop covering for your brother. You spent seven years in Hydebank. Are you going to give him the rest of your life?'

'No comment.' His voice a whisper.

'Ciaran, you can be free of him. Just tell me the truth, tell me what really happened. Then he'll be gone. He'll never touch you again. I promise.'

His hands shook. 'No comment.'

'All right,' Flanagan said. She allowed the room's dull quiet to settle over them for a few moments before she said, 'I have something to give you.'

She took the envelope from her pocket, held it in front of Ciaran.

He looked at her hand, asked, 'What's that?'

'Please take it,' she said.

Ciaran reached for the envelope, took it from her.

'It's a Crime Prevention Order,' Flanagan said. 'It says you're not allowed to associate with Thomas unless it's under direct supervision by your probation officer or someone specifically approved by me. I applied for the order in court this morning.'

Ciaran sat back in his chair. Stared at her. A cold hardness there now.

'After you leave here,' Flanagan said, 'you'll be allowed no contact with Thomas without prior arrangement with Miss Cunningham.'

'No,' Ciaran said, a slight shake of his head.

'That's the court's decision,' Flanagan said.

The shake of his head became slower, wider, along with a rocking motion.

'No,' he said.

'I'm sorry, that's all — '

The slap of his palm against his cheek reverberated in the room. He grabbed a handful of his own hair, pulled hard. Slapped himself again.

'Ciaran, stop.'

Flanagan looked to Ballantine, who stood and exited the room. The solicitor put an arm around

Ciaran's shoulder, whispered to him to calm down. Ciaran jerked his body loose. Flanagan reached across the table, tried to take Ciaran's hands. He pulled away, made a fist with one hand, drew it back, slammed it into his own jaw. Again, and again.

'Stop, Ciaran, please.'

Flanagan came around the table, tried to take him in her arms, but he writhed within her embrace, broke free. Blow after blow, fists, open hands, his head jerking with the force of them. The harder Flanagan tried to seize his arms, the harder he fought himself. Blood on his lips, smeared on his bared teeth.

The interview room door burst inward and four uniformed men rushed through, leg and arm restraints in hand. Flanagan backed away, let them take Ciaran. Like a boy caught in an avalanche. The solicitor fell from his chair to the floor, papers scattering. They worked with practised and dreadful efficiency. Within moments they had Ciaran face down on the floor, a knee between his shoulder blades, a hand pressing his head down into the linoleum, careful of his teeth. Velcro straps bound his calves, more holding his hands behind his back.

Then all was still and quiet, the solicitor and Flanagan backed into opposite corners, the only sound Ciaran's gasping breath.

'Get him to his cell,' Flanagan said.

The four officers lifted him, face down, carried him head first towards the door. Ballantine stepped aside to let them past. She looked back at Flanagan, wide-eyed.

'What now?' Ballantine asked as the solicitor rushed past her.

Flanagan did not reply. Ballantine followed her all the way to the canteen.

'What about the brother, ma'am?' she asked.

'We let him sweat,' Flanagan said, as she filled a paper cup full of coffee. 'Let him wonder what Ciaran's telling us. Let the worry set in.'

Ballantine fetched a tea for herself and joined Flanagan at the nearest table. 'Aren't you going to interview him?'

'Maybe,' Flanagan said. 'Maybe not. Won't make much difference. He'll give us a string of no comments. It's Ciaran I need to work on.'

'But he'll do the same,' Ballantine said. 'He'll do what the solicitor tells him, just say no comment to everything.'

'No. Away from the solicitor. On his own.'

'And then nothing he says is usable.'

'True, but that's not the point. The point is to chip away at this loyalty he has to Thomas. Wear it down until it breaks. Then he'll talk in front of the solicitor, under caution. Then he'll give up his brother.'

'And how are you going to do that?' Ballantine asked.

Flanagan did not answer. She drank her coffee in silence.

43

It's getting dark outside. If Ciaran rolls onto his back and cranes his neck, he can see through the small cell window. The light above is hard on his eyes, like glass fingers reaching inside his skull. He doesn't know how long has passed since they put him in here. Feels like hours.

He screamed for a long time, he remembers that.

Lying face down on the thin vinyl-covered mattresses they had placed on the floor, hands strapped behind his back, his ankles bound. He had thrashed and kicked as much as the strapping would allow, tried to bash his head against the concrete, but the mattresses had softened each blow. All he'd managed was to strain his neck, his shoulders, his lower back, his thighs. Eventually, he gave up and lay still.

Then a long stretch of nothing, the only noise that which echoed within his head. Bad thoughts. Dangerous thoughts.

Thoughts of Daniel Rolston bleeding in an alley.

Thoughts of Thomas's teeth.

Thoughts of Serena Flanagan's body. Her arms holding him, and the warm blades of her mouth.

Not very long ago, two uniformed police officers entered the cell. He lifted his head to see them.

'You calmed down any?' one of them asked.

Ciaran exhaled, let his body go limp.

'Good,' the policeman said. 'You feeling okay? Do you want to see a doctor?'

'I'm all right,' Ciaran said.

They said nothing more, left him there on the floor and closed the door behind them.

Now Ciaran's tongue moves behind his lips. He looks for the anger and the hate that had devoured him earlier that day, finds nothing but a sadness he can't quite grasp.

He startles at the sound of the door unlocking. He lifts his head again and sees Serena Flanagan step through carrying a tray. His heart kicks in his chest. Cold sparks in his stomach. He rolls to his side, humiliation swamping him.

She sets the tray on the bench that serves as a bed.

'Tea and toast,' she says. 'I remember how you like it. Lots of milk, lots of butter.'

Ciaran knows the two policemen are waiting outside to rush in if he does anything. He can't see or hear them, but he knows all the same.

'If you stay calm,' she says, 'I'll ask the officers to undo the strappings so you can eat. Will you try to stay calm for me?'

Years compress like an accordion and Ciaran is a child again. Alone and terrified in a cell like this one. This woman his only friend. The sole focus of his being. The one constant in his days, his only reason to keep breathing.

Ciaran rolls onto his other side, his back to her. He wants the toilet. He hopes he can hang on. He couldn't bear to sink any lower.

'How are you feeling?' she asks.

He wants to feel angry. He wants to hate her. But he can't.

'I'm okay,' he says, his voice thin and whispery.

'Are you still angry?'

'Dunno.'

'It's okay to be angry,' she says. 'Everyone gets angry sometimes. But it's not okay to hurt yourself. Or anyone else.'

Ciaran closes his eyes. He doesn't know what she wants him to say.

'I understand why you're upset,' she says. 'I know how important your brother is to you, and I'm not trying to drive you apart. But you must see why I got this order.'

'Are you sending me back to jail?' Ciaran asks.

'Not yet,' Serena says. 'First thing tomorrow morning I have a Risk Management Meeting with your probation officer and her area manager. They might want to go to the parole commissioner and ask for your release licence to be revoked. Then you'd have to go back to Hydebank. But I can ask them not to do that. If you'll talk to me. Not under caution, not officially, just talk like we're doing now. If you do that, I'll ask for your licence not to be revoked. Fair enough?'

Ciaran doesn't answer.

He hears her stand and come close, feels the pressure on the mattresses shift as she kneels down beside him. He can smell her now, soap and flowers and something else, the scent filling his head like it did seven years ago.

'Will you talk to me?' she asks.

'What about?'

'You,' she says. 'And Thomas.'

'All right.'

He feels her hand on his shoulder.

'Thank you,' she says. She takes a breath. 'You know, you spent two years in Hydebank without Thomas, and you managed. You can take a little time away from him now, can't you?'

Ciaran wants to tell her what those two years were really like. The fear constantly ringing inside him. The sense of being alone and adrift amongst the other boys. How at night he often imagined the feeling of a belt or a strip of bed sheet tightening around his neck. Ciaran knew how to do it, still knows, just tie one end to a door handle and sit down. That's all. If not for Thomas's visits, for the words and promises his brother whispered to him every time, Ciaran doesn't know what he would have done.

'Where is Thomas?' he asks.

'In another cell,' she says. 'Not in this block.'

'I want to see him.'

'Tomorrow,' she says. 'Under supervision. Depending on how things go between now and then.'

'I want to see him tonight.'

'That's not going to happen.'

Ciaran folds in on himself, gathers in his knees, his chin, curls like a question mark around his own frightened heart.

'You don't have to be afraid,' she says. 'Nothing bad is going to happen to you. You're safe here. You don't need Thomas. He can't hurt you while you're with me. I'll look after you.'

Can't hurt me.

The words resonate in Ciaran's mind as her hand returns to his shoulder. He closes his eyes. Focuses on the pressure there on his skin, the feel of hers through the fabric of the sweatshirt. Her fingertips move to his collar, then to the bare skin of his neck. He opens his eyes, turns his head to look up at her. His gaze holds hers for a moment.

Only for a moment, a crackling instant, then her fingers lift away like startled birds.

He can barely breathe.

Can't hurt me.

Don't need him.

That possibility glints like a candle flame in the darkness. The flame sputters, flickers, almost dies.

Then it steadies and glows.

Ciaran opens his mouth to speak, but the other policewoman appears at the door of the cell. 'Ma'am?' she says. 'Is everything all right?'

Serena moves away from him.

'It's fine,' she says. 'I'll call you if I need anything.'

The other policewoman hesitates, looks at Ciaran, looks at Serena, and backs out of the doorway.

Quiet for a while, then Serena says, 'Okay, I'm going to leave you now. The other officers will undo those strappings. You eat the toast and drink the tea. I'll come back in an hour. While I'm gone, I want you to think very hard about what I've said. About what you're going to say to me. All right?'

Ciaran nods.

Serena stands and walks to the door. She pauses there and says, 'You don't need him.'

He watches her leave and the two uniformed officers enter. They undo the straps while he lies very still.

One of them says, 'Good boy,' and pats his shoulder. 'Maybe get some sleep.'

The cell door closes and locks.

44

Ballantine waited along the corridor. Flanagan didn't slow her pace on the way to the temporary office she'd been given.

'Ma'am.'

Flanagan pretended she didn't hear as she reached her door.

'Ma'am.'

Louder. More insistent.

Flanagan exhaled and turned to the detective sergeant's voice. 'What?'

'Can I have a word?'

Flanagan opened her office door, stood back to allow Ballantine to enter, then followed her in. 'Well?' she asked as she closed the door behind her.

Ballantine stood at the desk, her arms folded, her fingers curling around her elbows, her gaze on the floor.

'Come on,' Flanagan said. 'We haven't got all night.'

'I saw the way you touched him,' Ballantine said.

'What do you mean?'

'The way you were stroking his neck.'

'Stroking?' Flanagan forced an indignant laugh. 'I wasn't stroking anything. I put my hand on his shoulder while I was speaking with him. A friendly gesture to relax him. To get him to talk to me.'

Ballantine shook her head, but kept her eyes downward. 'You were touching his neck. In an intimate way, with your fingertips.'

'Rubbish.'

'It's inappropriate,' Ballantine said. 'He's a very vulnerable young man, and you're playing games with him.'

'Enough,' Flanagan said, the edge of her voice sharpening.

'You can't exploit his feelings for you like — '

'I said, enough!'

Ballantine fell silent. She hadn't looked at Flanagan once.

'Now, I want you to continue questioning Thomas Devine. You know the areas I want covered, you know which approaches to take. We probably won't have him or his brother here for long, so there's no time for this nonsense. Understood?'

'Yes, ma'am.'

'All right,' Flanagan said. 'Go and do your job.'

Ballantine left without another word. Flanagan watched the door for a time before she said, 'Fuck.'

Anger burst in her, a childish rage. She walked a circle around the room, her fists clenched, wishing she had something or someone to punch. Instead she kicked the chair in front of her desk, barely budging it. Then she pushed it over, kicked it again.

'Fuck,' she said once more.

Stop it, she commanded herself. Grow up. She opened her hands, felt the heat where her nails

268

had dug into the palms, brought them together as if to offer up a prayer.

When calm had returned, or as near as she was likely to get, Flanagan breathed deep and thought about how she would use the remaining hours with Ciaran Devine. She looked at her watch and cursed again before lifting her mobile.

As she listened to the dial tone, a sense of déjà vu swamped her. Seven years ago, she made the same call for the same reason, like her life had turned in one long, wide circle.

When Alistair answered, she said, 'I'll be late home.'

'So much for easing back in,' he said, his voice sounding kind but exasperated.

'I know,' she said. 'I'm sorry. It's just this case. I've only so long to interview the DP before I have to let him go.'

'I understand,' Alistair said. 'What time do you reckon?'

'I don't know. Late. Maybe all night.'

Silence for a few seconds, then, 'The kids were asking for you.'

Flanagan covered her eyes with her free hand. 'Are they all right? How was school?'

'Do you really want to know?' he asked. 'Or are you just asking to be polite?'

'Don't,' she said.

'Don't what?'

'Don't use them against me like that. It's not fair.'

'Not fair? Are you . . . '

Alistair exhaled as he cut the sentence short

before he said something hurtful. She silently thanked him for it.

'Sneak in and give them a kiss for me,' she said.

'You could always come home and do it yourself,' he said.

'I'd like to,' she said. 'But I can't.'

'Yeah. Sure, we'll see you when we see you.'

'Okay. I love you.'

'Yeah,' he said, and the line died.

45

Ciaran dreams.

Hundreds of faces flash through his wandering mind. He knows few of them.

Thomas is calling from far away. Ciaran can't see him.

He is alone in a darkened corridor. Thomas's voice reverberates between the dull painted walls and scuffed vinyl tiles on the floor.

Where is this place? A hospital? A prison? A school? Whatever it is, Ciaran doesn't like it. It smells of toilets and disinfectant. He can feel how empty it is. This place should be full of people, bustling, working, talking. Instead it is quiet.

Apart from Thomas's voice, rising and falling.

Ciaran walks, realises he is barefoot, feels the tiles kiss his soles. He follows the voice around one corner, then another, and another.

It's darker here, deeper inside the building. Colder, the air heavier.

Up ahead, he sees a door with a window. Mesh in the glass like at the Young Offenders Centre. Light glowing sickly pale from within. The voice seeps between the door and its frame, carried by the light.

There are other doors along this corridor but Ciaran knows there are terrible things behind them. Bloody and painful things.

Ciaran draws closer. He sees a shape in the

window: Thomas, watching him approach, his mouth moving.

Ciaran reaches the door. He touches the glass. He can no longer hear Thomas's voice, but his brothers lips move regardless. The glass steams up from his breath. Ciaran sees the teeth behind the lips, glistening yellow-white.

Inside the room, beyond Thomas, is a bed. A hospital bed, a woman upon it.

Ciaran knows her, even though he hasn't seen her in many years. Except for dreams like this. His mother watching him, a smile on her lips.

Thomas is gone. Only a door between Ciaran and his mother. All he has to do is reach for the handle and turn it. Walk through to her.

That's all.

The handle is slippery on his skin. He can't grip it. It's too difficult. He tries and tries as his mother's eyes plead for him to come to her. Finally, he gets hold of the metal, presses down, and the door is gone and he is inside with her.

She lifts her arms to him, hands and fingers outstretched, come to Mummy.

He crosses the space between them without taking a step and is swallowed in her embrace. There on the bed, he melts into her, their arms and legs entangled and he is a child again, an infant, and she is the only woman in the whole wide world.

Her lips and breath on his infant ear: You don't need him.

I do, he says.

You don't.

I do, he's the big boy, I'm the baby, he has to look after me.

You don't need him. I won't let him hurt you again.

Ciaran opens his eyes to look at his mother. She has eyes just like Serena Flanagan's. And the same mouth and skin. And the smell like clean air and summer.

You don't need him, she says.

Then she is gone in a hard and burning light and Ciaran is falling, landing, jerking awake on the cell floor. He rolls onto his side, his arms cover his face, ready for his brother's teeth.

'Ciaran,' she says.

Serena Flanagan's voice.

He lowers his arms, finds her through the punishing brightness of the cell's fluorescent lighting.

'Are you ready to talk some more?' she asks.

As the confusion drifts away, Ciaran sits up on the mattress. His mouth is dry. He watches her, remembering the feel of her dream-embrace. He swallows.

'Ciaran?'

Ciaran says, 'I don't need him.'

46

'That's right,' Flanagan said.

He stared up at her from the floor, his eyes wide.

Just a child, Flanagan thought.

No, a grown man. Remember that, she thought. Whatever happens, remember that.

'Can I sit down?'

Flanagan waited for an answer. When none came, she went to the bench and sat down. The tiled concrete cold on her thighs, the mattress still on the floor with the others. Ciaran wrapped his arms around his knees.

'Tell me about before,' she said.

'Before what?'

'Before things went bad. When you and Thomas lived with your mother, before you were taken into care. Before your father died.'

'I don't remember him,' Ciaran said. 'Not really.'

'Nothing at all?'

Ciaran thought for a moment, his eyes distant, then said, 'He had hard fingers. I remember him holding my hand. His skin was dry and scratchy. And he smelled of cigarettes.'

'Do you remember when he died?' Flanagan asked.

'I remember the funeral,' Ciaran said. 'All the crying.'

'And after that?'

'We went to live in the house by the sea. Near

Newcastle. It belonged to Mum's parents. She got it when they died. It was good at first. Then Mum started to get sick.'

'Then tell me about the good part.'

Ciaran rested his chin on his knees, stared at something far away.

'She used to take us to this little beach, near the house. We used to look for crabs in the rock pools. Play hide-and-seek in the dunes. I used to laugh while we ran. I remember laughing so hard I couldn't breathe. Thomas used to laugh then too. He doesn't laugh any more.'

Flanagan hesitated for a moment, then lowered herself to the floor beside Ciaran, leaned her back against the bench. 'Have you ever gone back there?' she asked.

Ciaran shook his head. 'Thomas sold the house when he got out.'

'Did he share the money with you?'

'No,' Ciaran said.

'Doesn't that bother you?'

'No. I don't need any money.'

'Do you miss that house?'

'Sometimes.' He moved to a cross-legged position. 'The good times, anyway. Not after. Not when it got bad.'

Flanagan became aware of his knee touching her thigh, the small overlap of their bodies.

'Would you like to go back?'

'I wanted to, but Thomas said no. He told me it's empty, waiting to be knocked down. You can't get in.'

Flanagan watched him as she said, 'Maybe I could take you.'

He seemed shocked by the idea. 'You?'

She swallowed, a dry click in her throat. 'Yes. Why not?'

'Thomas wouldn't want me to.' He dropped his gaze.

'So? You told me you don't need him, remember?'

'But . . . ' His mouth opened and closed as he searched for an answer.

'We could go,' Flanagan said, leaning in closer to him. So close she could feel his warmth. 'Just you and me. All you have to do is tell the truth about what happened to Daniel Rolston, and to his father. Tell me what Thomas did, and I promise you and I will go to the seaside, where you used to live. Just talk to me.'

A sudden tremor through Ciaran's shoulders. 'But Thomas won't let me.'

'Thomas has no say in it.' Flanagan put a hand on his forearm. 'You don't need him.'

Tears rolled now, crystal beads racing on his cheeks. 'But he won't let me, he won't, he'll be angry, and he'll bite me.'

'Bite you?'

'He'll bite me if I'm bad,' Ciaran said, the words choked between sobs. 'He always bites me when I'm bad.'

Flanagan remembered the marks on Ciaran's forearm, now covered by his sleeves. She lifted her hand away, looked at his wrist, the bruising that crept beneath his cuff.

She knew what she wanted to do. That same impulse as long ago. But it was too dangerous.

She looked up at the camera. Imagined Ballantine watching, judging.

'Oh Jesus,' she said. 'C'mere.'

In spite of everything, she took him in her arms. Like so many years before. His body, at first unyielding, softened against hers. She felt the spasms of his torso as he wept, his cheek pressed into her neck. Like before. A child then, a young man now.

'Thomas won't let me go,' he said.

Every nerve in her body seemed to fire in volleys, fear tangling with emotions strange to her. The truth, she told herself. I will get the truth and I will have done the right thing.

For the truth, that's all.

'He will,' Flanagan said. 'I promise. I'll make sure he never touches you again.'

'You can't stop him.'

'Yes I can.'

'How?'

'I'll put him away,' she said, her lips finding his ear. 'I'll put him where he can never hurt you again. I promise you. But you have to trust me. Do you trust me?'

He nodded, his face burrowing deeper into the hollow between her shoulder and her chin. She felt his mouth move, the heat of his breath, as he whispered, 'Yes.'

For the truth. That thought echoed in her mind. Only the truth and nothing else.

Flanagan rocked him in her arms. 'Then tell me the truth. Tell me what happened in that bedroom with Daniel's father. Tell me who killed him.'

'I can't,' Ciaran said, his voice soft and thin like a child's.

'You can,' she said. 'If you trust me, then tell me. Then we can go to the seaside together. I promise, I swear on my life, I will take you there. Just tell me what happened.'

He became still and quiet. Through his skin, Flanagan felt something shift inside him, some change in his soul.

She eased back from him, her hands on his upper arms, her eyes locked on his. 'Ciaran, tell me.'

He took one deep breath. 'It was — '

'Flanagan.'

Her head snapped up, her gaze to the cell door. DSI Purdy, unshaven, a suit with no tie. Horror on his face. Ciaran inched away from her.

'Not now,' Flanagan said.

'Now.'

'Please,' Flanagan said, 'I'll come to your — '

Purdy's face contorted in rage. 'Right fucking now!'

His bellowing voice resonated and boomed in the cell.

Ciaran backed away, pushing with his hands and his feet, curled into a ball in the corner.

Flanagan stood, smoothed her clothing, went towards the door. She looked back over her shoulder, saw Ciaran staring back at her over his knees.

'I promise,' she said.

★   ★   ★

'What exactly are you playing at?' Purdy asked.

He had led Flanagan to her makeshift office and barked at her to sit, but he remained pacing on the other side of the desk. The clock on the wall read 1:34 a.m.

'Trying to get Ciaran's trust,' she said. 'There's nothing to stop me talking to him off the record, getting him to open up. Then I can use that when he's under caution.'

'Getting his trust. I see. So for him to trust you, you have to feel him up.'

'What?'

'You want to know what happened about an hour ago?'

Flanagan didn't answer.

'I'm just nodding off in bed, nice and snug, then my phone rings. Detective Sergeant Ballantine, awful sorry to disturb me at this time of night, wants a quick word.'

Flanagan's mouth dried. Dizziness and nausea followed. She gripped the arms of the chair.

'She's got a situation and she doesn't know what to do about it. Of course, I tell her to talk to you about it, but no, she can't do that because Detective Chief Inspector Flanagan is the fucking problem.'

'Sir, I don't know what DS Ballantine has told you, but — '

'Oh, she told me plenty. She told me she'd seen you touch a detained person in an inappropriate manner. She said you were going back in to talk to him some more, and she was worried about what was going to happen.'

'Please, sir, if you'll let me — '

279

'Of course I told her, don't be daft, Flanagan's a pro, she's as good as they come, she wouldn't do anything stupid like that. All the same, I got out of bed, drove up here, and had a look at the CCTV feed from that boy's cell.'

He leaned over the desk. Flanagan looked at the floor.

'And there's you and young Ciaran Devine getting all cosy on the floor.'

'Sir, I don't know what it looked like, but I can assure you nothing inappropriate happened. He was distressed, and I was comforting him. That's all.'

'Oh, he looked comfortable, all right.'

'He was getting ready to talk. If you hadn't interrupted, he would have told me the truth about what happened to Daniel Rolston's father.'

Purdy gave a dry crackling laugh. 'Oh yes, I know what you said to him earlier today, in front of the solicitor, on record.'

'It was a valid question.'

'Valid? You put it to him that he didn't kill his foster carer, that his confession was bullshit, that he was wrongly convicted. I listened to the interview. I heard you say it.'

'It's a line of inquiry that — '

Purdy's voice rose as his jowls quivered. 'It's a fucking lie that's going to land me in the shit.'

Flanagan blinked, shook her head in confusion. 'Sir?'

He stabbed at his chest with a finger. 'That was my case. Mine. And you're trying to make out I fitted up the wrong boy for it.'

280

'Sir, he confessed, there was no reason for you to — '

'If that conviction gets overturned, the blame goes on me.'

'I worked that case too,' Flanagan said. 'It was me who took the confession. I'm as much to blame as you are.'

'And I'm the one who'll take the grief for it. I'll be destroyed. You think I'm going to let you take a wrecking ball to my career?'

Flanagan forced calm into her voice. 'If Ciaran Devine didn't kill that man, then the truth has to come out.'

Purdy threw his arms wide. 'Why? Who's it going to help? They were both there in the room. They both went away for the murder. You get that boy to change his story, what difference is it going to make?'

'Maybe none, but what are we here for if not to get the truth? It won't get Ciaran back those seven years, but I'll have done my job.'

'Are you saying I haven't?'

'No, I — '

'Shut up and listen to me.'

'I — '

He leaned over the desk once more, his voice shaking now. 'I said shut up.'

Flanagan locked her hands together in her lap, clenched her jaw.

'Now, I'm taking this case away from you.'

Flanagan opened her mouth, but Purdy raised his hand to silence her.

'Don't breathe another fucking word, or so help me God, I'll have you in front of a misconduct panel. Clear?'

Flanagan nodded.

'Good. Now, you were supposed to be investigating a murder that took place at the weekend, not one that happened seven years ago. Given the lack of anything solid that ties those boys to the murder itself, I'm going to let them go before the morning. You will hand over all material you have relating to this case and provide any support requested to whomever the ACC and I appoint in your place. You will not make any further reference, to anybody, to their previous conviction other than the facts established by Ciaran Devine's confession and the evidence that was presented at trial. Do you understand me?'

'But — '

'Do you understand me?'

'Yes, sir.'

'Okay. Now get the fuck out of my sight.'

Flanagan marched along the corridor from her office, rage bound up like a fireball in her chest. She wanted to scream, to curse, but kept her mouth tight closed as she exited the building, even as the pressure of it built inside her. Furious tears and tremors escaped as she unlocked her car. Inside, she slammed the door, and screamed her throat raw.

47

Ciaran has been waiting and waiting for her to return. He's waited so long it's light outside. Somewhere in those hours he fell asleep, and revisited Mother-Serena in the hospital bed where she made him beautiful promises that he can no longer remember.

He knows she will return. She will come back and set him free. Free of this cell, and free of his brother. And she will take him to the seaside.

And what then?

Ciaran doesn't know, but the idea of it is bright and glowing in his mind when the cell door opens. He looks to the door, joy flowering in him, but it isn't Serena. Instead, it's a uniformed policeman and the other police-woman, the one with the long blonde hair and hard eyes.

'You're free to go,' she says.

'I'm waiting for Serena,' he says. 'I want to talk to her.'

'DCI Flanagan is no longer working on this investigation,' the policewoman says. 'You won't have any further contact with her.'

Ciaran's mind cannot absorb what the policewoman has told him. 'But I need to talk to her,' he says. He hears the quiver in his own voice.

'The Crime Prevention Order DCI Flanagan requested is still in force,' she said. 'You're to have no contact with Thomas Devine unless under supervision. For the time being, you're free to go.' She stepped away from the door, leaving a space exactly as wide as Ciaran. 'So go. Now.'

★ ★ ★

Mr Wheatley comes and gets him at six in the morning. He barely says a word as he drives along the motorway from Antrim, his eyes dark with fatigue.

As Mr Wheatley parks at the hostel, he says, 'The van will be here to lift the other boys in about ten minutes. If you're quick, you can still go to work today. If you don't, you'll probably get the sack.'

Ciaran says, 'Okay.'

'Good. Away you go.'

Fifteen minutes later, Ciaran waits with the other boys on the pavement. They don't speak to him, or even look at him. The van arrives, and they climb in. The seat next to Emmet is free, so Ciaran sits beside him once more.

'Jesus, did you forget your lunch again?' Emmet asks.

'Yeah,' Ciaran says.

'Well, I'm not sharing with you today.'

Ciaran doesn't answer as the van pulls away. He thinks only about Serena Flanagan and how she broke her promise.

They're all the same, Thomas would say.

All the same.

48

Cunningham waited at the long table in the boardroom listening to her boss's breathing. Edward Hughes sat at the other side of the table, his head nodding forward then jerking up again. He stirred himself, blinked, checked his wristwatch and said, 'Fifteen minutes.'

Cunningham didn't answer. The meeting was supposed to start at ten. Flanagan hadn't struck her as the type to miss appointments. She checked her own watch to be sure Hughes had got the time right.

Sixteen minutes, now.

She quietly thanked God when there was a knock at the boardroom door.

'Come,' Hughes said.

A man Cunningham didn't recognise entered, a file tucked under his arm. Mid-to-late fifties, around her boss's age. Hughes had frozen halfway out of his seat. He remained there, hunched over the table, staring at the new arrival.

'DSI William Purdy,' the man said. 'I'm here to talk about the Ciaran Devine case.'

Hughes finally stood upright, extended his hand. Cunningham did the same. As Purdy shook hers, she said, 'I was expecting DCI Flanagan.'

He released her hand. 'DCI Flanagan is no longer working on this case.'

'Why not?' Cunningham asked.

'It's an internal matter,' Purdy said as he took a seat at the end of the table. 'Can we get started?'

Cunningham remained on her feet. 'But DCI Flanagan knows Ciaran's case inside out.'

Purdy gave her a tight-lipped smile. 'Seeing as I led the investigation that resulted in Ciaran's conviction, I'd say I'm pretty familiar with it myself, wouldn't you?'

Cunningham studied him as she lowered herself to her seat, suddenly worried for Flanagan. Purdy had the demeanour of a man more concerned with the safety of his pension than with the moral obligations of his job. Had he pushed Flanagan aside for his own benefit? Or had she done something to deserve to be stood down?

Hughes cleared his throat. 'So, the purpose of this Risk Management Meeting is to establish whether Ciaran Devine poses a threat to himself or anyone else and, accordingly, if there are grounds for his release licence to be revoked. Paula, do you want to start?'

Cunningham swallowed before she spoke. 'This hinges entirely on the killing of Daniel Rolston. Ciaran and Thomas Devine are suspects in that killing, therefore — '

'Just a moment,' Purdy said. 'Sorry to interrupt, but it's a stretch to call them suspects given that the only thing we really have to connect them is some sort of an altercation at a shopping centre earlier in the day. We have nothing physical to put them at the scene of the killing, no CCTV footage, no witnesses who can place them there. All we've really got is supposition.'

'Supposition?' Cunningham echoed. 'Are you being serious?'

'Paula,' Hughes said, his tone a warning.

'Murder isn't something I joke about,' Purdy said, giving her a hard look.

Cunningham stared back, her concern for Flanagan deepening. 'You had grounds enough to arrest the Devines, interview them under caution. Now you're telling me it was just supposition.'

'DCI Flanagan had all of yesterday evening to turn something up. She didn't get a scrap out of either of them. Now, I've talked with the officers who searched Thomas Devine's flat and Ciaran Devine's room at the hostel. They took some clothes away, but there were no obvious traces from the murder, and no weapon. It'll be a day or two before the analysis of the clothes comes back, but when it does, I'd bet my house there'll be nothing.'

Cunningham shook her head. 'But they're the only possible suspects.'

'Based on what? That they had a row with the victim? There are at least two of Daniel Rolston's workmates that have had disagreements with him in the last few days, one of which got physical. Should I take them into custody too?'

'How can you be so wilfully blind?' Cunningham asked.

Purdy sat back in his chair, contempt on his face. He turned to Hughes. 'Are you going to let her talk to me like that?'

'Paula, enough,' Hughes said.

'No,' Cunningham said. 'It's not enough. It's not nearly enough. You can't dismiss this as if it's — '

'Stop, Paula.'

' — some punch-up outside a pub. A young man has lost his life. The last of his family. All of them wiped out by Thomas Devine and — '

'Thomas Devine was never convicted of murder,' Purdy said.

' — you're telling me there's not enough evidence?'

'Paula, please stop,' Hughes said.

'No, I won't stop, this is — '

Hughes's voice rang between the walls of the boardroom. 'Shut your mouth right now or I will take this case away from you.'

Cunningham closed her eyes and exhaled, tried to breathe away the anger. It didn't work: the rage still sparked in her. But when she opened her eyes again, she could at least pretend to be calm.

'All right,' Hughes said, 'now settle yourself.'

Cunningham nodded her assent.

'Good.' Hughes spoke to Purdy. 'So I take it you're not recommending Ciaran's licence be revoked.'

'No, I'm not,' Purdy said. 'I think it would do more harm than good at this stage.'

'Paula, you disagree?'

'I strongly disagree,' she said. 'Ciaran Devine and his brother are clearly a danger to themselves and to others. I believe Thomas Devine killed

288

Daniel Rolston and Ciaran is covering for him purely out of loyalty. I also believe Thomas Devine posted a threatening note through my door.'

Hughes leaned forward, his elbows on the table. 'But it's not Thomas Devine we're talking about sending back to prison. Even if your suspicions are proven to be true, it's Thomas who's the danger, not Ciaran.'

'That's not the point,' Cunningham said, but Hughes raised a hand to silence her.

'Now, both of you disagree on whether or not Ciaran's licence should be revoked, so it looks like it's up to me to make the decision.'

Cunningham's stomach felt heavy inside. She sat back, closed her notebook, resigned to the outcome.

'As I understand it, the Crime Prevention Order that DCI Flanagan got at court is still in effect. The Devine brothers are prohibited from seeing each other. And, in your opinion, Paula, it's Thomas Devine who presents a danger, not Ciaran. So I'm inclined to side with DSI Purdy on this, and I'm not going to recommend that Ciaran's licence be revoked.'

Cunningham got to her feet and gathered her things.

As she went to the door, she said, 'I just pray to God you don't regret this.'

49

Flanagan saw DCI Conn approach through the crowd outside the church. She braced herself.

'You were told to stay away from Julie Walker,' he said.

'Penny Walker was my friend, and I've as much right to go to her funeral as anyone else.'

She had stood at the back of the church for the service, crammed in with those who arrived too late to get a seat. The two coffins stood side by side at the top of the central aisle, flowers arranged on each. At the end of the first pew, Julie Walker and her boyfriend, both of them standing with their heads bowed.

Flanagan had swallowed her anger as the minister segued from his sermon to a droning hymn.

'At least stay out of Miss Walker's sight,' Conn said as mourners brushed past him. 'Show a little sensitivity.'

'I'll try,' Flanagan said, though in truth she didn't care one jot about sparing Julie Walker's feelings.

She remained among the stragglers, well away from the procession that moved away from the church at the top of the hill and down the slope to the terraces of graves. Penny had been quietly religious, rarely discussing her faith, but Flanagan knew she attended Sunday morning services here, dragging poor Ronnie along with her at Christmas and Easter.

Some of the members of the support group clustered near the front of the crowd. Flanagan had succeeded in remaining unnoticed by them. They would wonder why they hadn't seen her. She would never have to explain; she would not go back to the group again, tainted as it now was by the manner of Penny's death.

The procession paused as pallbearers swapped places, men young and old locking arms beneath the caskets. The older of them stoical, the younger with fear on their faces. Alistair had once told Flanagan about the first time he had carried a coffin at the age of nineteen, and how he had lain awake the night before his grandfather's funeral, terrified of slipping and falling while performing this sacred duty, how he pictured the coffin crashing to the ground in front of the horrified mourners.

'It was fine in the end,' he had said, 'but I had a hell of a bruise on my shoulder the next day.'

The sound of suppressed coughs and hundreds of shuffling feet all around as the pallbearers began the final leg of their short journey. The Walkers had a family plot on the southwestern edge of the graveyard. Green felt covered the mound of excavated earth beside it. A small digger parked beneath a tree a respectful distance away, a man in overalls leaning against it.

Flanagan could not make out the minister's words over the grave. She watched Julie Walker, the dryness of her eyes, Barry Timmons on her arm. Barry's face hollowed by fear. Flanagan felt a small stab of pity for him. He was not made for murder. One day he would crack under the pressure of his conscience; it was only a question of how many weeks, months or years that would take. Flanagan hoped he would go to the police and tell the truth rather than harm himself. But Barry Timmons looked like a coward, and she felt in her gut that he would take the coward's way.

'God help him,' Flanagan whispered under her breath.

The larger coffin was lowered first, then the smaller. A sob escaped Flanagan, surprising her. Grief at her friend being taken before she was ready. The grief slowly turned to anger. She resisted the shift at her centre for as long as she could, but it was no good.

A line formed as friends of the family went to express their condolences to the Walkers' sole surviving child. One after the other, hands were shaken, shoulders patted, heads bowed. With little thought of her actions, Flanagan joined the queue that wound down towards the graveside.

In a few minutes she was twenty feet away from Julie Walker, and DCI Conn had spotted her once more. He picked his way through the thinning crowd to Flanagan's side.

'What are you doing?' he asked, leaning in close, his voice low.

'Paying my respects,' Flanagan said as the line advanced.

He gripped her elbow. 'Come on.'

'Get your hand off me.'

His fingers tightened on her arm. 'I told you to

stay away, now for God's sake — -'

'Let go of me,' Flanagan said, 'or I will break your fucking nose right here in front of everybody.'

Conn stood silent for a moment, breathing hard. 'Don't think you'll get away with this,' he said before turning and walking back towards the church.

Less than a minute passed before Flanagan came face to face with Julie. The younger woman automatically extended her hand before realising who stood before her. Flanagan closed her fingers hard around Julie's, felt the sudden tension.

'It shouldn't have been like this,' Flanagan said. 'There was no need for it.'

Julie's gaze, her eyes laced with red, flitted across the mourners around them. 'I'd rather you hadn't come,' she said.

'I guessed so,' Flanagan said, 'but I came anyway.'

'All right. Now you can go.'

'There'll be no investigation,' Flanagan said. She gave Barry a glance. As he looked away, she said, 'Not unless something changes. Not unless someone tells the truth. Otherwise, well done. You got away with it. Not many do.'

Julie couldn't meet Flanagan's stare. 'Please leave now.'

'Yes, I'm going. I just wanted to make sure you know what I know. You got away with it, but you didn't go unnoticed. This will haunt you for the rest of your days. How will you live with it?'

Julie's features hardened as her eyes flashed.

'Please just fuck off.'

A hush all around, then a wave of murmurs.

Flanagan gave Barry Timmons a last smile before heading towards the church gates, ignoring the attention of those who watched her leave.

50

Using a trowel, Ciaran makes a hole in the loose earth about the size of his fist. Emmet presses the root ball down and in, the flowers wavering as he compacts the soil around them. Ciaran has lost count of how many they've planted. Dozens and dozens.

The sun is out and warm on his back, and its light reflects off the petals. Orange and pink glares that linger in his vision.

'You all right?' Emmet asks.

Ciaran says, 'Yeah,' and digs another hole.

'You weren't chatty yesterday, but you're even quieter today.'

Ciaran shrugs, keeps his eyes averted from Emmet's.

'Did you sleep last night? You look knackered.'

'I'm okay,' Ciaran says, his voice harder than he'd intended.

Emmet remains quiet for a while, but watchful. Then he asks, 'Is it true what the others said about you?'

'What others?' Ciaran asks.

'The boys in the van. They were talking about you on the way to pick you up.'

Ciaran lays the trowel on the earth. 'What did they say?'

'That you're the kid who was all over the news years ago. The kid who killed his foster carer.'

Ciaran held Emmet's stare. 'That's right.'

'Jesus,' Emmet says. 'But you're not like that any more. Are you?'

Ciaran does not reply. He picks up the trowel and starts digging again.

'All right,' Emmet says, 'no need to get the arse with me. I'll just keep my mouth shut.'

Ciaran has been distracted all morning. The day before, the digging had soothed his mind, flushed it out. Today it does not. Today Ciaran only thinks about her and how she left him in that cell and didn't come back like she promised.

She promised she would take him to the seaside, back to the old house.

The promise was a lie.

Just like Thomas had always said. No one can be trusted. They are the deceivers, all of them. They will cheat Us and hurt Us always. If They are not Us then They are against Us.

Waves of anger keep creeping up on Ciaran, so fierce they make him shake. Earlier, he said he needed a toilet break. The foreman had looked him up and down as if he was a fly crushed against the wall, then told him to be quick. Ciaran had gone to the portable toilet and locked himself in. He had covered his mouth with his hands and screamed, felt the pressure build in his head until he thought his skull might crack open.

It was not only her betrayal, her abandoning him, that caused the anger: it was that piece of paper that said he couldn't see Thomas. Now he feels alone and frightened.

Ciaran doesn't know what else to do, so he works.

296

His back and shoulders are sore from digging, but he ignores the discomfort. He feels no relief when the foreman calls the lunch break. He remains crouched, keeps digging as Emmet stands.

'You not coming?' Emmet asks.

'I've no lunch with me,' Ciaran says.

'I know. Have you any money?'

Ciaran puts his hand in his pocket, retrieves a few pounds in change.

'There's a shop down the way,' Emmet says. 'Go and get yourself something.'

Ciaran hesitates. He doesn't like going to shops.

'I told you, you're not having any of mine.'

As Emmet walks away, Ciaran's stomach growls. He gets to his feet and calls after Emmet. 'Which way?'

Emmet stops and points to the street behind Ciaran. 'Down there and turn right, I think.'

Ciaran nods a thank-you and slips the gloves from his hands. He walks in the direction Emmet pointed, past rows of houses built of beige brick. Small gardens, some neat and tidy, others overgrown and strewn with rubbish. A dog barks at him from a window. He turns right and keeps walking. After thirty yards or so he realises there's no shop.

He stops, looks around, and walks back the way he came.

At the end of the street, he pauses to get his bearings. The site and his workmates should be to his left. He turns right, looking for a sign, a flash of colour amongst the dreary homes. The road curves first one way, and then the other. A minute or so has passed when he stops, looks around again, turning in a circle. The houses all look the same.

Ciaran realises he can't remember which way he came. He'd lost track when he turned around. Fear rises in him. He doesn't even know what this place is called, let alone where it is. No one around to help him. He can't manage on his own. Thomas is right, Ciaran can't do anything for himself.

He should run. But which way?

Ciaran's breathing quickens, shallow gasps as his heart beats faster. He needs to run, get out of here. But which way? Thomas, which way do I go?

Thomas isn't here. Just choose a direction. That's all. Just choose.

Ciaran runs.

A jog at first, then faster. Fast as he can go. Legs and arms turning churning quickly-slickly. The scared driving him on.

As the road curves he stumbles off the footpath, between the parked cars, his boots slapping on the tarmac. His eyes are hot. Tears stream towards his temples, blown back by the breeze as he cuts through the air.

A car ahead, heading straight for Ciaran, but he doesn't see it, not really, not until it's close and he hears the tyres bite into the road as it slows.

Ciaran knows this car. As it stops just feet from him, he knows it, but he keeps running until his hands touch the bonnet. He stops there, breathless, feeling the engine's rumble through the metal and paint.

Tears come now, free and uncontrolled, waves hot on his skin, salty on his lips.

The driver opens the door and gets out.

Comes around to the front.

Thomas takes Ciaran in his arms.

★   ★   ★

They have been driving for half an hour before Ciaran speaks.

'What happened to your hand?'

Thomas flexes his fingers on the steering wheel. His left hand is wrapped in a handkerchief stained with red blotches. He has blood on his sleeve and trouser leg.

'Nothing,' Thomas says. 'I got bitten, that's all.'

'By what?'

'A dog. But it's all right. Forget about it.'

'We're not supposed to see each other.'

'Yeah,' Thomas says. 'That bitch gave me a letter too. Fucking bitch. I told you, didn't I? Always the same. All of them.'

'I should go back to work. Lunchtime's only forty-five minutes.'

'They can't treat us like that,' Thomas says. 'We can't let them keep us apart.'

'I want to go back to work.'

'I should be at work too. But I'm not. Why were you crying?'

'I was lost.'

'Well, you're all right now. I found you.'

'I want to go back.'

The seatbelt grips Ciaran's chest as Thomas brakes. The car skids and stops.

'We can't go back,' Thomas says. His hands shake until he grips the steering wheel tight enough to steady them. 'It's all fucked now. That probation officer and that cop made sure of it. Fucking bitches.'

Ciaran wants to tell him to stop calling them that. But Ciaran can't tell Thomas anything.

'Two years I waited for you,' Thomas says. 'Two years so we could be together. And I was good all that time. Now you're out and they're trying to break us up.'

Thomas leans forward until his forehead rests against the wheel. He wraps his arms around his head.

'I'm not well,' he says. 'These things in my head. They're making me sick. Making me stupid. Since you came out, I'm losing control. I was good for two years. Now you're back, and I'm losing it. I'm not thinking right. I shouldn't have gone to her house. I shouldn't have done that.'

Ciaran is afraid to ask, but he asks anyway. 'Done what?'

Thomas sits back. Closes his eyes as he breathes in and out. He shakes his head like he's freeing himself from something.

'Nothing,' he says. 'It's all fucked now, anyway.'

'It's your fault,' Ciaran says.

'What?'

Ciaran regrets the words as they leave his

tongue. He meant to only think it, not say it out loud.

'What did you say?' Thomas asks, a tremor in his voice.

'Nothing.' Ciaran stares straight ahead at the not-moving road.

Thomas's right hand lashes out, striking Ciaran's cheek. 'What did you say?'

'It didn't have to be like this,' Ciaran says. 'But you made it like this. It's your fault.'

Thomas sits very quiet and still for a time. His breathing the only sound in the car.

Eventually, he says, 'Give me your arm.'

Ciaran shakes his head. 'No.'

Thomas's hand moves again, but he pulls it back, inhales. 'Give me your arm. Now.'

'No,' Ciaran says.

Thomas grabs for Ciaran's wrist, but Ciaran whips it out of his reach. He fumbles at the door handle as he undoes his seatbelt.

'What are you doing?' Thomas asks.

Ciaran opens the door and gets out. Ignores Thomas calling after him. As, he walks along the road he hears the driver's door open, feet scuffing the ground. A hand on his shoulder. He shakes it off and keeps walking.

'Ciaran.'

He puts his head down, walks faster.

'Ciaran, stop.'

The hand on his shoulder again. Ciaran swipes it away.

'Stop, Ciaran. Talk to me. Tell me what's wrong.'

Thomas passes Ciaran, turns to him, blocks his path.

Ciaran slaps his brother across the cheek. Hard.

Thomas rocks on his heels, stares back at Ciaran.

'You did this,' Ciaran says, the tears coming again, his palm stinging. 'All of this. You did it.'

'I did it all for you,' Thomas says. 'So we could be together. That bitch Flanagan had to go and — '

'Don't call her that,' Ciaran says.

'Why not? That's what she is.'

'Don't,' Ciaran says.

'She's a bitch.' Hate twists Thomas's face until Ciaran can barely recognise him. 'Her and the probation woman. Both of them. Bitches. Just like Mum. They're all the same.'

'Don't call Mum a bitch,' Ciaran says.

'But that's what she was.'

Ciaran slaps him again. This time he leaves a glaring red mark beneath Thomas's eye. Thomas blinks three times. Steadies himself.

'She promised she'd come back for me,' Ciaran says, fresh tears erupting.

'Me too. But she went and killed herself with the drugs, so that was that.'

'In the cell. She said she'd come back for me if I talked to her.'

Thomas takes a step back. 'Flanagan?'

'She said she'd come back. She said she'd take me to the seaside.'

Ciaran cries so hard it blinds him. He brings his hands to his face, hides behind them. Arms slip around him. The familiar embrace. Thomas's lips at his ears.

'They'll always let you down,' Thomas says.

'But she promised.'

Thomas takes Ciaran's hands away from his face, wipes the tears from Ciaran's cheeks. 'Do you want to go and see her?' he asks, his voice very soft.

'We can't,' Ciaran says.

Thomas pulls Ciaran close again. 'Course we can. Remember I told you? I know where she lives. Do you want to go and see her? Do you? Do you want to do that?'

Ciaran lets his body go soft, sinks into his brother's arms.

'Yeah,' he says.

51

Cunningham cursed as she drove past her house, a Mini parked in her space.

Not that it was really her space, owning a house didn't mean you owned the road in front of it too, but generally the neighbours in the terrace of small homes stuck to the principle of respecting everyone else's few feet of tarmac.

'Fuck it,' she said, and pulled in three doors down. She didn't know the people who lived in this house, but there was usually a red Mondeo parked outside. It wasn't quite mid-afternoon, so they wouldn't be back for a good three hours. Once the Mini moved, she would come out and shift her Nissan back to where it belonged.

She locked the car and walked back to her gate. As she opened it, she made the hundredth mental note to herself to paint over the rust. It clanked shut, and she awaited the usual clamour of barking from inside the house.

No barking.

Cunningham paused and listened. No, nothing.

Worry, quiet but insistent, in her gut. She walked to her door, rummaging in her bag for her key. Still no barking. No silhouette through the frosted glass, charging up, batting at the door with its paws.

As Cunningham opened the door, the worry grew from a whisper to a frightened voice inside her. 'Angus,' she called. 'Angus?'

She pushed the door closed behind her, listening all the time. She stayed still and quiet, afraid to go any further into her own house.

A movement of cool air distracted her.

The clack-clack of the train on the Bangor line. Louder and clearer than it should be. The way it would sound if the sliding patio door leading from the kitchen to the yard lay open.

'Shit,' she said.

Cunningham walked along the hall, slow, one hand on the wall, until she reached the living room door. She saw the books first, scattered on the floor. Some of them with pages ripped out. And CDs, DVDs, the few photographs she kept, now behind the broken glass of their frames. She stepped across the threshold and saw the television lying face down where it had been tipped from its stand. A wet stain on the wall: the almost full wine glass she'd left on the coffee table last night.

Nothing stolen. Simply destruction for its own sake.

The shakes started then, wave upon wave. Feeling another breeze, she looked through to the kitchen, saw the patio door open, the lock twisted away from the frame. The tiled floor covered with broken glass and crockery.

'Angus?'

Perhaps he had run away. The door was open, he could have fled. But the gate beyond remained closed. Whoever had broken in and done this had scaled the back wall.

'Oh God, Angus.'

Upstairs, under her bed. That's where he always went when he was scared. Thunder, fireworks, her own angry outbursts. He always took refuge under the bed.

Cunningham returned to the hall and went to the bottom of the stairs. She called the dog's name once more, listened, then climbed towards the silence.

At the top, the bathroom door opened onto the same devastation. The mirror over the hand basin had been shattered. All of her small and personal things strewn and poured across the floor, puddles of shampoo and shower gel, tampons and cotton wool balls mired in them.

Cunningham allowed herself only a moment to take it in before moving to her bedroom. There, on the sill between the carpeted landing and the laminate wood floor of her room, she took one sharp breath.

Amongst the ruin, the scattered clothes, the torn sheets and exploded pillows, a pool of deep red spreading from beneath the bed.

'Oh no,' she said.

Cunningham stepped into the room, picked her way through the debris. She saw the thick-shafted screwdriver, its blade speckled with red. Her hand went to her mouth, her vision blurred by tears.

'Oh Jesus no,' she said and took small, slow steps to the bedside.

From beneath the bed, a bubbling exhalation ending in a high whine.

Cunningham dropped to her hands and knees, ignored the splashing of the blood, peered underneath. There, in the shadow, Angus lying on his side, his chest rising and falling with each shallow breath, his tongue lolling in pinkish-red sputum.

She reached under, scrabbling for him, got hold of his legs and pulled. Another whine at the pain it caused him. She gathered him in her arms, her feet slipping on the blood as she fought to get herself upright.

'Its all right,' she whispered in his ear. 'You're going to be all right.'

Cunningham didn't care about the open patio door as she ran to her car, the dog's blood soaking her clothes.

52

Fatigue had caught up with Flanagan as she drove home from the funeral. Thirty-six hours without sleep had weighed down her mind, like sand drifts behind her eyes. She had wound down the car's windows as she merged onto the motorway, let the rush of air wash over her, keeping the urge to sleep at bay.

The house felt more than empty when she let herself in by the back door. A quietness deeper than silence. The home she had renovated with her husband stood at the end of a country lane outside Moira, far enough from the M1 that the rumble of traffic seldom drifted over the fields. It had taken more than a year to get used to the stillness and dark out here. Both she and Alistair were townies — she from Banbridge, he from Dungannon — and they had been used to the constant intrusion of cars and street lights.

Now she relished the quiet. That dead-of-night emptiness as if the world held its breath. She still didn't like the darkness, but she had stowed that irrational fear away, put a wall around it. When she drove home from work each evening she felt the grubbiness of the job wear away, like dirt washed from beneath her fingernails.

Flanagan dropped her house and car keys on the kitchen table and contemplated fixing herself a gin and tonic. She checked her wristwatch and saw it had only just gone two, though it felt much later. Alistair would be home with the kids by four-thirty. The time between would be better spent catching up on some sleep, so she forgot about the drink and made her way upstairs.

The bedroom overlooked the back garden, a plain lawn with Alistair's best efforts at gardening spread around it. Poorly tended shrubs, a flower bed that never seemed to be free of weeds, and a patch for herbs that produced nothing of any real use. Every year, Alistair tried anew to raise the garden from the level of barely presentable to something more impressive, and every year he failed.

She pulled the blind, shutting out the view and the sunlight, and threw her jacket onto the chair by the bed. Kneeling down, she opened the wardrobe to reveal the safe bolted to its floor. She unclipped her holster and placed it and the Glock 17 inside, locked the safe door, and closed the wardrobe.

When she kicked off her shoes and flopped onto the bed, her limbs felt suddenly sore and heavy, as if she had run a marathon that morning instead of standing at the back of a draughty church. She rolled onto her side, closed her eyes, and tried not to think of Penny and Ronnie Walker or how they died.

Sleep took Flanagan within minutes, and she dreamed she held the pillow over Penny's face and whispered to her, shush, don't worry, it'll be over soon . . .

★ ★ ★

The chime and buzz of her mobile phone pulled her from the warm void, a tumbling, rolling sensation as she rejoined the world. She squinted at the time on the phone's screen. A little over ninety minutes had slipped away. The display said Paula Cunningham.

Flanagan blinked the last of the sleep from her eyes, cleared her throat, and brought the phone to her ear. 'Paula,' she said.

'He broke into my house,' Cunningham said.

'What?'

'I came home and found the place smashed up. Stuff thrown everywhere, things broken, drawers emptied.'

'You said, 'he'. Who do you mean?'

'Thomas Devine,' Cunningham said. Flanagan heard the tremor in her voice, knew she barely had control of herself. 'He did it. He tried to kill Angus.'

'Who's Angus?' Flanagan asked.

'My dog,' Cunningham said. 'Thomas Devine broke into my house and tried to kill my dog. I took him straight to the vet. It was a screwdriver into his side. It punctured his lung. The vet had to drain the chest cavity and reinflate the lung. He's lost so much blood. The vet doesn't know if he'll survive. That bastard did this.'

Flanagan eased herself upright, lowered her feet to the floor. 'Are you all right?'

'I'm okay,' Cunningham said. 'I'm shaking all over, but I'm fine.'

'I can come over if you want.'

'No. Thank you, but no. But can you lift Thomas? Question him?'

310

'You don't know for sure it was him.'

'Yes I do,' Cunningham said. 'And you know it too.'

'All right, maybe he left some physical evidence this time. Something that will put him away.'

'There was blood on the handle of the screwdriver. I saw it. There were fingerprints on that.'

'Okay,' Flanagan said. 'That's something. What did the responding unit say?'

Silence.

Flanagan asked, 'When you called the police to the house, what did they say?'

'I didn't,' Cunningham said, her voice suddenly small and far away. 'I called you.'

Flanagan sighed and covered her eyes.

'I needed to get Angus treated before anything else,' Cunningham continued. 'You're the only one who'll take this seriously. You know who we're dealing with. So I called you.'

'All right,' Flanagan said. 'Get off the line and dial the non-emergency number right now. Just get a car to your house as quickly as you can. I can't help you any more with this. I'm off the case.'

'I know. Your boss told me this morning. He talked my boss into not revoking Ciaran's licence.'

'I thought he might,' Flanagan said. 'Now get off the phone. Call the police.'

'Okay,' Cunningham said. 'Thank you.'

'Look after yourself,' Flanagan said.

A tone sounded in her ear and the line died.

'Shit,' Flanagan said to the empty room.

The idea of a gin and tonic resurfaced, even shinier than before. Half an hour to an hour before Alistair and the kids get home. Time to make the drink, maybe take it out to the garden, decompress a little.

Flanagan nodded as she made the decision. She got to her feet, eased into her slippers, and crossed to the window to open the blind. She blinked against the glaring sunlight then went to the stairs. They creaked under her weight as she descended. Tiredness still dragged at her mind, but she'd had enough sleep to get her through until tonight. Maybe she would check the fridge and the cupboards, cook something nice for Alistair and the kids. She seldom got the chance, Alistair mostly took that responsibility, and it'd help her unwind. Something with lots of preparation, something that required lots of pots bubbling and the oven humming, something to focus her mind on other than her work.

A smile found its way to Flanagan's lips as she opened the kitchen door.

She froze in the doorway.

Ciaran Devine stood on the other side of the table. His brother Thomas rummaged through the fridge. He turned to smile at her.

'Got anything to eat?' Thomas asked.

53

Ciaran stands still, as if his feet are locked to the floor. He stares at her. Thomas says something, but Ciaran can't hear. Tiny golden flecks of dust move through the light from the windows.

'You promised you'd come back for me,' he says.

Serena looks at him, fear and confusion on her face.

Then she turns and runs.

Thomas says something.

Ciaran watches her go for the stairs.

Thomas says something.

Ciaran turns to him. 'What?'

'Go after her.'

Ciaran runs. He's fast, always has been. He covers the distance between the kitchen and the stairs in seconds. Serena is stumbling at the top when he mounts the bottom step. He takes them three at a time as one of her slippers bounces past him. She disappears into a bedroom. He catches the door before it slams shut. She's diving for the wardrobe.

'Stop,' he says.

She doesn't. She opens the wardrobe, reaches for something on its floor. Something that beeps when she presses the buttons. A safe. He grabs her, pulls her away.

Serena slashes at him with her nails, scratches his forearm through his shirt. He raises his fist and she shrinks down, presses herself against the wall. She stares up at him, breathing hard.

'You promised you'd come back for me,' Ciaran says.

She shakes her head, her mouth opening and closing.

'What's in the safe?' Thomas asks from behind him.

She shakes her head again.

'What's in it?'

'Nothing,' she says.

Thomas crouches down beside her. 'You were in an awful hurry to get nothing.'

'What do you want?' she asks.

Thomas points to the safe. 'Is that where you keep your gun?'

'Please, just tell me what you want.'

'I want you to unlock the safe, but don't open the door. Then I want you to move away from it.'

'There's nothing in there,' she says.

'Open the safe.'

'No.'

'Open it or I'll tell Ciaran to hurt you.'

She looks back up to Ciaran. 'He won't,' she says.

'Oh, he will,' Thomas says. 'He'll hurt you. He'll do whatever I tell him to do.'

'He won't,' she says again. 'Not me.'

'Ciaran,' Thomas says, and Ciaran knows what he has to do.

He kicks her hard beneath her ribs. Feels the give in her flesh, the expulsion of air.

She folds in on herself, curls into a ball, coughing and groaning.

Ciaran watches her, wants to take it back. He wishes he didn't have to hurt her.

Thomas laughs. 'Told you. Now open the safe.'

Serena gets to her hands and knees. 'No, I won't.'

'Ciaran,' Thomas says.

Ciaran doesn't move.

Thomas says his name again, his voice harder.

Ciaran kicks her in the side, feels the flex of her ribs, almost feels the pain himself. Once more, she curls into a ball. Coughs, her face red, spit hanging from her lip.

He wants to crouch down, take her in his arms like she did for him, tell her he's sorry, so sorry. But he can't.

'Open the safe,' Thomas says.

She shakes her head.

Thomas reaches down, grabs her hair, lifts her face up to meet his. 'Ciaran will beat you to death if he has to. And after that, we'll wait for your husband and your children to come home, and then he'll do them too.'

'No,' she says. 'He's not a killer. I know the truth. I know it was you killed Daniel Rolston and his father. You let your brother take the blame to save yourself. Now whatever you need to do, you go on and do it.'

A laugh starts in Thomas's belly and works its way up to his mouth. 'You know nothing,' he says.

'I know you,' she says, the words forced between her teeth.

Thomas laughs harder, then goes very quiet.

He watches her for a moment, then says, 'Tell her, Ciaran.'

Ciaran doesn't know what to say. His mouth is dry.

Thomas looks up at him. 'Go on, tell her.'

Ciaran takes a step back, rubs his hands on his jeans, feels suddenly ashamed. Like when Thomas made him tell that girl in the park about playing with himself.

He hates Thomas. He loves Thomas.

He doesn't know what to do.

Thomas's face darkens. His voice softens. 'Tell her.'

Ciaran's legs are shaky. He sits on the edge of the bed. The whole world feels bigger and brighter, the air thicker, the light harsher than he can ever remember it being. He takes a breath. Then another.

'I killed Mr Rolston,' Ciaran says.

'I don't believe that,' Serena says. 'I never believed that. Don't take the blame for him any more, Ciaran, please don't.'

'But I did kill him,' Ciaran says. 'I took the book thing, the iron cat, and I smashed him on the head. He stopped moving after the first couple of times, but I kept going.'

Ciaran remembers the feeling, the hard skull going soft as it collapsed under the force of the blows. The heat of the blood, on his hands and arms, and in his veins.

Serena shakes her head. 'No, Ciaran.'

'Tell her why,' Thomas says.

'Because Thomas told me to. He said Mr Rolston would hurt him again if I didn't.'

316

'There was never any proof of that,' Serena says. 'I don't believe Mr Rolston ever touched your brother. Did you ever see him touch your brother?'

'Thomas told me he did,' Ciaran says. 'Thomas doesn't tell me lies.'

'Oh God, Ciaran, he's been lying to you your whole life. He's been using you. Can't you see that?'

Thomas says, 'Tell her about Daniel.'

'Oh Christ,' she says.

'I had to do it,' Ciaran says.

'You didn't,' she says. 'Please tell me you didn't do it.'

'I had to. He was going to make trouble and put us in jail again. Except it'd be the big prison, and I wouldn't be able to see Thomas.'

She covers her face with her hands.

'Tell her how you did it,' Thomas says.

'We watched him,' Ciaran says. 'We followed the bus in Thomas's car. We saw him get off in town. Then I stayed with him. Far enough away so he didn't see me. But I saw him. I watched him getting drunk in the park. There were too many people to do it then. The police came and talked to him. I followed him through the streets until he went into an alley. I snuck up behind him. With a knife from the supermarket. I didn't mean to do it so many times but once it started I couldn't stop.'

Ciaran remembers now, the whirling rush of it, the knife in his hand. In and in and in and in, sometimes the blade meeting bone, sometimes not, until Daniel went still and quiet, and then in

317

and in again because there could never, will never be enough, not ever.

Serena sits huddled against the wall, one hand covering her eyes, the other pressed against her side. He wishes Thomas hadn't told him to hurt her.

'You promised you'd come back for me,' Ciaran says.

She lets her hand drop. Her eyes are red and wet. 'I wanted to, but I couldn't. My boss took me off the case, told me to leave. I swear to you, I would've come back if I could.'

Thomas smiles. 'She disappointed you, didn't she, Ciaran? She was all talk, pretending to be nice to you, and then she goes and leaves you alone. That's why you had to come and see her now. Isn't that right?'

'Yeah,' Ciaran says. 'You told me you'd take me to the seaside.'

She stares at him for a moment, breathing hard, then she says, 'It's not too late. We can still go. We can go now if you want.'

'She's lying again,' Thomas says. 'Trying to get you to trust her. Then she'll try to turn you against me.'

'It's too late,' Ciaran says.

'No,' she says, getting up onto her knees, her hands reaching out to him. Then she points across the room. 'In that drawer, the top one, right at the back. Underneath the other papers.'

Ciaran looks to the chest of drawers. It looks old, chips and scratches in the dark-stained wood. 'What?' he asks.

'The letter,' she says. 'Remember you sent it to

me? I kept it. Because I cared about you, Ciaran, I always did.'

'She's lying,' Thomas says. 'She never gave a shit about you.'

Ciaran stands and crosses the room to the chest. There are two drawers at the top. He points to the left. 'This one?'

'The other one,' she says.

'Leave it,' Thomas says.

Ciaran ignores him, opens the drawer. It's full of jewellery boxes, hairbands, clips, a sewing kit. He reaches in to the back, to a stack of envelopes and folders. He lifts them out. Letters from insurance companies, a car registration form, birth certificates, medical cards.

'I said, leave it.' Thomas is getting angry now, Ciaran can hear it in his voice. Still he ignores him.

'It's hidden in an envelope,' Serena says. 'It's addressed to me, marked from the Family Planning Clinic.'

Ciaran finds the envelope, opens it, reaches inside. His hand closes on another smaller envelope, and he slips it free. There, upper-case letters in his own childish handwriting.

TO SERENA
THE POLICE STATION
LISBURN

He doesn't hear Thomas cross the room, is startled when the envelope is snatched from his fingers. Thomas stuffs it into his jacket pocket.

'That's mine,' Ciaran says.

Thomas pays no attention. 'Now,' he says, hunkering down beside Serena once more. 'Enough messing about. Open the safe.'

'No,' she says.

Thomas looks back to Ciaran. 'She tried to break us apart. You saw that letter from court. She wants to keep us apart, and we can't let that happen.'

Thomas takes a small knife from his pocket. A kitchen knife, the kind you'd use for peeling an apple. Its blade is shiny new. It cuts the air. Thomas holds the knife by the metal, the handle towards Ciaran.

Ciaran pauses.

He hates Thomas. He loves Thomas.

Ciaran reaches for the knife.

'All right,' Serena says. 'I'll open it.'

Ciaran turns the knife in his hand. The blade glints in the sunlight from the window. He tests its edge with his thumb. It leaves a line of tiny red beads on his skin.

She crawls to the safe, takes a breath, puts her finger to the keypad.

'Remember,' Thomas says, 'unlock it, but don't open it. Move away as soon as you've put the number in.'

She presses a number. Then another. And another.

She presses a fourth. The safe whirrs and clicks. The door opens an inch.

'Serena?' a voice calls from downstairs. 'You up there?'

Thomas looks to the bedroom door.

54

Now.

Flanagan threw the safe door back and grabbed for the holster. She thumbed the catch off, wrapped her fingers around the Glock's grip, tried to turn, bring the pistol back up, but Thomas fell on her.

His hands clutching at the pistol, her grip too strong to break. She fell back into the wardrobe, Thomas's weight upon her, the hard corners of the safe digging into her back. Clothes and hangers fell from the rail above, snaring them both.

Teeth slummed the skin of Flanagan's neck and cheek, seeking a hold to tear at the flesh. She whipped her head from side to side, denying Thomas purchase. His hands closed on hers, on the pistol.

So strong.

She gasped as she resisted, but he forced her pistol's muzzle up until it pressed beneath her chin. His weight bore down on her, crushing the air from her lungs. She tried to bring her knee up to his groin but it only thudded against his thigh. She pushed with her feet, tried to lift her body, but her soles skidded on the slick floor.

His fingers crept towards the trigger guard, forced their way between hers. The muzzle pressed harder beneath her jaw. His fingers squeezed. The pistol jerked.

A click.

She felt his body soften with surprise.

One chance before he realised the Glock's chamber had been empty.

She released the pistol with her right hand, let her arm drop, slammed the heel of her hand up and under his jaw.

His head rocked back, compressing the nerve cluster at the base of his skull, and he fell away from her, stunned. Before he could recover, she rammed her elbow into his nose, felt the hot spurt of blood on her forearm.

Flanagan fumbled for the Glock, found it, scrambled to her feet, brought the pistol up, her finger on the trigger, ready. She swung her aim between Ciaran and Thomas as she backed away to the corner opposite the wardrobe where she could keep both of them within range.

Ciaran stood rooted to the floor, his arms by his sides, his mouth wide, terror in his eyes. The knife still in his right hand. Thomas coughed and groaned, spat blood on the floor as he got to his hands and knees.

'Fucking bitch,' he said, the words blunted by the damage to his nose.

'Ciaran, drop the knife,' Flanagan said. 'Do it now or I will shoot you.'

Thomas tried to get to his feet, but stumbled. Flanagan moved her aim to him. 'Stay down.'

He ignored her, used the bed to haul himself upright. 'Fucking bitch,' he said, spraying the bedding with red. He took Ciaran's arm, said, 'Let's go.'

From downstairs, Alistair's voice. 'Serena? You

322

all right up there? I thought I heard banging.'

'Don't move,' Flanagan said.

Footsteps on the stairs.

Thomas guided his brother towards the door.

'Stop,' Flanagan said. She raised her voice. 'Alistair, don't come up here.'

From the landing, 'What?'

Thomas bundled Ciaran to the other side of the room.

Alistair at the door.

Flanagan's finger left the trigger. The brothers between her and her husband. She couldn't fire and be certain of not hurting him.

Ciaran's hand moved.

Metal flashed.

Alistair gasped and fell.

Flanagan said, 'Oh no.'

She leapt across the room to the doorway as Alistair crumpled against the frame. The thunder of the brothers' feet on the stairs.

'Jesus,' he said, staring wide-eyed at the growing red stain on his abdomen. 'Jesus.'

'Okay,' Flanagan said, 'it's not as bad as it looks. Stay calm.'

She had no idea how bad it was, but she had to staunch the bleeding. She grabbed a pillow from the bed, shook the case free, balled the cotton up, and pressed it into his stomach.

Between groans of pain, he said, 'The kids. They're downstairs.'

'Shit,' Flanagan said. 'Keep pressure on it.'

She lifted her pistol and stepped over her husband, ran for the stairs, down, calling her children's names. As she reached the hall, she found Ruth in the kitchen doorway.

'Mum, who were those men? What's going on?'

Flanagan took Ruth's shoulders even as she flinched from the gun.

'Did they touch you?'

Ruth shook her head. 'No.'

Flanagan heard an engine roar, tyres scattering gravel.

'What about Eli? Where's Eli?'

She looked over Ruth's shoulder into the kitchen, saw Eli standing by the table, his fingers knotted together with worry. 'Mum, what's wrong?'

Flanagan went to the back door, closed and locked it. 'Ruth, take Eli to your room, lock the door and don't open it to anyone but me.'

Eli protested. 'Mum, I don't want to — '

'Just go. Now.'

She ran past them both, back upstairs, stopped at the airing cupboard and grabbed an armful of towels. As she returned to Alistair, she dropped the Glock to the floor and took the soaked pillowcase from his belly. She put one of the towels in its place.

'Press it down, tight,' she said.

Flanagan stepped over Alistair once more, fetched her phone from the bedside locker, and turned back to him.

'Stay awake,' she said as she hit the emergency icon on the phone's home screen. She hunkered down beside her husband. 'Don't fucking die on me. If you do, if you leave me alone with two kids, I'll bloody kill you again myself.'

55

Thomas pushes the car hard through the roundabout. Ciaran feels the front end struggle for grip as Thomas jerks the wheel left to exit onto the main road. The sign says this is the way to the airport. Are they going to get on a plane?

Ciaran's hands shake like jittering pink spiders in his lap. One hand has red speckles on it. The knife lies in the footwell by Ciaran's feet.

A laugh escapes Thomas, high and edgy. Blood still drips from his nose into his lap. Not broken, he'd said, but bruises are already forming beneath his eyes. He accelerates past the filling station, swerves into the other lane, passes a lorry and a van.

'Where are we going?' Ciaran asks.

'I don't know,' Thomas says. 'But we need to change cars. We haven't got long before they start looking for this one. We need to get onto the back roads.'

'I don't want to hurt anyone else,' Ciaran says.

'We'll probably have to.'

'Why?'

'Because they'll be coming for us,' Thomas says. He spots a right turn, signed for Maghaberry. Ciaran knows that name. There's a prison there. Thomas steers into the box junction. 'Whatever we do, they'll come for us. We can run for a while, find somewhere to hide, but they'll catch up with us eventually.'

He makes the turn onto the narrower road, green all around them.

'We shouldn't have touched Daniel,' Ciaran says.

'He shouldn't have been stirring things up. He brought it on himself.'

'We wouldn't have to run if we'd left him alone.'

Thomas takes a left turn off the road, onto a lane barely wide enough for one car.

'Yeah, but he wouldn't leave us alone, would he?'

'I don't want to go back inside,' Ciaran says.

Thomas slows the car to a halt, puts it out of gear as he pulls the handbrake.

'Me neither,' he says. 'So what are we going to do about it?'

Ciaran doesn't have an answer, just stares at his hands.

'They'll come for us,' Thomas says, 'and we can either fight or let them take us. Me, I'd rather fight. Because when they take us, it'll be to a real prison. Not like we had before. Maghaberry, near here. Proper walls and bars. And the other prisoners. They won't be kids. They'll tear you to pieces.'

Ciaran leans forward. He hides his face.

Thomas puts a hand on the back of his neck, strokes it, gentle like a big brother should be.

'It didn't have to be like this,' Ciaran says.

'Yes it did. It was always going to end up this way. We started down this road when you killed Mr Rolston. We were both fucked from then on. No point crying about it now.'

Ciaran has no tears left. 'You told me to do it. You made me.'

'I can't make you do anything,' Thomas says. 'We talked about this. Anything you do, you do it yourself.'

'I wish I'd never done it,' Ciaran says. 'I wish . . . '

'You wish what?'

'Nothing.'

'Tell me.'

'I wish we hadn't been taken from Mum. I wish she hadn't been sick. I wish she was still alive.'

'Wish all you want, it's not going to change anything.' Thomas leans over, puts his arm around Ciaran's shoulder, brings him close. 'Look, all we have is each other. No one will ever love you more than I do. No one will ever love me more than you do.'

'I hate you,' Ciaran says.

He can't see his brother's face. He feels him stiffen, then his arms go soft.

'That's all right,' Thomas says. 'Sometimes loving someone's the same as hating them. There's no reason to it. It just is. Look, I waited two years for you. I could've done anything, but I kept myself right so I could be here when you got out. All the things I kept to myself, kept tied up inside me. Now you're here and we can do what we want.'

'But I don't want to hurt anyone,' Ciaran says.

Thomas lifts Ciaran's head in his hands, places dry losses on his eyelids, and says, 'Want's got nothing to do with it.'

327

He lets go of Ciaran, puts the car in gear, and moves off.

★ ★ ★

Twenty minutes to find the right place.

An old bungalow at the end of an unkempt driveway, hidden in the hollow between the fields. A ribbon of smoke from the chimney even though it isn't cold. Greying net curtains at the windows.

'Old people live here,' Thomas says.

He pulls the car up to the iron gates. 'Get out and open them,' he says.

Without a word, Ciaran does as he's told. Like a good boy. The gates squeal as he pulls them wide. One side has to be wedged by a concrete block to keep it in place. Thomas drives through and parks alongside an ageing blue car with a Ford badge. As Ciaran walks up the driveway he sees Thomas wipe at his nose and lips with a tissue, checking himself in the mirror for traces of blood. Then he climbs out of the car and joins Ciaran at the front door.

Somewhere inside the house, a dog barks. A small one, by the sounds of it.

Thomas doesn't like dogs. Ciaran watches him pick at the cloth still wrapped around his hand.

Before they can ring the doorbell, a small, hunched form appears behind the frosted glass of the door.

'Who's that?' a voice calls. An old man's voice, high and cracked.

The door has a lever handle, probably locked

328

from the inside, level with the letterbox.

'We're from the council,' Thomas says.

'What do you want?'

'We're from the dog control office. We've had a complaint about a dog that lives on this property.'

'What sort of complaint?'

'About barking,' Thomas says. 'We've had a complaint about the noise.'

'What are you talking about? Sure, no one lives close enough to hear anything.'

'Well, that's the complaint we've had, and we have to investigate. You'll need to open the door.'

'Put your identification through the letterbox,' the old man says.

Thomas looks down at the letterbox.

'My ID's attached to my wallet. I'm not putting my wallet through the letterbox. How do I know you'll give it back? You'll have to open the door.'

'My arse, I will. Now piss off and close that gate behind you.'

'All right, I can get the police here, if that makes you feel better. But I have to warn you, they might seize the dog. You don't want that, do you?'

'Tell you what, son, I'll just call the cops myself.'

The form moves away from the door.

Thomas crouches down, slips his hand through the letterbox, reaches to the left, towards the lock. He grunts as he strains. The barking grows louder, and Ciaran hears paws scrabbling on a hard floor. Thomas hisses in pain and pushes harder.

From inside, 'Here, what do you think you're at?'

The shape returns to the other side of the glass, ghost-like arms trying to grab at Thomas's. Thomas grins. Ciaran hears the click-clack of the lock opening, then Thomas pulls his arm free. He stands, presses the handle, pushes the door, but the old man pushes back on the other side. One good shove, and the old man lies sprawled on the hall floor, the door bouncing off the wall.

Ciaran follows him inside.

'Your car keys,' Thomas says to the old man, kicking the dog away. 'Now.'

56

Cunningham took the invoice from the locksmith and closed the front door behind him. She walked back through the scattered debris in her living room to her kitchen, careful of the shattered glass and crockery, and took a seat at the table. She'd have made herself a stiff vodka tonic if she'd had anything left to drink it out of.

A cry, then. Just a minute or two of wallowing.

She'd changed out of her work clothes as soon as she returned home, felt the weight of Angus's blood soaked into their fabric as she stuffed them into the washing machine. It hummed and sloshed in the corner, pink water inside.

She pulled the packet of tissues from her pocket, dabbed one on her cheeks as she sniffed.

Her phone vibrated on the table, the vet's number on the display.

Cunningham grabbed it, brought it to her ear. 'Yes?'

'Paula? It's Sinéad Mooney from Mooney and Smyth's — '

'Yes, I know, what's wrong? Is Angus all right?'

'Yes, he's doing well. I just wanted you to know he's perked up and taken some water.'

Fresh tears from the relief, followed by a needle of shame at her impatience with the vet. 'Okay,' she said. 'Thanks for letting me know. And thank you for all you've done.'

'Don't mention it,' the vet said. 'I'll be in

touch if anything changes.'

Cunningham thanked her again and hung up.

She sat still and quiet for long minutes, the washing machine the only sound, wondering how to get her house back in order and where to start. The pair of policemen had been polite and efficient, but she knew they could do little. For all they knew, this was just another burglary like the dozens of others they saw in a week. She gave them Thomas Devine's name, but it seemed to mean little to them.

Her phone vibrated again.

Number withheld.

She answered it.

'Hello, is that Paula Cunningham?'

She hesitated, then said, 'Yes.'

The caller identified himself as a reporter from the news desk at one of the Belfast dailies. 'I wondered if you could comment on the Devine brothers.'

'What?'

'I'm sure you saw the news this evening. Or maybe heard on the radio?'

A cold feeling low in her stomach. 'No, I didn't.'

'They're wanted in connection with an incident at the home of a senior PSNI detective. One person is seriously injured, and the brothers are missing.'

'Oh Christ,' she said. 'Was it Flanagan?'

'It was DCI Flanagan's home,' the reporter said. 'Just between you and me, it's not been made public, but her husband got knifed. The cop's all right. She was involved in the Rolston murder the brothers were put away for, so that's presumably why they came back for her. Unless you know something I don't.'

The reporter waited while she looked at her repaired patio door.

'Do you?' he asked.

'How did you get my number?' she asked.

'Have you any comment to make?' the reporter asked. 'Is there anything you know of that's been held back?'

'How did you get my number?' she asked again.

'Any comment?'

Cunningham hung up and dropped the phone on the table.

The washing machine came to the end of its cycle, water gurgling in its drain, then silence. She felt the air cold on her neck, the house alive with its own breath, its own soft voice.

Telling her to get out, she was not safe here.

Five minutes, and she had a bag packed and in the boot of her car.

Any hotel in town would do.

57

DSI Purdy entered the ward, looking around. Flanagan didn't wave to get his attention. She didn't feel much like being sociable with him. Nevertheless, he spotted her along the corridor, seated on the row of vinyl-covered chairs outside the Intensive Care Unit. Her blouse still clung to her stomach, its fabric soaked with patches of deep red.

'Well?' he asked as he approached.

'He's going to be all right,' Flanagan said. 'No organ damage, thank God.'

She hoped the same was true for her. She had been to the bathroom once since coming to the hospital, and there had been blood in her urine. It might have been wise to visit A&E herself, but she wanted to be here, not stuck in a waiting room with dozens of other walking wounded.

Purdy sat down beside her. 'Where are the kids?'

'Alistair's sister has them.'

'Good,' he said. 'And you should stay away from home tonight.'

'I'm not going anywhere,' Flanagan said. 'This is where I'll be sleeping tonight. Or trying, anyway.'

He sat quiet for what seemed an age, fidgeting, adjusting his tie, twining and untwining his fingers. When he eventually took a breath, ready to speak, Flanagan closed her eyes.

'I suppose I owe you an apology,' he said.

He waited for an answer, probably expecting her to say no, not at all. Flanagan opened her eyes, but kept her mouth shut. He cleared his throat.

'I shouldn't have turned them loose,' he said.

'No, you shouldn't.'

'But your behaviour was inappropriate, and I was right to take you off the case.'

'Who's taking over?' she asked.

'The ACC has stepped in,' Purdy said, 'taken it off my hands. It's a manhunt now. The murder investigation can wait.'

'And how is this manhunt progressing?'

'It's not. The Devine brothers have vanished in a puff of smoke. No sightings of the car.'

'They'll have dumped it,' Flanagan said, 'taken another.'

'There have been two reported hijackings and one creeper theft this evening, two in west Belfast, one in Craigavon. Nothing that looks like our boys. They've no friends, no family. No one they'd run to. They could have made for the border. The Garda have been notified and asked to keep a lookout.'

'The house they lived in before they were taken from their mother,' Flanagan said. 'It's not far from Newcastle. Ciaran talked to me about it, said he wanted to go there.'

Purdy shook his head. 'That was left to Thomas. He sold it when he got out of Hydebank.'

'It's still empty. Ciaran told me. It's the nearest thing they have to a home.'

'I can't see it. Not if they don't have access to the property.'

'That's where they'll be,' Flanagan said, more to convince herself than Purdy.

'All right,' Purdy said. 'I'll pass it along, make sure a local patrol has a look.'

He stood, put his hands in his pockets, shuffled his feet, glancing towards the exit.

Flanagan looked up at him, no patience for awkward pauses. 'You have something to say. Go on and say it.'

Purdy exhaled. 'Now's not the time.'

'Bloody say it.'

She felt heat on her cheeks, knew she shouldn't speak to her superior in such a way. But it was too late now.

Purdy stepped closer, leaned in, spoke in a hushed tone. 'I was right about Ciaran Devine. The confession was sound seven years ago, and it's sound now. I always knew it was. You shouldn't have had to find out exactly how sound the way you did, but there's no helping that now. You shouldn't have questioned my professionalism.'

Flanagan nodded. 'Fair enough. And you shouldn't have let them go.'

Purdy's shoulders slumped. 'All right. I'll keep you posted.'

He walked towards the exit, paused, and turned.

'We'll get them,' he said. 'They can't hide for ever.'

Flanagan did not reply. She watched him leave, the ward doors closing behind him.

She knew in her gut she would see Ciaran Devine before he and his brother were captured. It was only a question of when.

58

Ciaran watches Thomas pace the floor of the kitchen, back and forth, like the caged tigers in the zoo he'd seen as a child. Anger spits from Thomas like flares from the sun. It seems to Ciaran that it will ignite the air around him.

The table is still here. The same table their mother sat at when Ciaran last saw her. He sits there now feeling the damp in the air creep into his lungs, chill him from the inside out.

Ciaran doesn't know if the old man is alive or dead.

They left him bleeding on his hall floor, the dog running in frantic circles. Ciaran's knuckles still hurt, the skin cracked, blood in the creases. Maybe Ciaran's. Maybe not.

Thomas drove, first towards Belfast, then he followed the signs for Castlewellan and Newcastle. It wasn't the shortest way, but it was the way Thomas knew. It took a long time, journeying in silence. Lots of time to think.

Except Ciaran didn't like the thoughts he had, so he closed his eyes and chased them away. Eventually, as the sky turned from grey to dark purple, Thomas pulled in to a church car park.

'It's about two miles,' he said, taking the torch from the glovebox, the one he'd lifted from the old man's house. 'We can walk.'

Ciaran stayed behind his brother all the way, carrying the plastic bag with the food they had bought at a filling station. Thomas had made Ciaran go to the counter and pay, even though he didn't want to. They'd notice the bruises on my face, Thomas had said, so Ciaran had to do it. The walk felt longer than two miles, but then Thomas might have taken some wrong turns. He didn't say if he did, just kept walking like he knew everything there ever was to know.

Ciaran remembered then that he once believed that of Thomas. That his older brother was the wisest, cleverest, bravest boy in all the world, who knew the answer to every question that Ciaran could possibly think to ask.

He didn't know how old he was when that idea crumbled and fell away. Some time after they'd been put in Hydebank. And by then it was too late.

It was full dark by the time they reached the lane that curved between the trees with its small house at the end. A head-high wall surrounded the property, and a chain link fence had been erected in the gateway.

The sign said:

DOWN COASTAL PROPERTIES
BUILDING SITE
DANGER: KEEP OUT

Ciaran couldn't see beyond the fence.

'Have they knocked it down?' he asked.

'No,' Thomas said, 'it's still there. Here, help me up.'

Thomas went to the wall, reached up to the top, and pulled. Ciaran put his hands under

Thomas's feet, pushed against them, boosted his brother up. Thomas sat astride the wall and reached down.

'Come on,' he said.

On the other side, they walked along the driveway, gravel and weeds beneath their feet. Ciaran made out the shape of the house, a simple two-bedroom construction, pebble-dashed, sash windows. Hanging baskets still by the door, whatever had been in them long dead.

A bar had been screwed to the front door and its frame, a padlock attached.

'We'll try the back,' Thomas said.

The darkness thickened around the side of the house, their path obstructed by overgrown bushes and shrubs. Thorns pierced Ciaran's clothing, scratched his cheek. Something fled through the growth, sped away into the night, leaves rustling as it went.

At the back of the house, knee-high grass moved in waves through the torchlight. Ciaran remembered playing here, sun hot on his skin. There had been a path, now lost in the flowing grass, leading to the iron gate in the rear wall. The gate that he and Thomas would run through, and the trees, and on across the field until they reached the dunes.

'Do you remember?' he asked out loud.

'What?' Thomas trained the torch's beam on the back door.

'We used to go that way to the beach,' Ciaran said. 'Before Mum got sick.'

'I don't remember anything before she got sick,' Thomas said as he took the jangling keys from his pocket. He searched through them, tried one in the lock, then another, grunting at the effort of turning it.

Ciaran heard a snap and a click. He watched Thomas's fingers go to the handle, press it down, and push. A sound like a sticking plaster being peeled from skin as the door opened. The smell of mould carried by cold air currents.

'Here we are,' Thomas said.

Now Thomas paces, his shoes whispering on the old stone floor.

Ciaran's eyes have adjusted to the dark. Blue moonlight through the window allows him vision enough to see his brother's fury.

'What do we do now?' Ciaran asks.

Thomas doesn't answer as he turns at one wall, marches to the other, turns again.

'What do we do?' Ciaran asks again. 'Do we just wait?'

'Shut up and let me think,' Thomas says.

Once again Ciaran wonders if Thomas might be coming apart. The idea terrifies him, so he brushes it aside. Thomas cannot lose control. Because if Thomas is not in control, then all the world is madness.

'Are we going to live here?' Ciaran asks.

'Maybe for a day or two,' Thomas says. 'Then we have to move. Maybe go south. Cross the border at Newry. We'll have to get another car, though.'

Thomas stops pacing, stands still at the centre of the room. Ciaran realises his brother is shaking, small tremors in his fingers.

'Maybe we should eat,' Ciaran says, indicating

the bag on the table.

Thomas pauses, then says, 'All right.'

He sits down opposite Ciaran and switches on the torch. The beam illuminates his face from beneath, makes it look even thinner than it really is. He places the torch on the table, lights up the bag of food. Thomas opens the bag, removes the loaf of bread, the packet of ham, the pot of raspberry jam, the two-litre bottle of water. He wipes the tabletop with his sleeve, scraping away a decade of dust. It's no good, the table is still dirty. He takes the plastic bag, splits it along its two outer seams, and spreads it flat across the table.

'There,' he says.

Ciaran's stomach grumbles.

Thomas removes two slices of bread from the packet and places them flat on the torn plastic bag, then unscrews the lid of the jam jar. He stops, quandary clear on his face.

'I've nothing to spread it with,' he says.

Ciaran removes three knives from the coat slung over the back of his chair, the ones he'd taken from the old man's house. Only one is sharp enough to use for a weapon. He hands one of the blunt knives to Thomas.

Thomas spreads jam on the two slices of bread and gives one to Ciaran. As they eat in silence, Ciaran's mind travels back to this very place, many years ago. Sitting where Thomas sits now, eating jam sandwiches that his mother made.

Ciaran wonders if he was happy then. Certainly it was a better time than any other he could remember. Those rare minutes when he had her all to himself. When she was the only woman in the world, and he the only boy.

Light rolls across the kitchen ceiling.

Ciaran reaches out for the torch to stop it falling to the floor. Then he realises it hasn't moved at all.

Thomas stares over Ciaran's shoulder, at the window.

Ciaran turns to look, sees the car headlights in the lane.

Thomas switches the torch off and says, 'Someone's coming.'

He stands and goes to the window, peers through the grime and cobwebs.

'It's a cop car,' he says.

'Can you see?' Ciaran asks.

'No,' Thomas says. 'But it's cops. Has to be.'

He goes back to the table and lifts the sharpest knife. His eyes glint in the darkness.

'What are you doing?' Ciaran asks.

'What do you think I'm doing?' Thomas says. 'I'm going to fight. And so are you. We're not going back inside.'

Ciaran stands quiet.

'What?'

Ciaran says nothing.

'Say it.'

'We don't have to fight,' Ciaran says. 'Not if they don't find us.'

Thomas leans on the table, the knife in his right hand, breathing hard.

The rumble of an engine draws close, the sound of tyres on loose stone.

'Lock the back door,' Ciaran says. 'They don't

know we're here. If we hide, they won't know without breaking in.'

Thomas hesitates.

'Lock the door,' Ciaran says.

Thomas stands up straight, wavers like he might fall over, then runs to the back door, finds the key, turns it in the lock. Ciaran gathers the things from the table, bundles them up in the coat, shoves them under the sink. They run to the staircase that cuts the house in two, slip into the alcove beneath it. Thomas takes Ciaran in his arms, holds him close.

Ciaran can see the front and back windows from here. The light on the ceiling has stopped moving, died along with the noise of the engine. A car door opens and closes. Then another.

New, sharper lights flickering across the room. They have torches.

A metallic rattle as they try the fencing that blocks the gateway.

Voices and radio crackle.

Ciaran's breathing, soft and even, Thomas's quivering and ragged.

From outside, a grunt, followed a second or two later by heavy boots landing on the ground. Then another pair, and cursing, and laughter.

'... not fit for ...'

'... take a look ...'

'... get out of here ...'

Feet crunching on gravel, coming closer, closer.

Torch prints skitter and dash across the walls and ceiling.

A giggle creeps into Ciaran's mouth. From

nowhere, it forces his lips apart, air from his lungs. He puts a hand to his mouth, but the giggle escapes nonetheless.

Thomas's body shakes, Ciaran feels it in his embrace, and a laugh bursts from him too as a policeman appears at the window, torch and nose pressed to the glass. They ease back further beneath the stairs.

'Shh,' Thomas hisses, but he can barely contain his own laughter.

Like little boys playing hide-and-seek.

Like children.

Another cop at the window, peering in alongside the other, the light from their torches moving from one dust-shrouded object to the next.

Ciaran snorts, and he feels Thomas's hand slip over his mouth.

'Stop it,' Thomas whispers.

Still Ciaran shakes in his arms.

'Stop.'

The policemen leave the window. Ciaran listens. Hears footsteps pass the front door and fade. Ciaran breathes hard, recovering from his fit of laughter.

'Quiet,' Thomas says. 'They haven't gone yet.'

Soon lights flicker against the bushes through the window over the sink. Footsteps and voices approaching the back door. A rattle as one of the cops tries the handle. Then they appear at the window, hands cupped around eyes, torchlight bouncing across the room once more.

One of the beams dances close to the brothers' hiding place. Thomas pulls Ciaran back, further still, until they press against the wall. Ciaran feels the damp of the brickwork seep through his shirt. He shivers.

'Nothing here,' one of the cops says, his voice muffled by the glass. 'Come on. Might make the Chinese before it closes. Otherwise it's bloody sandwiches from the filling station.'

'Aye, let's go,' the other cop says.

They leave the window, go back in the direction they came from, their footsteps receding.

Thomas releases Ciaran from his embrace, crawls away from him, out from under the stairs. He stays on his hands and knees as he crosses to the front window. Placing his fingers on the rotten wooden sill, he peeks through the glass.

Ciaran comes to his side, looks out. The cops trudge back towards the makeshift gate, discussing the Chinese takeaway's menu, and whether or not their chips are any good.

As one helps the other back over the wall, Ciaran stands and says, 'Told you.'

'Get down,' Thomas says. 'If they look back this way, they'll see you.'

Ciaran lowers himself to the floor, sits down cross-legged. 'In the morning, when it gets light,' Ciaran says, 'can we go to the beach?'

'Yeah,' Thomas says.

59

Flanagan squeezed Alistair's hand.

'You're going to be fine,' she said. 'It'll hurt like hell, and you'll have to take it easy for a while, but you're going to be okay. You were very lucky.'

'Funny, I don't feel lucky,' he said, his gaze fixed on the ceiling.

The monitor above the bed kept a mute watch over them both, lines zigzagging across its face, a clip on Alistair's finger tethering him to the machine.

'I suppose not,' she said.

'Are the kids all right?'

'They're a bit shaken up. Worried about you. But they're fine. Your sister has them.'

Alistair went quiet, closed his eyes, but Flanagan knew he was not chasing sleep.

'Talk to me,' she said.

He shook his head.

Flanagan reached out, wrapped her fingers around his forearm. 'For Christ's sake, this isn't the time for keeping — '

'You brought this to our door,' he said.

She took a breath, went to retort, but decided to hold back, give him room to say what he wanted to say. She owed him that much.

'Jesus, our children. They were right there. What if those crazy bastards had decided to hurt them? How would you live with yourself?'

Flanagan let go of his wrist, brought her hands together in her lap, looked down at the floor.

'I struggle enough with worrying about you,' he said, 'if you're going to come home at night, or if you're going to get shot or stabbed or God knows what. But I thought that was as far as it went. I never thought it would come home with you. I never thought you'd put our children in danger.'

'I didn't put — '

'Shut up,' he said, the words spat at her with such venom that she recoiled in her seat. 'You did this. Those men came to our home, our children's home, for you. And I am so fucking angry at you right now and I don't know what to do.'

His tears came then, shocking them both.

Flanagan stood, brought her fingertips to his cheek. 'Alistair, please, I'm sorry.'

He opened his eyes, looked up at her. 'I know I'm not being fair to you, but that's the way I feel. Let me be angry.'

She bent down and kissed him, his eyelids first, tasting salt, then his cheek, then his lips. He reached up, put his arm around her shoulders. They stayed like that for a time, freezing out the bustle and chatter of the hospital, the electronic whirr of the machinery around the bed, until Flanagan knew only the warmth of him, the softness of his lips, the coarse hair of his beard, the sudden but familiar scent of him cutting through the clinical smells of the ward.

Her phone rang, breaking it all.

348

Flanagan leaned back, said, 'I have to take this.'

He nodded.

'I'm sorry,' she said.

'Go on.'

She took the phone from her pocket, checked the display. Purdy's mobile. She left the side ward, stepped into the darkened corridor, brought the phone to her ear.

'I heard from Newcastle,' Purdy said.

'And?'

At the station, a nurse looked up from her lamplit paperwork. Men and women snored and moaned in the general wards behind her. She pointed to the doors at the far end of the hallway. Flanagan nodded and headed towards them.

'A patrol had a look, but the place is all locked up. No sign of a forced entry, all the windows and doors intact. Our boys aren't there.'

Flanagan hit the button on the wall to release the double doors. They wheezed open, and she stepped through. She paced the floor in front of the elevator bank.

'Are they sure?' she asked. 'Did they look inside?'

'They're sure,' Purdy said. 'They had a good look through the windows, I'm told. No sign of any disturbance whatsoever.'

'Didn't they go into the house?'

She heard Purdy suppress a sigh.

'How could they? The place is locked up tight. They'd no warrant and no grounds to force entry. The Devines aren't there. It was a good shout, Serena, but it was wrong. I'll let you know if anything changes.'

'All right,' Flanagan said. 'Thank you.'

'Okay. Now, how's Alistair?'

'He's stable and out of ICU. Listen, I need to go.'

Flanagan hung up before Purdy could answer. She pressed the call button by the door to be readmitted to the ward, watched the nurse through the glass as she reached for the release. The doors opened, and Flanagan went back to Alistair's side ward, whispering her thanks to the nurse as she passed.

She pushed the door to Alistair's room open an inch or two and put her eye to the gap. His chest rose and fell in a steady rhythm, his breath whistling in his nose, his eyes moving beneath the lids. Within moments the whistling in his nose turned to a throaty snore.

Flanagan allowed the door to ease closed, then rested her forehead against the cool painted wood. I should go in to him, she thought, hold his hand while he sleeps. Be there for him when he wakes.

Or I should go to my children.

These are the things I *should* do.

Flanagan turned and walked back past the nurses' station, along the hall, to the double doors. Once more, she pressed the green button. Once more, she walked through.

Her mobile phone, still in her hand.

She called the direct line to her station. Hit the elevator's down button.

'This is DCI Flanagan,' she said. 'Put me through to Newcastle.'

60

Ciaran watches spiders through the glass. Dozens of them outside, webs spun into the corners of the frames. Fat black things. A moth is snared, and its struggles bring out the killer from its secret place. The spider carries the moth towards its corner, where it turns it, wraps it up tight, stores it for later.

Thomas dozes in a chair with his feet up on the table. Crusts and crumbs of bread litter the tabletop. The rest of the loaf is wrapped up tight. For later.

Ciaran can't imagine a later, a time after now, any more than the spiders can picture their own future. He wonders if there will be a tomorrow.

He doesn't think so.

The world is grey, crossing the border between the night and the morning. And cold. Ciaran has been shivering for hours. Thomas wouldn't let him light a fire in the old wood burner, said someone would see the smoke and come looking.

But at least now he can see, dim as it is. The kitchen with its old enamel sink, the cupboards with tattered curtains instead of doors. He folds one back, sees the collection of cups and plates that had been here when he was a child. A Superman bowl, plate and cup set that Mum had bought in a pound shop, thinking he would like it. He didn't, really, but he never told her so.

Beyond the table, the old couch so battered and worn that Mum had covered it in throws with patterns made up of stars and moons and zodiac signs. Mum had liked that sort of thing. She read books about astrology and the power of the mind.

Ciaran wonders why someone hadn't taken all this away. All this worthless rubbish. What good could it be to anyone? He supposes whoever bought the house will clear it all out before they knock the place down and build new homes on the site.

He feels a sudden grief for this building, and for the life he had here, however brief.

And for his mother.

One last look around, to remember.

Beyond the foot of the stairs, a door leading to the living room. Ciaran opens it, steps through. The stained net curtains make the light all milky. In the corner, the old television, tipped onto its back. It was ancient back then, and barely worked. That and the VCR. The cabinet it stood upon housed the collection of videos Mum had bought from charity shops. Cheap, she said, because everyone wanted DVDs, but the old videotapes were just as good.

Ciaran looks through them, fingering the spines of the cases. *The Lion King, The Little Mermaid* (Thomas said it was for girls, but Ciaran liked it), *The Iron Giant, FernGully, Star Wars, Batman*.

Before Mum got sick, all three of them would watch films in here on a Saturday night. Ciaran liked the cartoons best, but Thomas liked the superheroes. Mum didn't mind, so they took turns. Sometimes, if she had the money to buy it, she made popcorn, and they would eat it from her big flowery bowl.

Ciaran wishes she hadn't got sick. He wishes she hadn't died and they could still watch films here together.

Ciaran wishes he could go back and start again. Make everything different.

He feels heat in his eyes, and a thickening in his throat.

Before the tears can come, he leaves the room and mounts the stairs. There is mould, speckly black, on the wallpaper. The stairs creak under his weight.

At the top are three doors, all open. In the middle is the bathroom. Tape is stretched over the toilet and basin, red letters shouting DO NOT USE. Ciaran and Thomas have gone out in the garden.

To the left, Mum's bedroom.

Ciaran steps inside, breathes in the air. He had hoped he might still be able to smell her. He can't: only damp and mould odours fill his head. Her bed, stripped bare, the mattress half on the floor. Empty wine bottles, coated with dust, on the dressing table she got from a dump. Clothes strewn on the floor.

He goes to them, hunkers down, picks up a pink and white patterned blouse. He tries to remember it on her, but can't. He brings it to his nose, inhales. Nothing.

She is gone and gone and gone and gone.

Like she'd never ever been at all.

Again, tears threaten. He drops the blouse, wipes his eyes with the back of his hand, and gets to his feet.

Across the way, the room he and Thomas shared. The interior visible from here.

Part of him wants to close that door, go back downstairs. But the other part of him wants to see. Needs to see.

He crosses the small landing, pushes the door fully open.

Memory sparks in his mind. Flashes of things he doesn't want to remember.

Two single beds at opposite sides, both stripped down. Plain wallpaper, emulsioned over. The scrawlings of two young boys in crayon and pencil and pen. Pictures, words, wild slashes. Some make sense, most don't. Ciaran won't read any of it. He knows his mind won't withstand it.

He remembers. Even though he can hardly bear it, Ciaran remembers.

Thomas in the night, getting out of his bed, padding the few feet across the floor, climbing under Ciaran's blankets. Thomas's hard hands, sharp nails.

And his teeth. Always his teeth.

Biting hard.

Do what I say or I'll bite you again.

Please don't.

Do it or I'll bite you again.

I'll tell Mum.

Tell Mum and I'll kill her dead and it'll be your fault for being a tell-tale-tit and then I'll bite you anyway.

Ciaran cannot hold the weight of the memory, and he sinks to his knees. The tears will come now whether he wants them or not. He weeps for the little boy who lay awake in that bed every night waiting for his brother who would surely come with his teeth and his nails.

Time slips past unknown to him. He wraps his arms around himself, rocks, a child once again, helpless and afraid.

Almost without him noticing, another pair of arms joins them. A cold embrace, Thomas's chest on his back. Then Thomas stands, takes his hand, leads him to the bed, lays him down. Ciaran faces the wall. Thomas's weight settles in behind him. They embrace like so many times before, one body curving with the other, arms and legs tangling.

'It's all right,' Thomas says. 'I'll look after you. I always do.'

'Can we go to the beach now?' Ciaran asks.

'Yes,' Thomas says.

61

Flanagan waited in the station's reception area, the duty officer eyeing her from beyond the glass. She checked her watch. The officers who'd checked the house were due in from patrol at five. It was quarter past now. The clock above the reception desk concurred.

Her gaze travelled across the familiar range of public information posters that were pinned to the noticeboards. Warnings of the dangers of alcohol abuse, appeals for good citizens to inform on the criminals amongst them, illustrations of the catastrophic consequences of speeding.

As she read the messages beneath each glaring image, her eyes grew heavy and her head nodded forward. She jerked awake, inhaled sharp, cool air. Ignored the duty officer's curious yet disapproving stare.

The drive from Belfast had taken an hour and a half, including the detour she took to Moira to change out of her bloody clothes. She had examined the flowering bruises around her abdomen, tender to the touch. Fatigue had nagged at her on the way, and she resorted to winding the windows down and whooping and singing at the top of her voice to keep herself awake. Only the thought of strong coffee at the end of her journey kept her focused on her destination.

Of course, when she asked for some, the duty

officer told her the vending machine wasn't working.

'Haven't you got a kitchen and a kettle?' she had asked.

The duty officer had bristled and said, 'Yes, for the staff at this station.'

Flanagan's head dropped again, and once more jerked upward as if pulled by a string from above.

A telephone rang, and the duty officer answered it. Flanagan strained to hear what he was saying. After a few moments, he hung up and called, 'They're on their way now, ma'am.'

'Thank you,' Flanagan said as she got to her feet.

The doors leading into the station whirred as they unlocked, and two uniformed officers stepped through.

The older of them introduced himself as Sergeant Robert Nelson, and his colleague as Constable Sean Meehan. Flanagan showed them her warrant card and they nodded in deference to a superior, even though she had no authority over them.

'You checked out a property along the coast during the night,' she said.

'Yes, ma'am,' Nelson said. 'There was no one there. It looked like there hadn't been for years. I'm guessing some developer bought the place and ran out of money before they could do anything with it.'

'But you didn't go inside,' Flanagan said.

'We went over the wall and had a look through the windows on the ground floor,' Nelson said.

'Strictly speaking, we shouldn't even have done that without a warrant, seeing as it's private property. The windows were thick with dust, but we could see inside well enough to tell you there hasn't been a sinner in that place for years.'

Flanagan thought for a moment. Nelson seemed as sure as he could be that the house had not been disturbed. But *she* needed to be sure.

'I need you to take me there,' she said.

The officers looked at each other, then Nelson spoke once more. 'No can do, I'm sorry. I've got a pile of paperwork to get through, then I've to get home and let the wife away to work. I'm taking the kids to school. I'm sure someone from the next shift can take you.'

Meehan sighed and opened his mouth for the first time. 'I can do it, so long as we don't take too long. My girlfriend's expecting me home.'

'Thank you,' Flanagan said. 'So, shall we go?'

★ ★ ★

Meehan said little on the drive, and Flanagan was glad of it. The further from town they travelled, the more the certainty that had brought her here crumbled into doubt. These officers weren't fools. They had done the task that had been asked of them, and now guilt grated on her for implying by her arrival that they hadn't.

Winding roads criss-crossed between country-side and shore as they travelled north, passing through Dundrum, then south skirting the army base at Ballykinler.

Eventually, Meehan said, 'Up here,' and steered into a single-track lane that ran between clusters of trees, leaves glowing red and brown in the early light. A walled property appeared, its gateway barred by a chain link fence adorned with warnings to keep out. Just as they had described.

Meehan drew the car up close to the fence.

'Looks as empty as it did last night,' he said.

'It probably is,' Flanagan said. 'Look, I know you checked thoroughly and I've no business dragging you out here again. But I need to be sure. I don't expect you to understand, but that's the way it is.'

Meehan yawned and wiped his eyes. 'It's not up to me to ask about the whys and wherefores, ma'am. I just do what I'm told. Want to take a look?'

Flanagan opened the passenger door and climbed out. At the other side of his car, Meehan yawned again and put his cap on. 'I'll go first, will I?'

Flanagan nodded.

He went to the lowest part of the wall, which was still up to his chin, and grabbed hold of the top before jumping and hoisting himself up.

'I'm afraid I'm not so agile,' Flanagan said.

Meehan reached down and pulled her up, and she privately thanked God that she'd worn jeans. She rested at the top for a moment, a hand to her side and the bruises beneath her clothing, breathing hard.

'You all right, ma'am?' Meehan asked, concern on his face.

'Fine,' she said. 'Let's go.'

He lowered Flanagan down on the other side then jumped down after her, one hand keeping his cap in place.

Flanagan stood and observed for a moment, noting the patches of pebble-dashed rendering that had cracked and fallen away, the stout padlock on the door, the grime on the windows. Then she walked along the path, to the step, and examined the padlock. It showed no sign of having been tampered with, nor the latch it bound shut. No one had tried to force the door. She went to the window to the left, cupped her hands around her eyes, and peered in through a gap in the net curtains.

An upturned television, tatty furniture, mould and decay. She could almost smell it from out here. Meehan came to her side, tall enough to see over the top of the sagging line that held the curtains. He said nothing, but Flanagan knew he was thinking, told you so.

She walked past the front door to the other window. A couch directly in front of her, a sink and cupboards at the other side, and a table and chairs in the middle.

On the table, a loaf of bread, crusts, an empty water bottle, a jam jar.

Flanagan stepped back, indicated that Meehan should look through.

He did so and said, 'Fuck me pink.' He glanced at her and said, 'Sorry.'

Flanagan couldn't be sure if he was apologising for his language or for not seeing before what he saw now. It didn't matter either way.

360

'Move away from the window,' she said. 'Draw your weapon.'

Meehan backed towards the corner of the house, pulled his Glock from its holster. Flanagan drew her pistol, ducked past the window, came to Meehan's side.

In a hushed voice, he said, 'There's a back door with no padlock. We tried it last night, but it was locked.'

'Come on,' Flanagan said, stepping past him.

She stuck close to the gable wall as she walked to the rear of the house, her shoulder brushing loose chips of stone and rendering onto the moss-covered concrete path. Meehan's boots crunched on them as he followed.

Flanagan edged towards the corner, leaned slowly out, her pistol leading. The garden stood empty save for the jungle of grass and overgrown shrubs. She made her way to the window that overlooked the sink, glanced inside, then dashed past. Meehan did the same, then joined her at the back door, he at one side, she at the other.

She reached for the handle, pressed down.

The door opened an inch.

'Jesus,' Meehan said, his voice small and low in his throat. Flanagan noticed the tremor in his hands, his Glock aimed skywards. 'Are they armed?'

'Knives, maybe. No firearms as far as I know. Right, I'll take the rear corners,' Flanagan said. 'You take the forward. Ready?'

Meehan swallowed and nodded.

Flanagan kicked the door and entered,

swinging her pistol left and right to ensure the corners were clear. Meehan came behind. She ducked down, peered under the table, pulled back the curtains over the larger cupboards while Meehan checked under the stairs.

'Clear,' Flanagan said.

'Clear,' Meehan said.

They went to the foot of the stairs, and the open door beyond. Meehan kept the muzzle of his pistol trained on the landing above while Flanagan checked the room with the overturned television. She noted the scattered videotapes: children's films, mostly.

'Clear,' she said.

As they climbed the stairs, Meehan leading, Flanagan felt a growing certainty that they were alone in this house. The Devines had surely been here, but not now.

But they might be, she scolded herself. Don't talk yourself into a mistake.

A moment s glance confirmed the bathroom was empty, then she entered the bedroom to the left. A double bed, the mattress half off, wine bottles everywhere, clothes discarded on the floor. Their mother's room, her illness still ringing from the walls.

Flanagan backed out, crossed the landing into a room with two single beds at opposite sides. Madness scrawled on the walls.

'They're not here,' Meehan said, holstering his pistol.

Flanagan wanted to say she had no desire to be here either, the cold dampness of the place crawling beneath her clothing, the air tainted by something else, something darker she could not define.

'But they've been here recently,' she said. 'At least now we know that much. They could have headed south along the coast from here, crossed the border at Newry. I'll call it in from your car.'

She turned to the window overlooking the back garden.

A path so dense with grass and weeds she had not noticed it at ground level. Now she saw it led to an iron gate in the rear wall. A gate that stood open, the branches and long grass around it pulled aside.

'When you and Sergeant Nelson were here last night,' Flanagan said, 'did you open that gate?'

Meehan came to her side and followed her gaze. 'No, ma'am,' he said.

'Come on,' she said, making for the stairs.

62

Ciaran and Thomas stand at the water's sighing edge. Spray from the sea makes cold points on Ciaran's cheeks. The wind burns his skin. Grey out there, stretching all the way to touch the sky. Clusters of rocks hem this small beach in, a hundred yards of sand trapped between wet black walls. Orange and yellow buoys dip behind the waves a hundred yards out, reappear with the next swell, and then they're gone once more. Over and over, coming and going.

'Is it like you remember?' Thomas asks.

'I think so,' Ciaran says, but he really isn't sure. This place has been a dream to him for years. A fragment of a memory. Smells and colours.

A question has been hiding behind Ciaran's lips for hours. Now he asks it.

'Did Mr Rolston really do those things to you? Did he really touch you?'

Thomas exhales, the sound of it lost in the rushing air around them. 'Does it matter?'

'Yes, it does,' Ciaran says.

'Well, what do you think?' Thomas asks.

'I think you were afraid,' Ciaran says. 'But not of Mr Rolston. I think what Daniel told me was right. I think you saw me and Daniel were getting to be friends, and you couldn't stand it. I think you got me to kill Mr Rolston because you were afraid of losing me.'

Thomas folds his arms across his chest. 'Maybe,' he says. 'Or maybe I just wanted to watch someone die. To see what it felt like.'

Ciaran shivers as he looks out to sea and thinks of the lives he destroyed. His own among them.

'So all this because you wanted to see what it felt like,' he says.

'Maybe,' Thomas says. 'I don't know. I don't remember any more. I just remember he'd been lecturing me, telling me I needed to work hard at school, you and me didn't have to be nothing just because we were orphans. He said he was an orphan too, and he'd done all right. He said I didn't have to be angry all the time. And he kept on and on, every day, nagging at me.'

Thomas makes his hand a claw, drags his fingertips across his scalp and forehead.

'And every time he sat me down and started talking it got all hot inside my head, all noisy and confused, so I couldn't even think properly.'

The muscles in Thomas's jaw bulge, his words squeezing and hissing between his teeth.

'And I just wanted him to shut up and leave me alone. That's all. Just to leave me alone.'

He clenches his hands into fists, his shoulders rising and falling, his lips sealed shut now, his nostrils flaring. Then he breathes out, his hands drop loose to his sides, and he laughs once.

'Not everything has to have a reason. Sometimes stuff just happens.'

Thomas reaches into his jacket pocket. He takes out the envelope that Serena had hidden in her drawer. He goes to open it.

'Don't,' Ciaran says.

Thomas removes the single sheet of file paper from the envelope. He lets go of the envelope, and the wind carries it away. Ciaran sees his own spidery handwriting, the tumble of words, some of them crossed out, some of them underlined.

'Do you want me to read it to you?' Thomas asks.

'Please don't,' Ciaran says.

He crosses the few feet of sand to his brother, tries to grab the paper, but Thomas snatches it away from his reach.

'Dear Serena,' Thomas says as he backs away, the page held before him.

'Stop it,' Ciaran says, following.

'I want to say thank you for taking care of me in the police station,' Thomas says.

'Stop.'

'I was very scared, but you made me feel better.'

Ciaran dives for the page, but Thomas stumbles. He loses his grip on the paper and it flutters away, up into the wind, higher and higher. Out over the water.

As Thomas laughs, Ciaran walks away.

63

Flanagan reached the bottom of the stairs in seconds, turned, headed for the back door then ran along the path, kicking her way through the grass and weeds.

'Ma'am, wait,' Meehan called from behind.

She ignored him and walked through the gate, her pistol still ready in her hands. She stopped, listened. Only the call of gulls overhead, the rustling of the salty breeze through the thin line of trees. And not far ahead, the rumble and rush of the Irish Sea.

'Should we go back to the car?' Meehan asked.

'No,' Flanagan said.

She picked her way through the trees and into a field. The ground rose to a crest, a low wall of loose stones at the top. She walked up the slope and rested her hands on the wall as she scanned the rise and fall of the grassy dunes on the other side. Beyond them the sea, dark and angry.

Flanagan threw one leg over the wall, let her body follow. Stonework dug into her bruises and she swallowed a groan. Meehan came behind.

'You think they're out here?' he asked.

'Quiet,' Flanagan said. 'Listen.'

Only the crash of waves on the beach, the screech of the birds. The wind came in strong, carrying spray with it.

She descended into the bowl of the first dune, beckoned Meehan to keep up. At the bottom,

367

her shoes ploughing through loose sand, she lost sight of the sea. She climbed to the next grassy rise, her thighs protesting at the effort of pushing against the soft footing. The sea again, and a few yards of beach. Empty but for washed-up seaweed and stones.

The drop revealed a channel on the other side, a small sluggish stream of run-off water that twisted through the dunes towards the tide. Flanagan splashed along it, the sandbanks rising all around, grass leaning away as the wind strengthened.

The stream turned one way, then the other, seeming to take them no closer to the open. The wind funnelled through the channel, gathering speed, bringing water to her eyes. She lifted a hand up to shield them. At last the sea came into view, and something creamy white fluttering across the sand. An envelope, one Flanagan recognised. The envelope the brothers had taken from her drawer.

It drifted past, propelled by another gust of wind, and she turned to follow its trajectory towards the dunes behind her.

She saw Ciaran Devine withdraw the blade from Meehan's neck and let the policeman fall at his feet.

64

Ciaran watches her raise the gun and point it at him.

Her mouth moves. She shouts something, but he can't make out the words because the wind is battering against his ears. The blood on his hand goes from hot to cold.

She shouts again, jerks the gun at him.

Ciaran steps over the policeman, his feet splashing in the stream, comes closer to her. He shakes his head, raises his free hand to his ear, tells her he can't hear what she's shouting.

She steps back, shouts again, and this time he understands.

'Drop the knife,' she says. 'Stay where you are and drop the knife.'

Ciaran stops, but he keeps the knife in his fingers.

A sadness pierces him. It was always going to be her, wasn't it? No matter how hard he wished for it to be different, it was always going to be this way.

He takes another step, watches her finger move to the trigger, the wrinkles on her knuckle thinning and fading as she applies pressure. Do it now, he thinks.

No, tell her.

'Do it now,' he says, but his words are swept away by the wind. He barely hears them himself.

He shouts now, his body bending at the effort. 'Do it now!'

'No,' she shouts back. 'I won't. Don't make me. Drop the knife, Ciaran, please.'

Another step.

'Shoot me!'

She shakes her head. 'No, Ciaran. Drop the knife.'

Some absent part of Ciaran's mind wonders if she will shoot Thomas too, and as if summoned by the idea, Thomas appears behind her.

She notices Ciaran's gaze has left her, and glances over her shoulder to see what he sees. She swings her gun around, but not fast enough. Thomas drives the hand-sized stone into her temple and she falls down. Her gun tumbles end over end and lands in the stream.

A grin of animal triumph splits Thomas's face until he looks like a devil in a Halloween picture. He crouches down, leans over her as she blinks the blood away from her eyes. Ciaran can barely hear her groan.

Ciaran crosses the ground between them, stands over Serena and his brother.

Thomas raises the stone to him. Ciaran sees the blood on it, the strand of hair whirling in the wind.

'Finish her,' Thomas says.

Ciaran reaches for the stone, as much from instinct to obey his brother as from any desire of his own. He pulls his hand back, empty.

'No,' he says.

'Do it,' Thomas says. 'Like you did to Mr Rolston. Do it before she recovers.'

It's too late. Already she lifts her head, tries to get her arms and legs moving, to get away.

'No,' Ciaran says. 'Not her.'

Thomas tries to push the stone into Ciaran's hand. 'Do it or I'll bite you.'

'No.'

'Do it or I'll bite you hard.'

Ciaran swallows. He takes the stone from Thomas's hand, feels its weight. He thumbs the bloody patch, sees the red on his skin. Then he throws the stone away, past Thomas, out towards the beach.

Thomas stands, glares at him.

At their feet, Serena turns on to her stomach, gets to her hands and knees, crawls towards the sea. While Thomas stares hard into Ciaran's eyes, she gets to her feet, staggers a few yards, drops to her knees, climbs up again.

Thomas shakes his head, snatches the knife from Ciaran's hand, and walks after her. As he closes on her, he raises the knife, ready to bring it down.

'No!' Ciaran shouts.

Thomas swings the knife, but she sees him coming, twists away, her arm up. The blade catches on her sleeve. Ciaran hears her cry out as she falls back onto the sand.

He runs, arms and legs whirling.

Thomas raises the knife again. Serena raises her hands. Thomas laughs.

Ciaran's body collides with his brother's.

He hears the air driven from Thomas's lungs. He glimpses metal out of reach. They roll on the sand, arms and legs tangling, the shock of cold as they fall at the lip of the sea. Ciaran comes to rest on his side, his chest against Thomas's back, his arms wrapped tight around him.

Thomas reaches back, drags his nails down Ciaran's face. Ciaran snaps at the fingers with his teeth, feels skin and bone between them, hears Thomas squeal.

He climbs on top of his brother, pins his arms with his knees, balls his fists together, lifts them over his head.

'No more!' Ciaran screams.

He brings his fists down, feels Thomas's nose crunch beneath them. The blood sprays outwards like a red angel on Thomas's face. Then a wave comes, rushes over him, washes the blood away. The cold hits Ciaran's thighs, almost shakes him loose, but he holds on.

Thomas coughs and gags, spits water and blood. Ciaran raises his hands again, brings them down once more. Thomas turns his head, and the blow skims his cheek.

'No more!' Ciaran screams again.

Thomas calls his name, but it's lost in the crash of another wave.

But Ciaran hears his name anyway.

Not from beneath him, but from the beach. He turns.

Serena stands at the edge of the water.

'Ciaran, stop,' she shouts. 'Please stop.'

65

The water swallowed Flanagan's ankles, the cold making her gasp, trapping her pleas in her chest. Ciaran stared back at her, centuries of pain written on his young face.

She caught her breath, shouted, 'Ciaran, let him go.'

Thomas's eyes, mouth and shattered nose broke through the foaming water, and she heard him suck in air. He threw his weight to the side, taking advantage of Ciaran's distraction, and they both rolled into the surf.

Ciaran cried out at the shock of it. Flanagan struggled further out, her feet disturbing loose sand. The next wave reached her calves, already sending shivers through her back.

Thomas got to his feet, shaking water from his head, his entire body quaking. His breathing hard and ragged.

Flanagan knew the signs. The first stage, hyperventilation, followed soon by a deadening of the limbs as the body conserved heat by pulling blood to the core.

Ciaran up on his knees, Thomas looming over him. Another wave took Ciaran down as Thomas grabbed for him, and they sprawled in the water once more.

The same wave washed around Flanagan's thighs, so cold, so cold, but she pushed on, they were so close, if she could get between them . . .

Ciaran burst from the water, filled his lungs with air and reached down for his brother. He grabbed one handful of hair, another of collar, and hauled Thomas up.

Flanagan said, 'Stop,' but the word was choked in her throat by a wave that submerged her to the groin. She felt her body's temperature drop, cold to the bones of her. God knew how the brothers felt, in up to their chests now.

Ciaran's eyes met hers.

'Stop,' she said.

Ciaran pulled Thomas back through the tide, further out, each wave taking more and more of them until only his shoulders showed above the water.

Thomas still in his grasp, spitting and coughing.

As Flanagan watched from only feet away, Ciaran wrapped his left arm around Thomas's neck, kept hold of his hair with his right hand. He pushed Thomas under, held him there.

Thomas's hands above the water, flailing.

Flanagan reached for them, but her fingers touched something else, something that clung to her hand. Sodden paper, the ink running and smearing. The letter that had remained hidden like the shameful secret it was for seven years.

Then a wave took her, pushed her back to shore. Salt water filled her mouth and nose. Her feet lost contact with the sand, and she prayed to God she would not drown. She prayed to see her children again. And Alistair, poor Alistair.

Her knees ploughed into sand, then her hands, and she pushed up, face out of the water, coughing, hacking, her lungs feeling ready to burst from her chest. She got to her feet, staggered towards the beach, fell again, vomited in the surf.

She turned and looked back out to sea.

Ciaran's head above water, Thomas's hands clawing at his face.

66

Ciaran's feet are lifted from the sand, his body weightless.

Thomas's nails tear at his skin.

Ciaran doesn't mind.

Thomas kicks, tries to throw his body one way then the other.

Ciaran doesn't mind.

He is cold deep down to his centre, cold like he has never felt before.

Ciaran doesn't mind.

He would wish for it to be different, but he knows now that wishes are useless, worth no more than the air expelled in their making.

His feet touch the bottom once more, and he pushes back, further out. A wave rolls over his head, the cold complete and total now, every part of him racked with it.

His mouth is free of the water again and he gulps air, so hard and fast.

Another wave and he breathes salt water. It hurts.

Ciaran doesn't mind.

Thomas isn't moving any more, floating like a doll in Ciaran's arms.

Ciaran doesn't mind.

The shakes have stopped. Ciaran's arms and legs are heavy, like stone, dragging him down. It hurts. The cold hurts.

Ciaran doesn't mind.

Bright sparks inside his head, flashes so brilliant they burn away everything he knows.

Ciaran doesn't . . .

67

Flanagan crawled, spitting bile on the wet sand. Shivering so hard she could barely control her limbs.

She pulled the memory from the muddy chaos of her mind.

First aid. Hypothermia. Once out of the water, remove clothing immediately.

She struggled to her feet, pulled at her waterlogged jacket. It clung to her, refused to come away. She pulled again and it peeled off like icy skin.

The sand hit her hard as she fell, kicking the air from her straining lungs. Shoes off, toeing them from her feet. Reached down for the socks, pulled them away. Unbuttoned her trousers. They stuck to her legs, and she writhed and kicked until they were past her thighs, down to her ankles, then off. She pulled her sweater over her head.

Cold turned to pain, and she howled against the wind.

Flanagan got to her feet once more, looked back to the waves, searched for a sign of them. No head above the surf, no gasping for air. No hand reaching from the water. Both of them lost in the rolling grey. A violent shiver almost felled her again and she stumbled and tripped towards the channel with the stream and Constable Meehan's blood.

She found him there, lying on his back, the sand around him turning dark reddish-brown.

Flanagan fell to her knees beside him, fumbled for the radio fixed to his stab vest, hit the panic button, signalled every officer within range to come now. She remembered her training, how the microphone would remain open for a few seconds. Location, she'd been taught. Repeat the location over and over in case the GPS couldn't find them.

'Beach,' she said through chattering teeth, knowing her voice crackled in some operator's earpiece. 'Behind the house. Find the car. The house. Follow the path. The beach.'

She could say no more, her lungs unable to support the words. She felt for Meehan's throat, her fingers slick in the blood, too numb to feel a pulse even if it was there.

His eyelids flickered. He gasped. Alive. Alive, thank God.

And his body warm.

Flanagan searched his pockets until she found a handkerchief. She pressed it against the wound in his neck.

She wrapped her body around his, drew the warmth from him, knowing the last of it might be draining away.

68

Meehan lived.

Flanagan would be thankful for that for the rest of her days.

While they transferred him from Downe Hospital in Downpatrick to the Royal Victoria in Belfast, she spent twelve hours in A&E at Downe, swaddled in heated blankets.

She had wanted to stay on the beach until they found the bodies, but the paramedics wouldn't allow it. The shivering eased after four hours, but the nurses in the A&E ward insisted that she stay wrapped up as they brought her cup after cup of hot sugary tea. One kind nurse tended to the wound on Flanagan's temple while she drank. Then the cut on her arm where the knife had snagged her sleeve. No stitches, nothing deep enough. They wouldn't let her sleep while they observed for signs of concussion.

Six hours after she left the beach, a sergeant came to the A&E bay and told her a coastguard crew had found the bodies, still entwined, snared in a lobster line not far from shore. He left Flanagan alone, and she said a small prayer, asked God to forgive Ciaran Devine.

That night, DSI Purdy came to bring her home. He brought a bag of clothes he'd taken from his wife's wardrobe. None of it matched, but Flanagan didn't complain as she squeezed her feet into the slippers.

'I don't want to go home,' she told him as they headed west towards the motorway. 'I want to go to the Royal. To see Alistair.'

'I think visiting's over,' Purdy said.

'You think that'll stop me?'

He fell quiet then, and the hum of his car lulled her to the edge of sleep, her head propped on her hand.

'I've had enough,' Purdy said.

Flanagan jerked awake. 'What?'

'I'm done,' Purdy said. 'I'm going to retire. I've fulfilled my thirty-year contract, so there's nothing to stop me. I'm not far off sixty, and I'm still in decent shape. I might as well get out now, take my pension and run. Make the most of my dotage.'

Flanagan smiled. 'You don't play golf, do you?'

'Christ, no.'

'Not too late to start.'

'Yes it bloody is.'

He had more to say, Flanagan could tell. She kept her silence and waited.

As they reached the southern outskirts of Belfast, the skeletal RISE sculpture at the Broadway junction came into view. Two globes, one within the other, a latticework of steel and light sparkling against the dim orange glow of the city. At last, Purdy spoke.

'I made some bad decisions. I suppose everyone does, now and then. But there've been too many recently. Some of those decisions hurt you. And I'm sorry.'

'You don't have a monopoly on mistakes,' Flanagan said. 'God knows, I've made enough.'

381

She thought of the blade entering her husband's flank. The shock on his face. His anger at her for bringing this upon his family.

Minutes later, Purdy stopped his car a few yards from the hospitals main entrance.

'Thank you,' Flanagan said.

'Least I could do,' he said. 'Don't forget, meeting with the ACC at eight a.m. The Ombudsman's office at ten. You've a lot of statements to give.'

Flanagan gave a weary nod.

'Don't worry,' Purdy said. 'I'll stand by you. It'll be tough, but you've been through worse.'

'True,' Flanagan said.

She touched his arm, got out of the car, and walked to the entrance.

Patients ambled here and there, having abandoned their wards to sneak late night cigarettes outside. They looked like shuffling zombies, in thrall to their glowing embers and blue smoke.

Flanagan took the lift to Alistair's floor, found the doors to his ward locked as she expected. She pressed the bell.

The nurse at the far end of the hall, visible through the windows, ignored her. Flanagan pressed the button again. And once more.

At last, the doors opened and Flanagan stepped through. The nurse met her halfway along the hall. A different woman, not kind-eyed and understanding like last night.

'Visiting's over at eight-fifteen,' she said.

'I need to see my husband,' Flanagan said. 'Please.'

'No, the policy's quite clear, and it's up on the

door. No visitors after the allotted time.'

'You don't understand,' Flanagan said, blinking the heat from her eyes as she willed herself not to cry now, not now, not after all this. 'You don't know what I've been through.'

The nurse folded her arms across her chest and shook her head. 'I can't make exceptions, I'm sorry.'

Flanagan reached for the lump in her pocket: her wallet, sodden with water, sealed in a zip-lock bag. She removed the wallet, opened it, showed the nurse her soaked warrant card.

'So?' the nurse said. 'Being a police officer does not give you special privileges.'

Flanagan exhaled. 'Look, I'm going to my husband. You can try to stop me, you can call security, do whatever the hell you want, but I'm going to him. Easiest thing is to just let me past, then the whole ward won't get woken up.'

The nurse unfolded her arms, put her hands on her hips. She chewed her lip as she watched Flanagan. 'All right. Ten minutes, then out. And don't ever threaten me again or I'll have you barred from this ward. Understood?'

Flanagan nodded, said, 'Understood.'

She found Alistair held within the soft glow from a lamp over the bed. He snored, a gentle rattle as he breathed. The kind of snore he made when he'd had a drink. Morphine, probably, she thought.

She lifted the chair from the corner, brought it close to the bed. His hand warm in hers, she sat down, leaned forward. Rested her head on his shoulder.

The nurse woke her ninety minutes later, told her it really was time to go now.

★ ★ ★

By the following afternoon, Flanagan ached with fatigue, her mind dulled by hours of recounting events to one impassive face after another. She told it all as it had happened, no embellishment, no excuses, no hiding her own mistakes.

During her brief break for lunch she called Alistair's sister, who would bring Ruth and Eli home that evening. The idea of holding them filled Flanagan's heart and gave her the will to get through the rest of the day.

After that, she called Paula Cunningham, and heard traffic sounds when she answered. Outside her hotel having a cigarette, she said.

'I didn't know you smoked,' Flanagan said.

'I'd quit,' Cunningham said. 'Now I've un-quit. Given the circumstances, I think I'm entitled.'

Flanagan brought her up to date on what had happened. Cunningham gave a despairing sigh.

'It means you're safe now,' Flanagan said. 'You can go home.'

'That house will never be my home again,' Cunningham said. 'Besides, I could get used to hotel living. Room service, late bar, all that. While Angus is still with the vet, I'll hang out here. I've got a little room on my credit cards to blow through, so I might as well make the most of it.'

They said farewell, promised to keep in touch,

384

but Flanagan knew it was an empty oath.

She had left her car keys with a constable at the hospital, and the eager young man had volunteered to drive the car to Lisburn this afternoon. It had gone four when Flanagan hauled herself towards the station exit, her thoughts focused first on her children, then a bloody good night's sleep.

'Before you go,' Purdy called from along the corridor.

Flanagan's shoulders slumped in spite of herself. She turned to him.

'There's a chap has called in. He's insisting on talking to you.'

Flanagan sighed. 'Can Ballantine do it?'

Purdy shrugged. 'You and only you, he says.'

'Who is it?' she asked.

'Barry Timmons. That Walker woman's boyfriend. The one you — '

'Yes, I know,' Flanagan said. 'Where?'

Flanagan found him in the interview room. When he saw her enter, tears sprang from his eyes. His hands shook. He swallowed, a click in his throat.

'Barry,' she said. 'I think you have something to tell me.'

Acknowledgements

Once again I am beholden to the village of people who helped me raise this particularly difficult child. My heartfelt thanks to all the following:

Somebody once described my agent Nat Sobel to me as 'one of the great men of publishing', and I can't argue with that. Both he and his partner in crime, Judith Weber, have been the best guides an author could hope for. And all the good people at Sobel Weber, as well as Caspian Dennis and all at Abner Stein for their constant support.

As ever, I couldn't do this without my editors Geoff Mulligan and Juliet Grames, and the wonderful people at Vintage Books and Soho Press, including Alison Hennessey, Bronwen Hruska, Paul Oliver, Fiona Murphy and many more.

I owe special thanks to Steve Cavanagh and Paul McCusker for their insights into the opposite ends of the youth justice system, from entrance to exit. I have taken liberties with the procedures here and there, and have doubtless made mistakes, but be aware that such diversions from reality are entirely of my own making and are no reflection on the expertise of these gentlemen.

The generosity of the crime fiction community never ceases to amaze me. Writers, readers, bloggers, reviewers, all have shown me tremendous kindness, and I am grateful.

As before, a large portion of this book was written in my local library, and librarians and booksellers have been among my greatest champions. God bless libraries and independent bookstores because I wouldn't have a career without them.

The supportiveness of my wider family circle has been invaluable over the last few years, and there have been several moments where I might have given up on this writing lark if not for those closest to me: My children, Issy and Ezra, and my wife Jo, who have given me more than I could ever deserve.

We do hope that you have enjoyed reading this large print book.

Did you know that all of our titles are available for purchase?

We publish a wide range of high quality large print books including:
Romances, Mysteries, Classics
General Fiction
Non Fiction and Westerns

Special interest titles available in large print are:
The Little Oxford Dictionary
Music Book
Song Book
Hymn Book
Service Book

Also available from us courtesy of Oxford University Press:
Young Readers' Dictionary
(large print edition)
Young Readers' Thesaurus
(large print edition)

For further information or a free brochure, please contact us at:
Ulverscroft Large Print Books Ltd.,
The Green, Bradgate Road, Anstey,
Leicester, LE7 7FU, England.
Tel: (00 44) 0116 236 4325
Fax: (00 44) 0116 234 0205